GHOST
NOCTURNES

series editors
Michael Eury   Marilee Hord

collection editor
Lynn Adair

collection designer
Teena Gores

collection border art
Monty Sheldon

collection design manager
Brian Gogolin

GHOST™
NOCTURNES

story
Eric Luke

art
Adam Hughes
Mark Farmer **Tom Simmons**
Karl Story **Jason Martin**
Casey Jones **Paul Guinan**
Colleen Doran **Tom Grummett**
Terry Dodson **Lee Moder**
Gary Martin **Ande Parks**

cover painting
Russ Walks

coloring
Chris Chalenor **Lovern Kindzierski**

lettering
Steve Haynie

DARK HORSE COMICS®

publisher	**Mike Richardson**
executive vp	**Neil Hankerson**
vp of publishing	**David Scroggy**
vp of sales & marketing	**Lou Bank**
vp of finance	**Andy Karabatsos**
general counsel	**Mark Anderson**
creative director	**Randy Stradley**
director of production & design	**Cindy Marks**
art director	**Mark Cox**
computer graphics director	**Sean Tierney**
director of sales	**Michael Martens**
director of licensing	**Tod Borleske**
director of operations	**Mark Ellington**
director of m.i.s.	**Dale LaFountain**

Published by
Dark Horse Comics, Inc.
10956 SE Main Street
Milwaukie, OR 97222

May 1996
First edition
ISBN: 1-56971-150-X
1 3 5 7 9 10 8 6 4 2
Printed in Canada

This book collects issues #1, #2, #3, and #5 of the
Dark Horse comic-book series *Ghost™*.

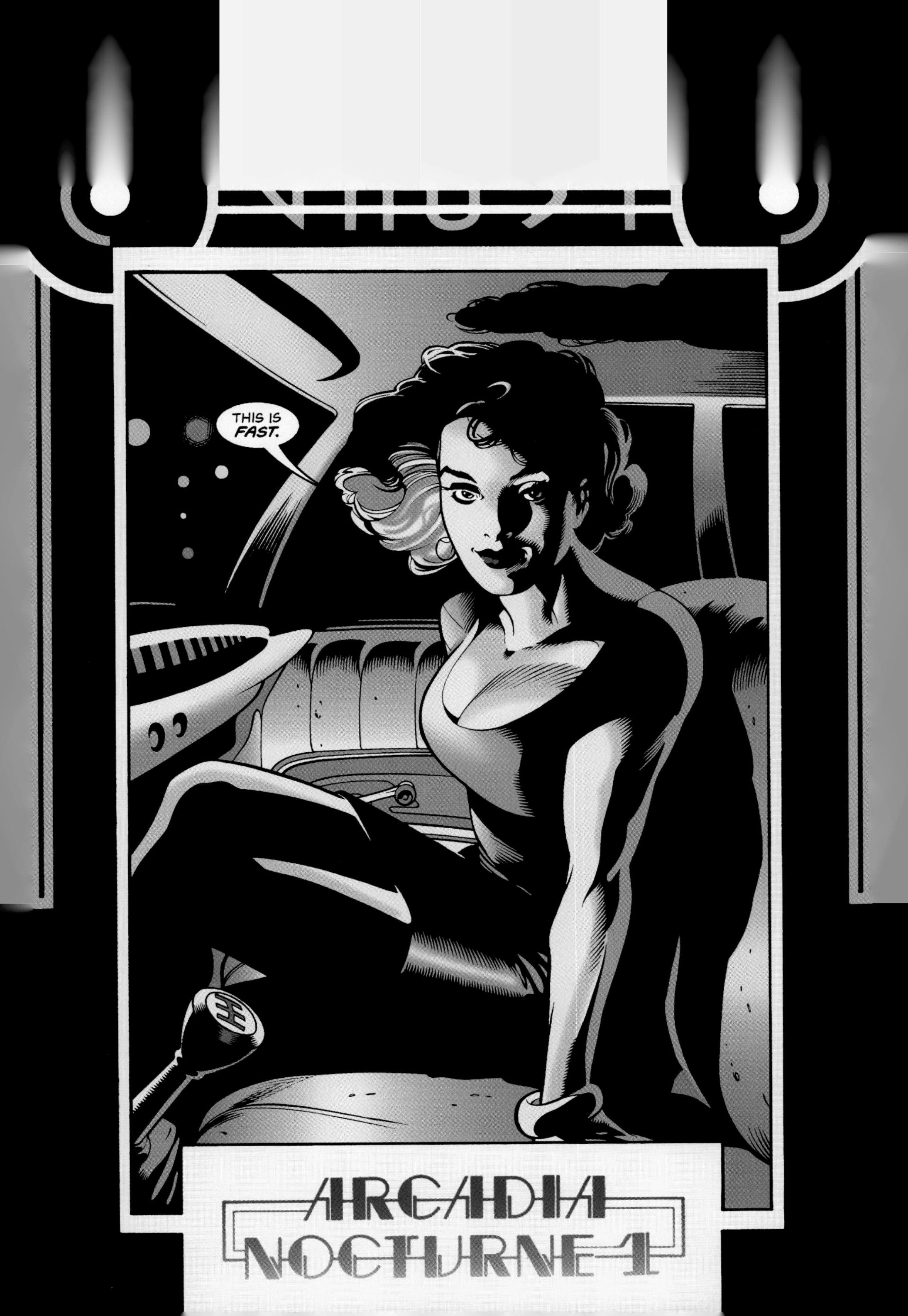
THIS IS FAST.
ARCADIA NOCTURNE 1

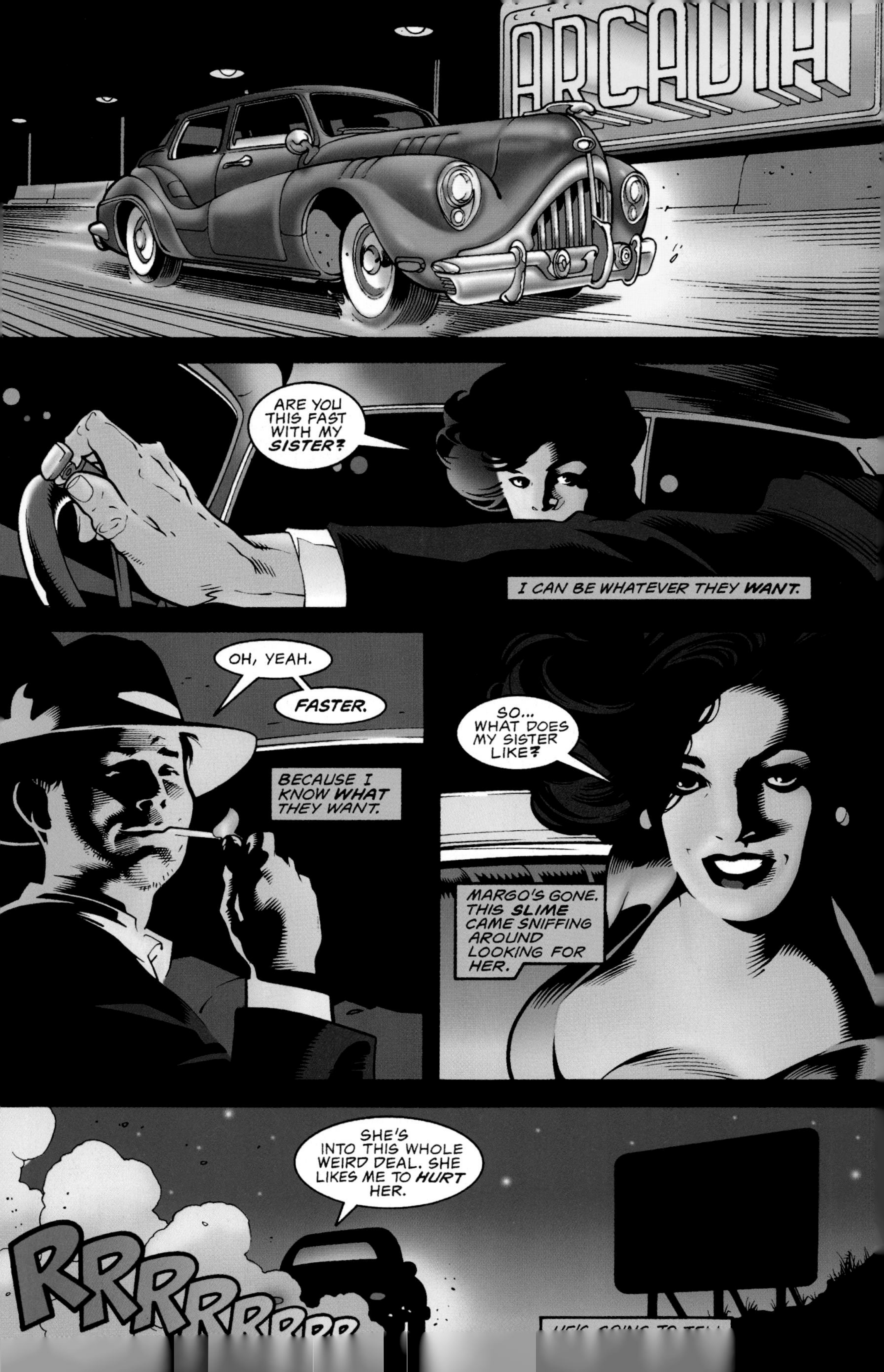
ARCADIA
ARE YOU THIS FAST WITH MY **SISTER?**
*I CAN BE WHATEVER THEY **WANT.***
OH, YEAH.
FASTER.
*BECAUSE I KNOW **WHAT** THEY WANT.*
SO... WHAT DOES MY SISTER LIKE?
*MARGO'S GONE. THIS **SLIME** CAME SNIFFING AROUND LOOKING FOR HER.*
SHE'S INTO THIS WHOLE WEIRD DEAL. SHE LIKES ME TO ***HURT*** HER.

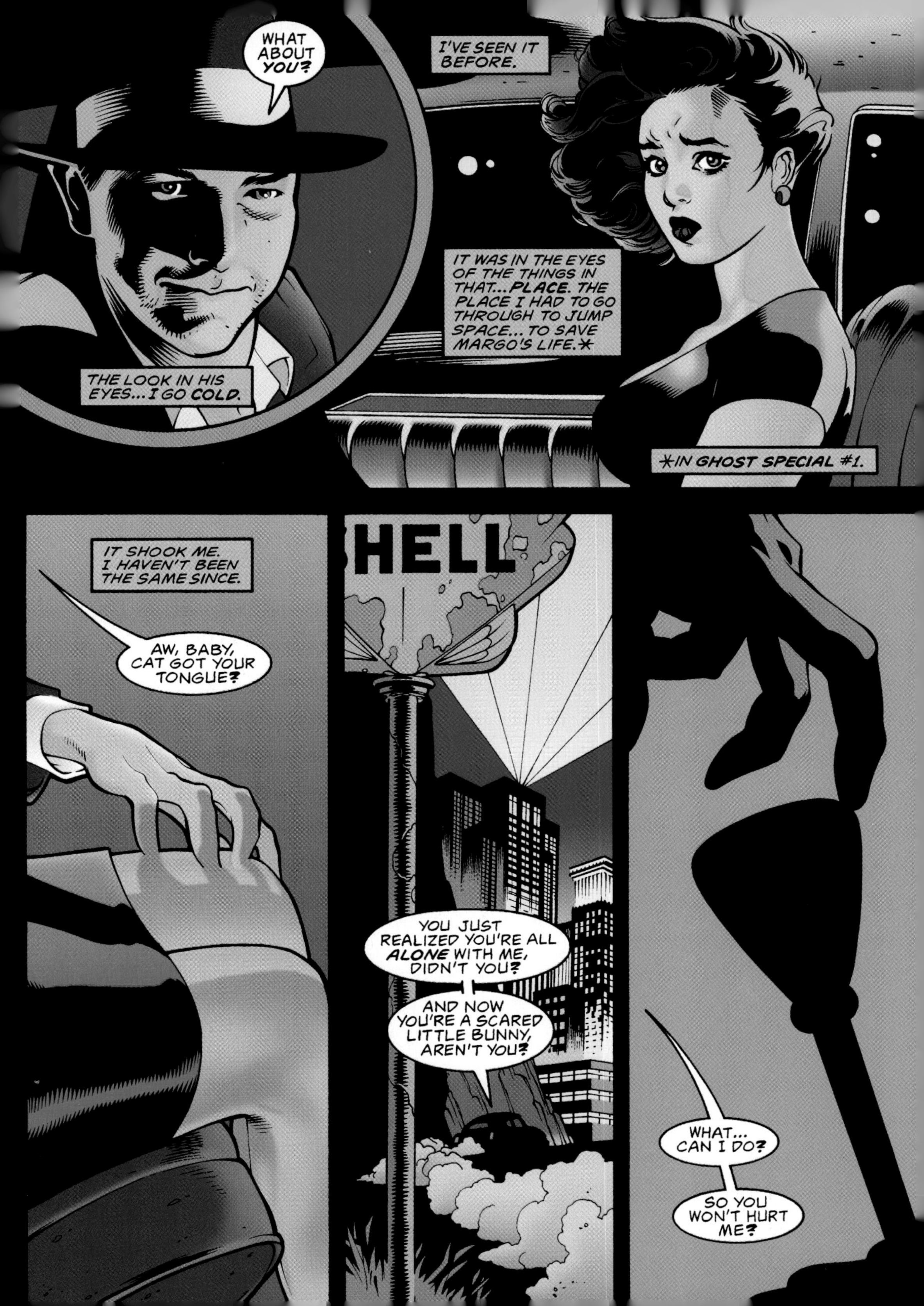

WHAT ABOUT YOU?
THE LOOK IN HIS EYES... I GO COLD.
I'VE SEEN IT BEFORE.
IT WAS IN THE EYES OF THE THINGS IN THAT... PLACE. THE PLACE I HAD TO GO THROUGH TO JUMP SPACE... TO SAVE MARGO'S LIFE.*
*IN GHOST SPECIAL #1.
IT SHOOK ME. I HAVEN'T BEEN THE SAME SINCE.
AW, BABY, CAT GOT YOUR TONGUE?
HELL
YOU JUST REALIZED YOU'RE ALL ALONE WITH ME, DIDN'T YOU?
AND NOW YOU'RE A SCARED LITTLE BUNNY, AREN'T YOU?
WHAT... CAN I DO?
SO YOU WON'T HURT ME?

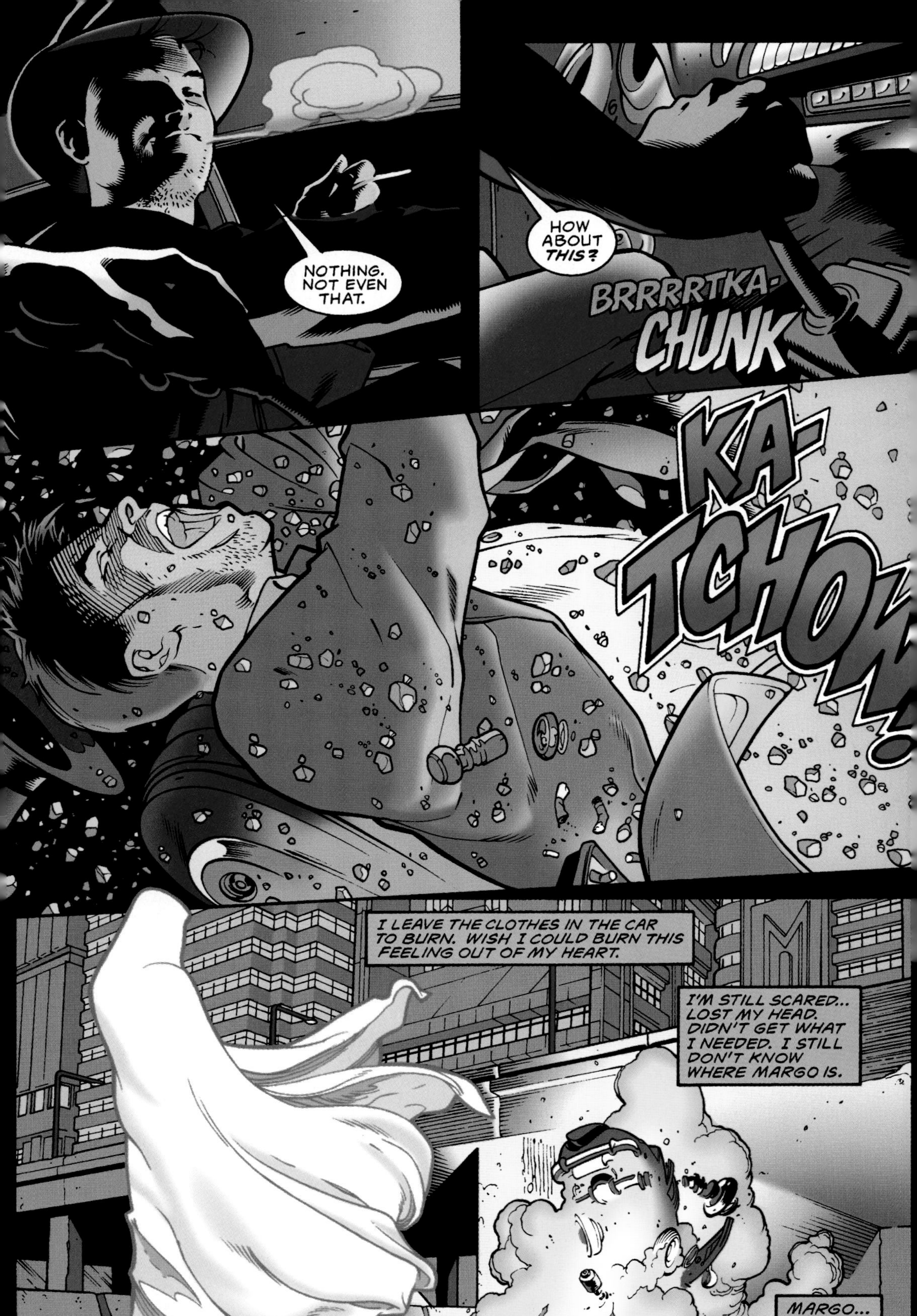
NOTHING. NOT EVEN THAT.
HOW ABOUT THIS?
BRRRRTKA-CHUNK
KA-TCHOW!
I LEAVE THE CLOTHES IN THE CAR TO BURN. WISH I COULD BURN THIS FEELING OUT OF MY HEART.
I'M STILL SCARED... LOST MY HEAD. DIDN'T GET WHAT I NEEDED. I STILL DON'T KNOW WHERE MARGO IS.
MARGO...

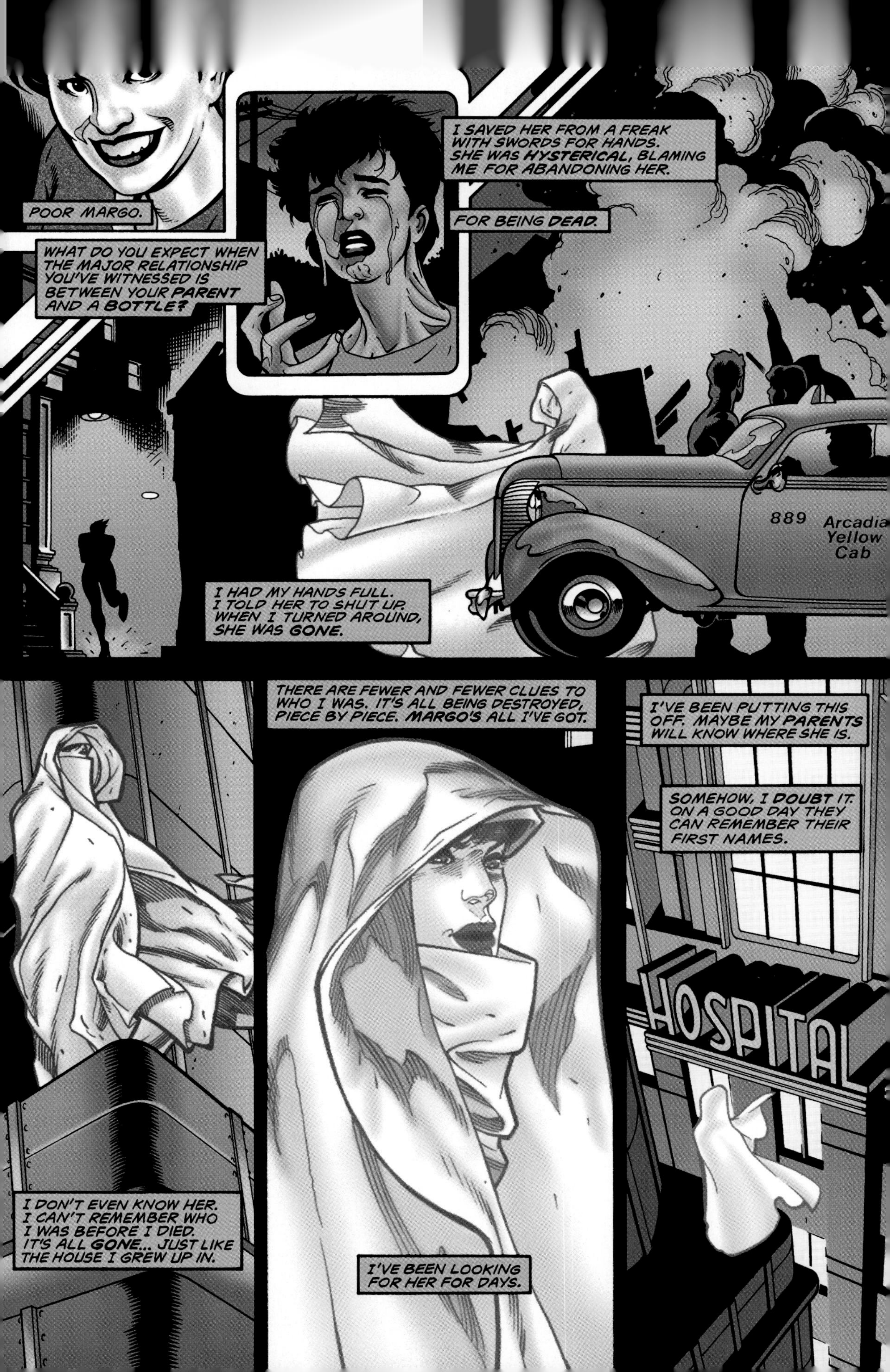

POOR MARGO.
WHAT DO YOU EXPECT WHEN THE MAJOR RELATIONSHIP YOU'VE WITNESSED IS BETWEEN YOUR PARENT AND A BOTTLE?
I SAVED HER FROM A FREAK WITH SWORDS FOR HANDS. SHE WAS HYSTERICAL, BLAMING ME FOR ABANDONING HER.
FOR BEING DEAD.
889
Arcadia Yellow Cab
I HAD MY HANDS FULL. I TOLD HER TO SHUT UP. WHEN I TURNED AROUND, SHE WAS GONE.
I DON'T EVEN KNOW HER. I CAN'T REMEMBER WHO I WAS BEFORE I DIED. IT'S ALL GONE... JUST LIKE THE HOUSE I GREW UP IN.
THERE ARE FEWER AND FEWER CLUES TO WHO I WAS. IT'S ALL BEING DESTROYED, PIECE BY PIECE. MARGO'S ALL I'VE GOT.
I'VE BEEN LOOKING FOR HER FOR DAYS.
I'VE BEEN PUTTING THIS OFF. MAYBE MY PARENTS WILL KNOW WHERE SHE IS.
SOMEHOW, I DOUBT IT. ON A GOOD DAY THEY CAN REMEMBER THEIR FIRST NAMES.
HOSPITAL

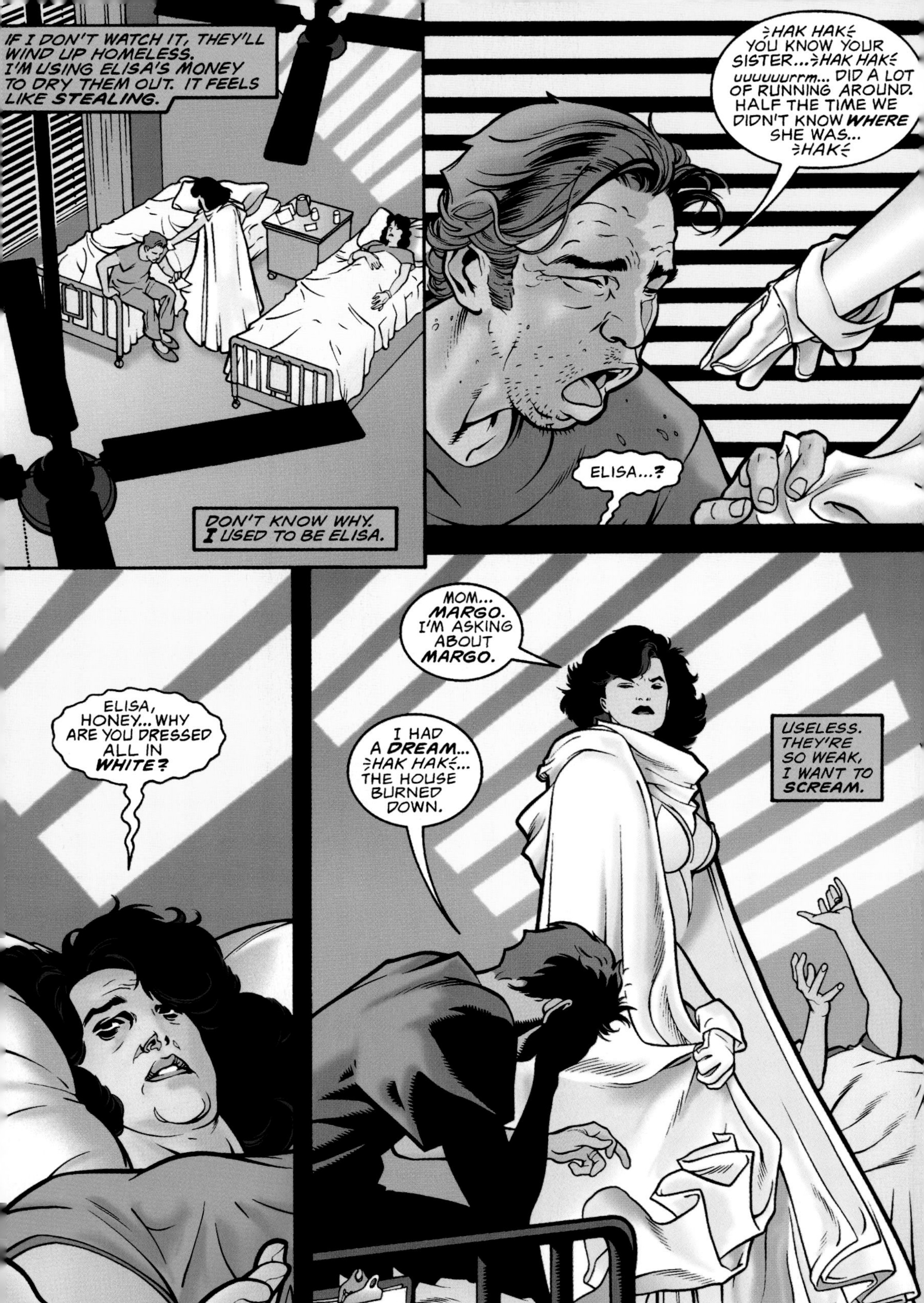
IF I DON'T WATCH IT, THEY'LL WIND UP HOMELESS. I'M USING ELISA'S MONEY TO DRY THEM OUT. IT FEELS LIKE STEALING.
DON'T KNOW WHY. I USED TO BE ELISA.
HAK HAK YOU KNOW YOUR SISTER... HAK HAK uuuuuurrm... DID A LOT OF RUNNING AROUND. HALF THE TIME WE DIDN'T KNOW WHERE SHE WAS... HAK
ELISA...?
ELISA, HONEY... WHY ARE YOU DRESSED ALL IN WHITE?
MOM... MARGO. I'M ASKING ABOUT MARGO.
I HAD A DREAM... HAK HAK... THE HOUSE BURNED DOWN.
USELESS. THEY'RE SO WEAK, I WANT TO SCREAM.

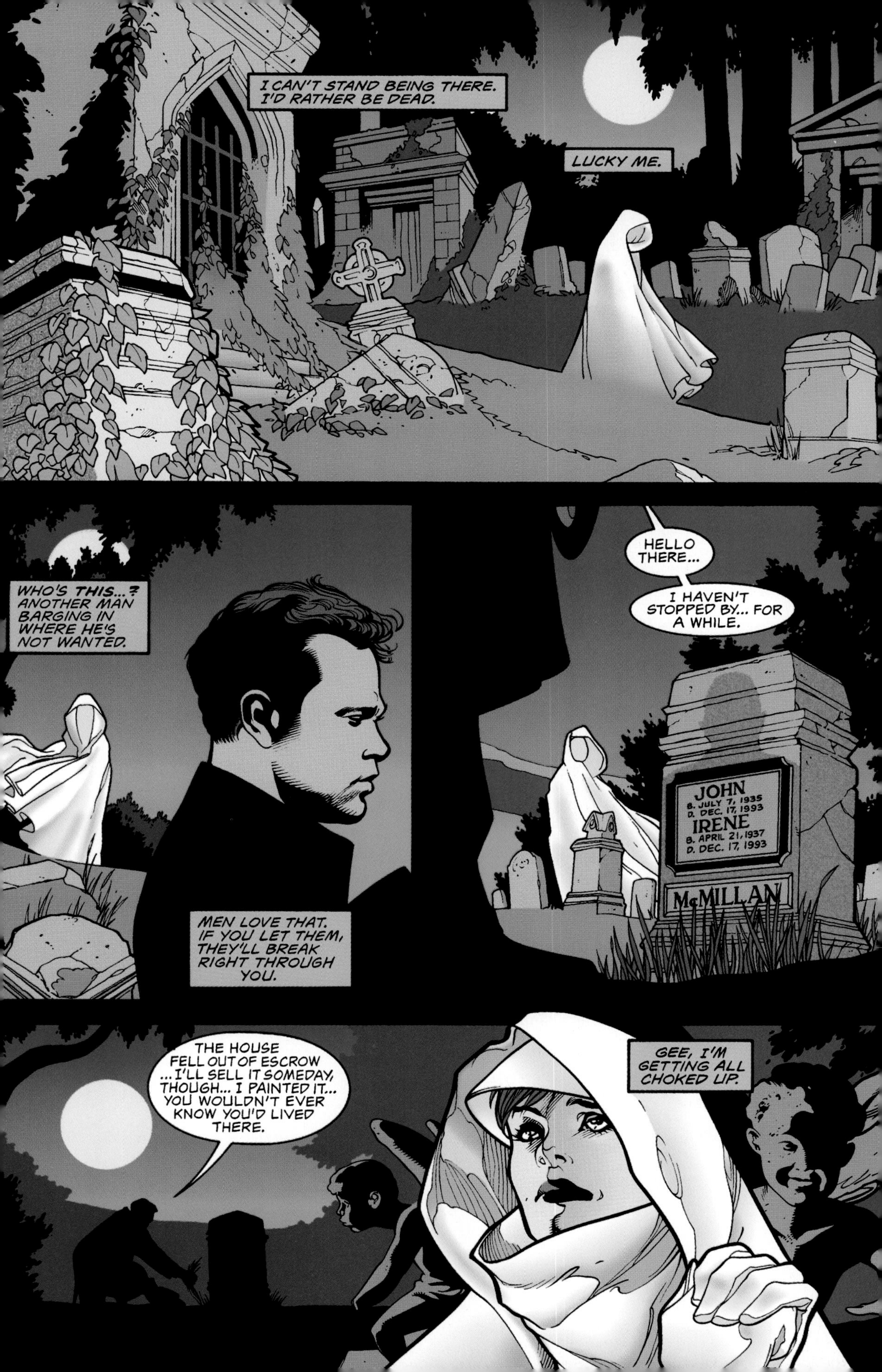
I CAN'T STAND BEING THERE. I'D RATHER BE DEAD.
LUCKY ME.
WHO'S THIS...? ANOTHER MAN BARGING IN WHERE HE'S NOT WANTED.
MEN LOVE THAT. IF YOU LET THEM, THEY'LL BREAK RIGHT THROUGH YOU.
HELLO THERE...
I HAVEN'T STOPPED BY... FOR A WHILE.
JOHN
B. JULY 7, 1935
D. DEC. 17, 1993
IRENE
B. APRIL 21, 1937
D. DEC. 17, 1993
McMILLAN
THE HOUSE FELL OUT OF ESCROW ...I'LL SELL IT SOMEDAY, THOUGH... I PAINTED IT... YOU WOULDN'T EVER KNOW YOU'D LIVED THERE.
GEE, I'M GETTING ALL CHOKED UP.

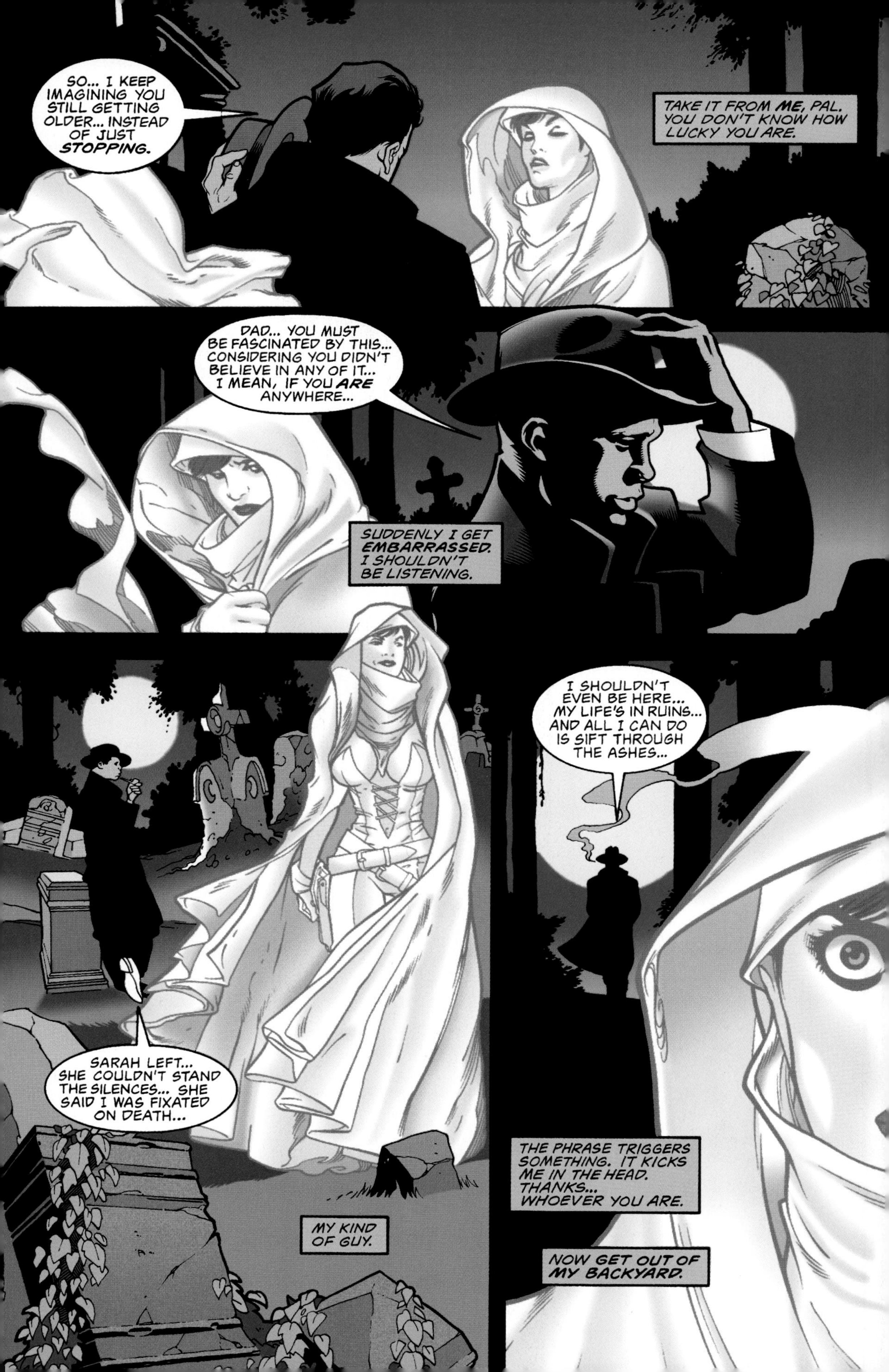
SO... I KEEP IMAGINING YOU STILL GETTING OLDER... INSTEAD OF JUST STOPPING.
TAKE IT FROM ME, PAL. YOU DON'T KNOW HOW LUCKY YOU ARE.
DAD... YOU MUST BE FASCINATED BY THIS... CONSIDERING YOU DIDN'T BELIEVE IN ANY OF IT... I MEAN, IF YOU ARE ANYWHERE...
SUDDENLY I GET EMBARRASSED. I SHOULDN'T BE LISTENING.
SARAH LEFT... SHE COULDN'T STAND THE SILENCES... SHE SAID I WAS FIXATED ON DEATH...
MY KIND OF GUY.
I SHOULDN'T EVEN BE HERE... MY LIFE'S IN RUINS... AND ALL I CAN DO IS SIFT THROUGH THE ASHES...
THE PHRASE TRIGGERS SOMETHING. IT KICKS ME IN THE HEAD. THANKS... WHOEVER YOU ARE.
NOW GET OUT OF MY BACKYARD.

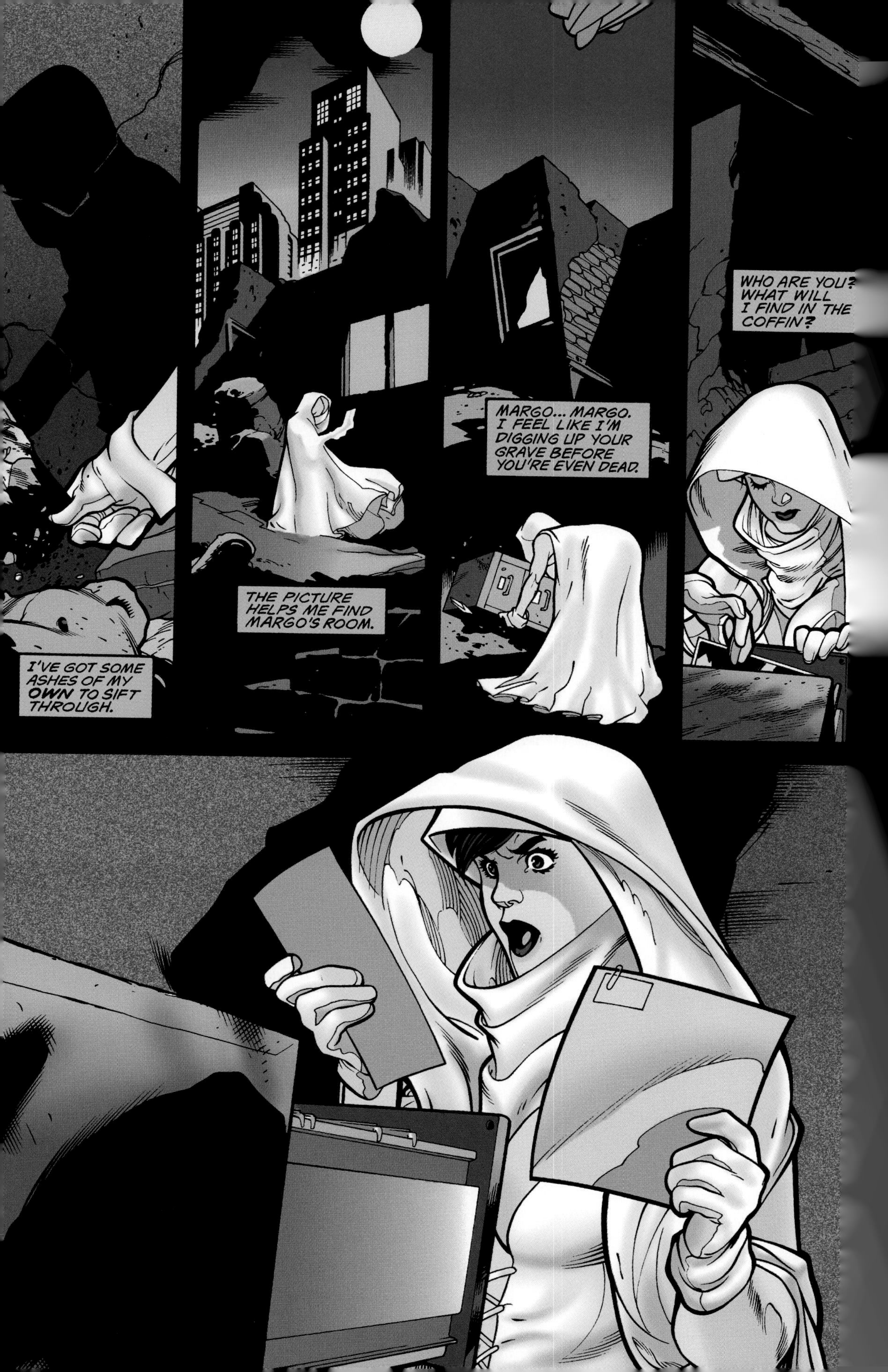
I'VE GOT SOME ASHES OF MY OWN TO SIFT THROUGH.
THE PICTURE HELPS ME FIND MARGO'S ROOM.
MARGO... MARGO. I FEEL LIKE I'M DIGGING UP YOUR GRAVE BEFORE YOU'RE EVEN DEAD.
WHO ARE YOU? WHAT WILL I FIND IN THE COFFIN?

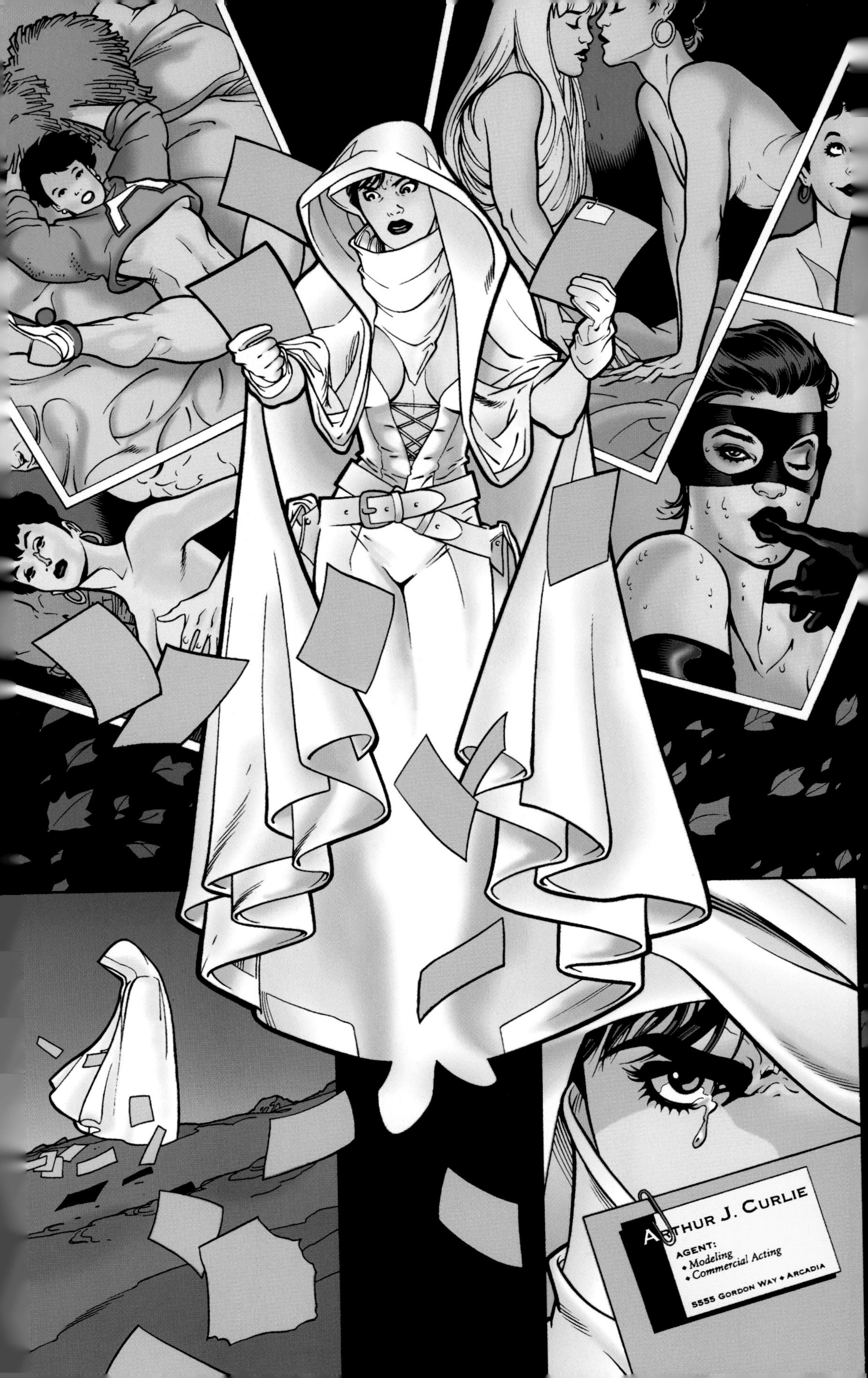
ARTHUR J. CURLIE
AGENT:
• Modeling
• Commercial Acting
5555 GORDON WAY • ARCADIA

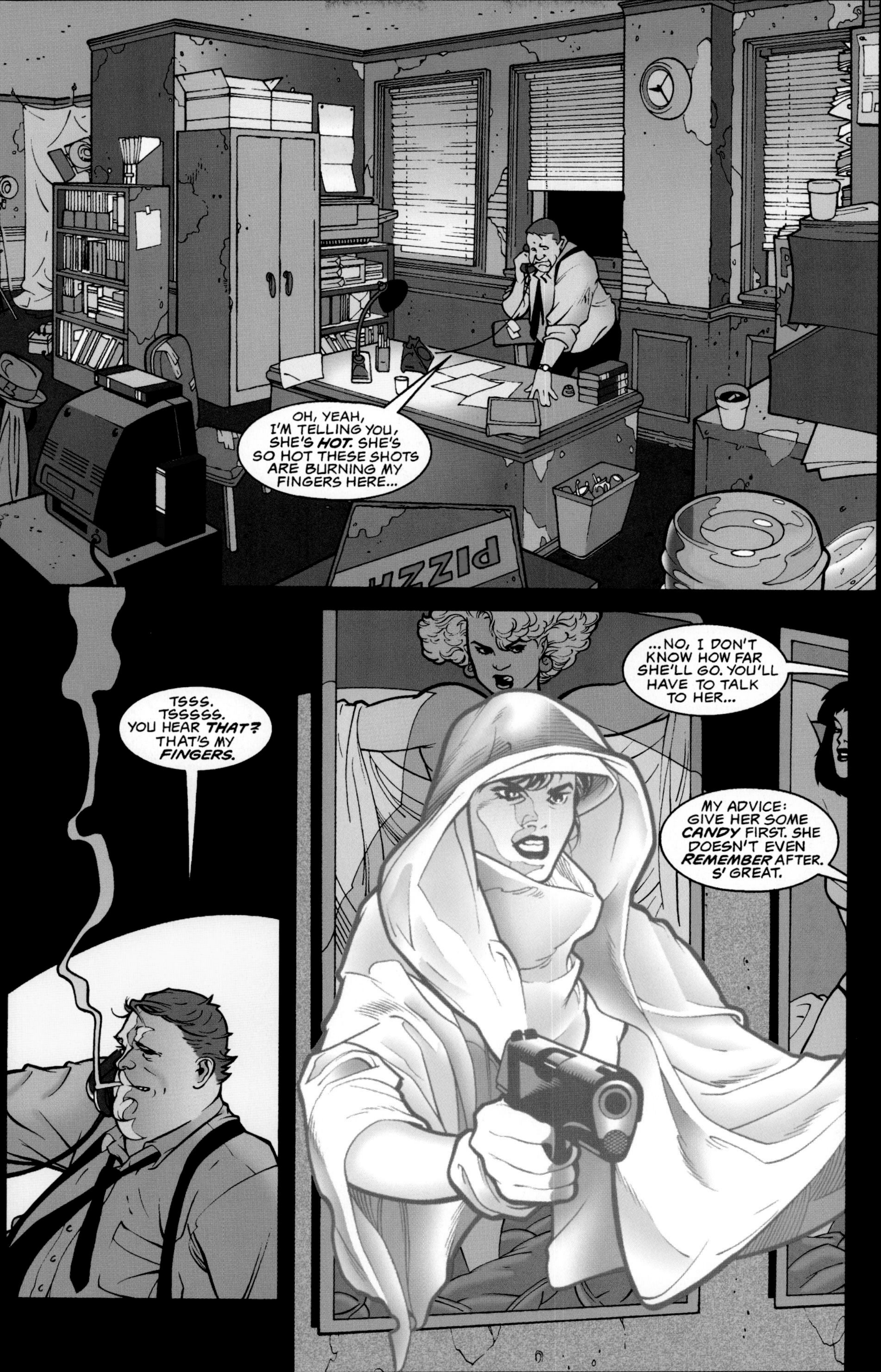

OH, YEAH, I'M TELLING YOU, SHE'S HOT. SHE'S SO HOT THESE SHOTS ARE BURNING MY FINGERS HERE...
PIZZA
TSSS. TSSSSS. YOU HEAR THAT? THAT'S MY FINGERS.
...NO, I DON'T KNOW HOW FAR SHE'LL GO. YOU'LL HAVE TO TALK TO HER...
MY ADVICE: GIVE HER SOME CANDY FIRST. SHE DOESN'T EVEN REMEMBER AFTER. S' GREAT.

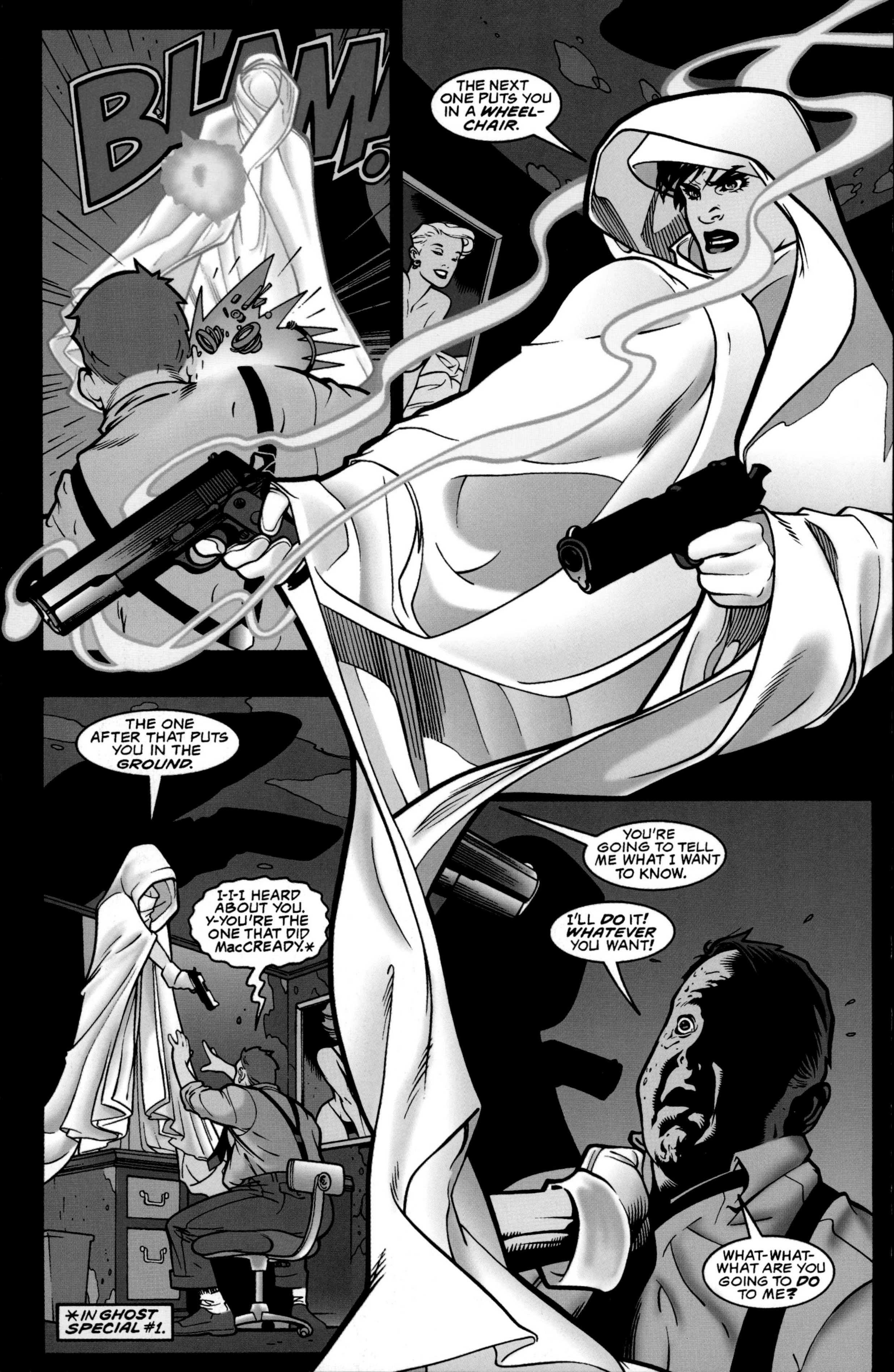
BLAM!
THE NEXT ONE PUTS YOU IN A WHEEL-CHAIR.
THE ONE AFTER THAT PUTS YOU IN THE GROUND.
I-I-I HEARD ABOUT YOU. Y-YOU'RE THE ONE THAT DID MacCREADY.*
YOU'RE GOING TO TELL ME WHAT I WANT TO KNOW.
I'LL DO IT! WHATEVER YOU WANT!
WHAT-WHAT-WHAT ARE YOU GOING TO DO TO ME?
*IN GHOST SPECIAL #1.

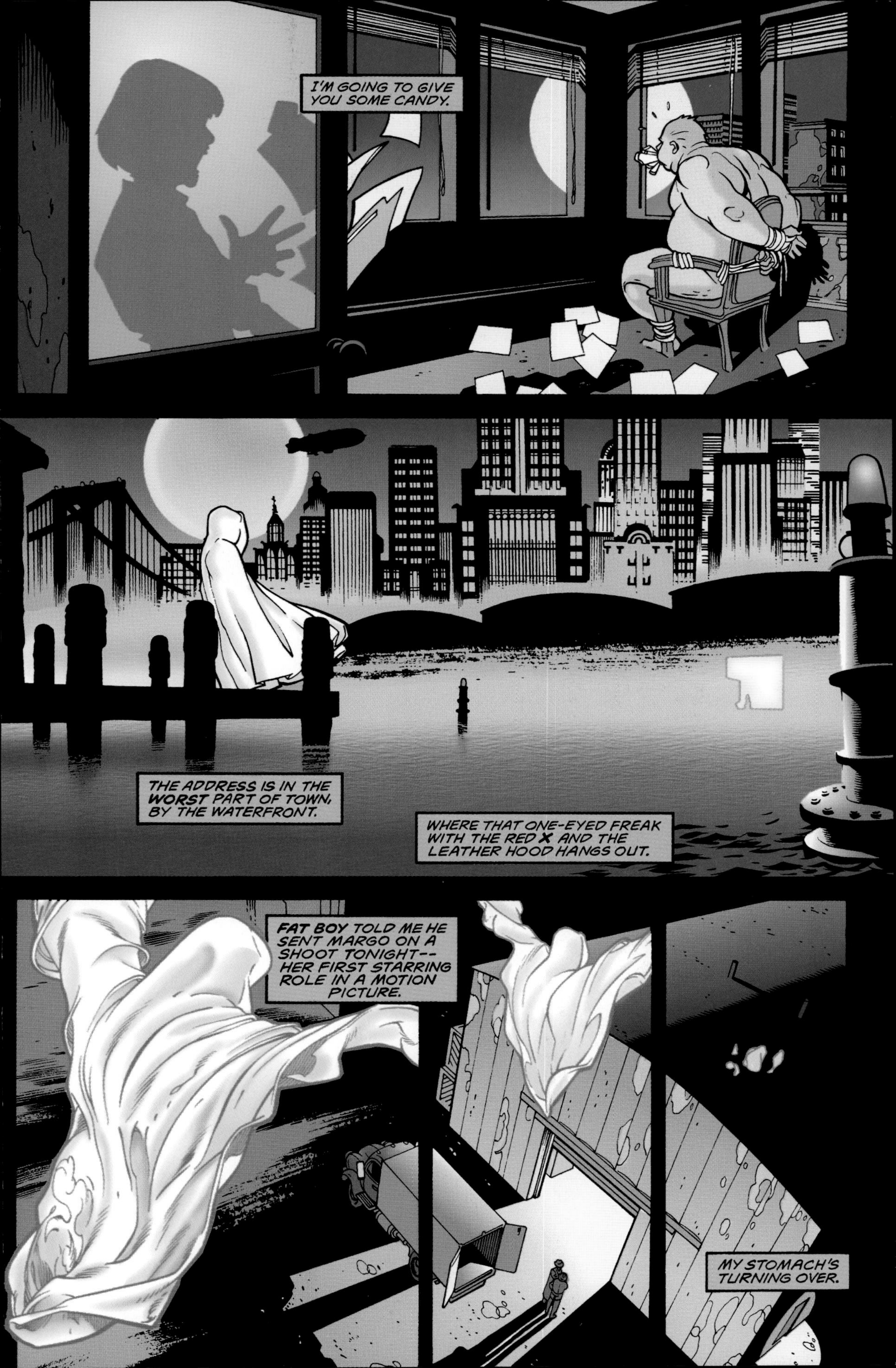
I'M GOING TO GIVE YOU SOME CANDY.
THE ADDRESS IS IN THE WORST PART OF TOWN, BY THE WATERFRONT.
WHERE THAT ONE-EYED FREAK WITH THE RED X AND THE LEATHER HOOD HANGS OUT.
FAT BOY TOLD ME HE SENT MARGO ON A SHOOT TONIGHT-- HER FIRST STARRING ROLE IN A MOTION PICTURE.
MY STOMACH'S TURNING OVER.

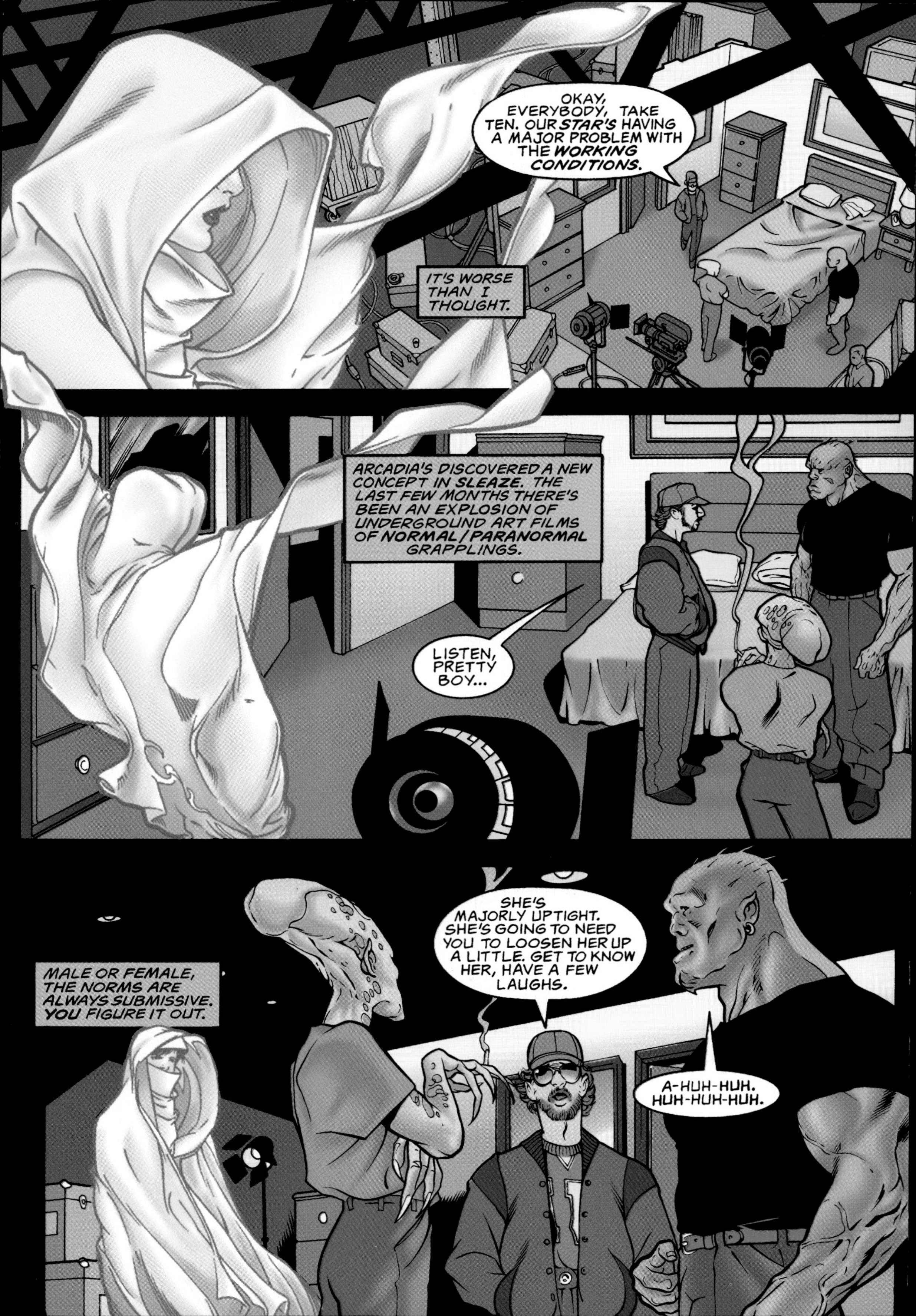
OKAY, EVERYBODY, TAKE TEN. OUR STAR'S HAVING A MAJOR PROBLEM WITH THE WORKING CONDITIONS.
IT'S WORSE THAN I THOUGHT.
ARCADIA'S DISCOVERED A NEW CONCEPT IN SLEAZE. THE LAST FEW MONTHS THERE'S BEEN AN EXPLOSION OF UNDERGROUND ART FILMS OF NORMAL/PARANORMAL GRAPPLINGS.
LISTEN, PRETTY BOY...
MALE OR FEMALE, THE NORMS ARE ALWAYS SUBMISSIVE. YOU FIGURE IT OUT.
SHE'S MAJORLY UPTIGHT. SHE'S GOING TO NEED YOU TO LOOSEN HER UP A LITTLE. GET TO KNOW HER, HAVE A FEW LAUGHS.
A-HUH-HUH. HUH-HUH-HUH.

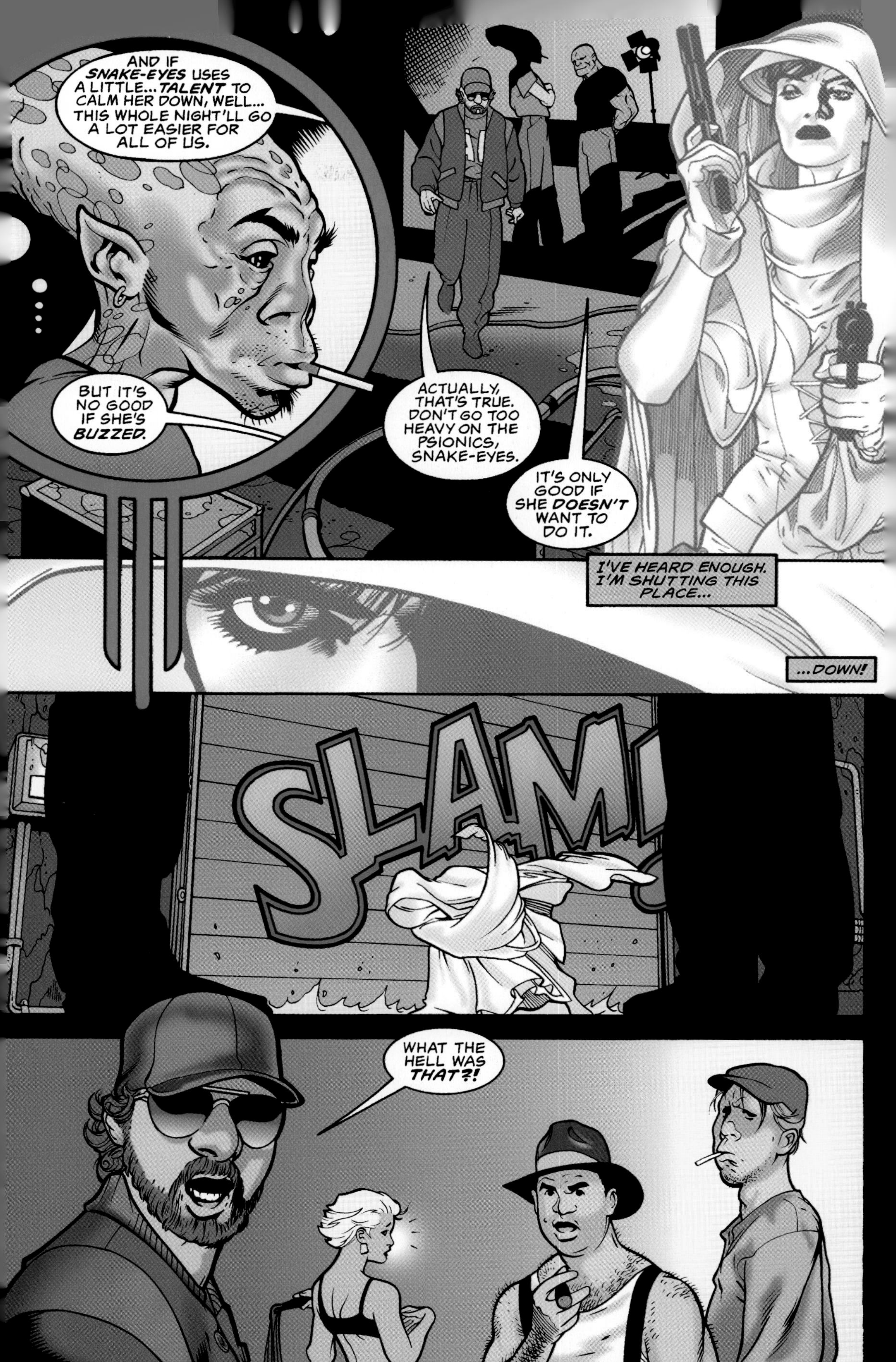

AND IF SNAKE-EYES USES A LITTLE... TALENT TO CALM HER DOWN, WELL... THIS WHOLE NIGHT'LL GO A LOT EASIER FOR ALL OF US.
BUT IT'S NO GOOD IF SHE'S BUZZED.
ACTUALLY, THAT'S TRUE. DON'T GO TOO HEAVY ON THE PSIONICS, SNAKE-EYES.
IT'S ONLY GOOD IF SHE DOESN'T WANT TO DO IT.
I'VE HEARD ENOUGH. I'M SHUTTING THIS PLACE...
...DOWN!
SLAM!
WHAT THE HELL WAS THAT?!

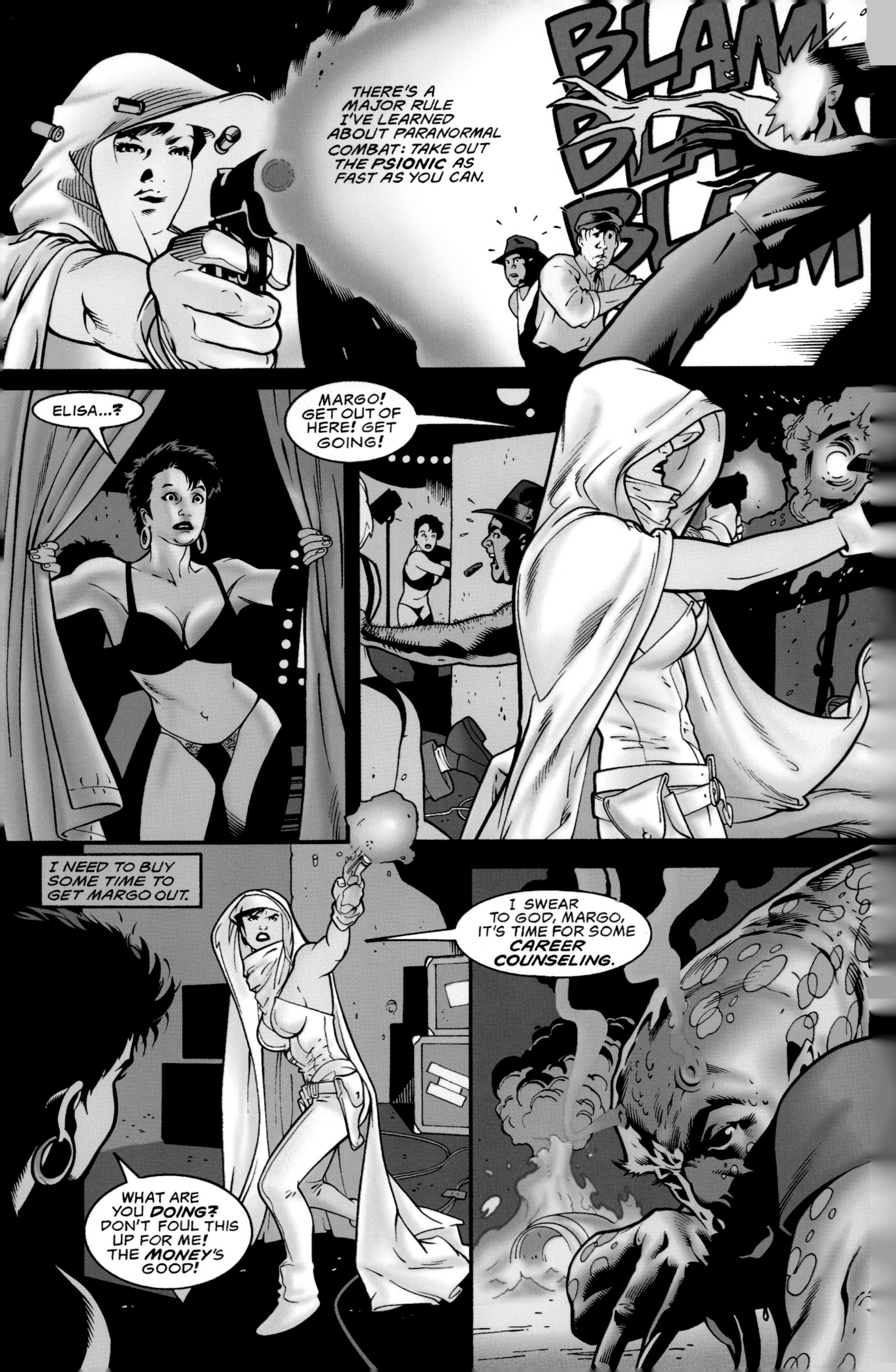
THERE'S A MAJOR RULE I'VE LEARNED ABOUT PARANORMAL COMBAT: TAKE OUT THE PSIONIC AS FAST AS YOU CAN.
BLAM
BLAM
BLAM
ELISA...?
MARGO! GET OUT OF HERE! GET GOING!
I NEED TO BUY SOME TIME TO GET MARGO OUT.
WHAT ARE YOU DOING? DON'T FOUL THIS UP FOR ME! THE MONEY'S GOOD!
I SWEAR TO GOD, MARGO, IT'S TIME FOR SOME CAREER COUNSELING.

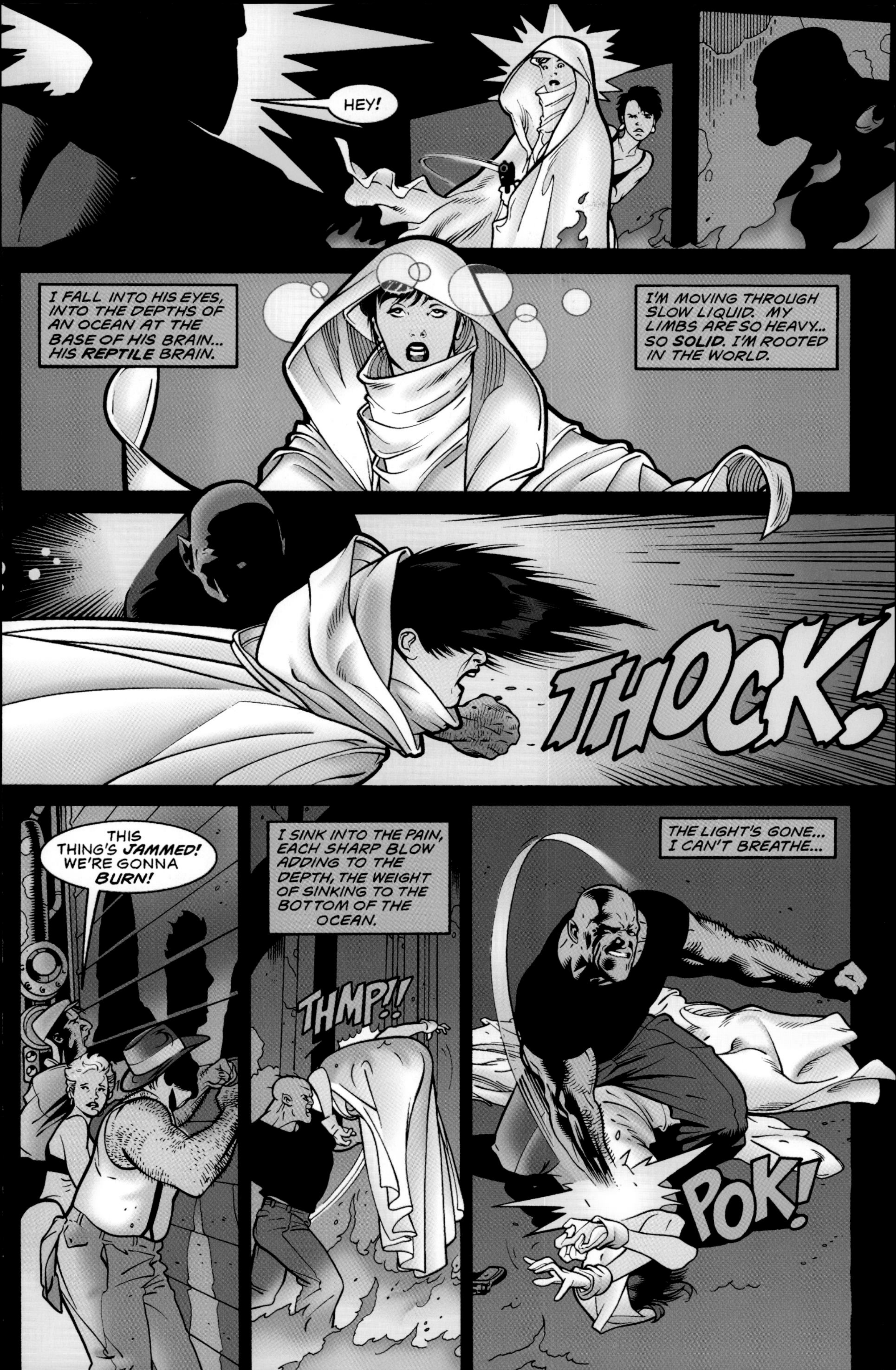

HEY!
I FALL INTO HIS EYES, INTO THE DEPTHS OF AN OCEAN AT THE BASE OF HIS BRAIN... HIS REPTILE BRAIN.
I'M MOVING THROUGH SLOW LIQUID. MY LIMBS ARE SO HEAVY... SO SOLID. I'M ROOTED IN THE WORLD.
THOCK!
THIS THING'S JAMMED! WE'RE GONNA BURN!
I SINK INTO THE PAIN, EACH SHARP BLOW ADDING TO THE DEPTH, THE WEIGHT OF SINKING TO THE BOTTOM OF THE OCEAN.
THMP!!
THE LIGHT'S GONE... I CAN'T BREATHE...
POK!

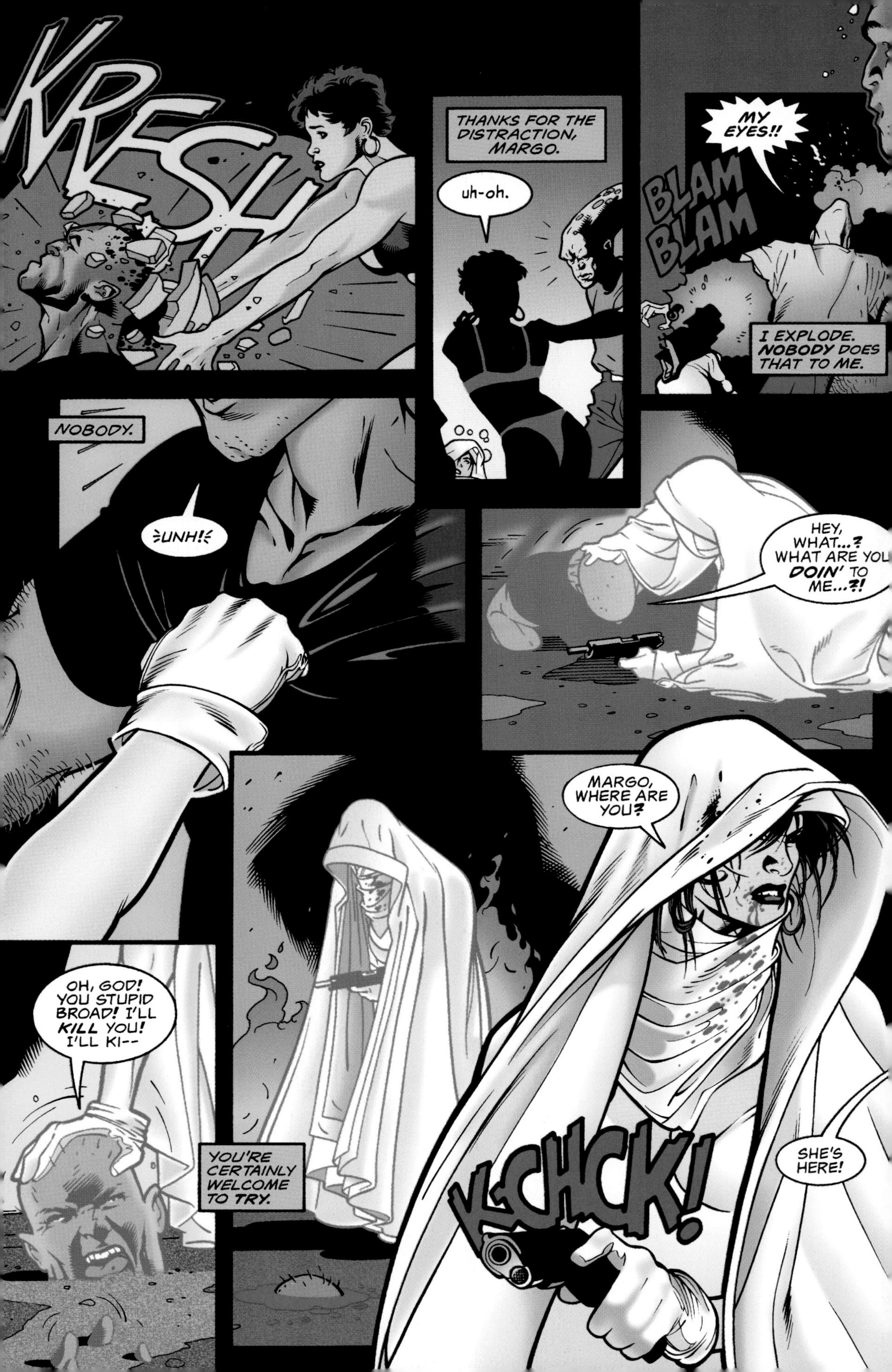
KRESH
THANKS FOR THE DISTRACTION, MARGO.
uh-oh.
MY EYES!!
BLAM BLAM
I EXPLODE. NOBODY DOES THAT TO ME.
NOBODY.
UNH!
HEY, WHAT...? WHAT ARE YOU DOIN' TO ME...?!
MARGO, WHERE ARE YOU?
OH, GOD! YOU STUPID BROAD! I'LL KILL YOU! I'LL KI--
YOU'RE CERTAINLY WELCOME TO TRY.
KLCHCK!
SHE'S HERE!

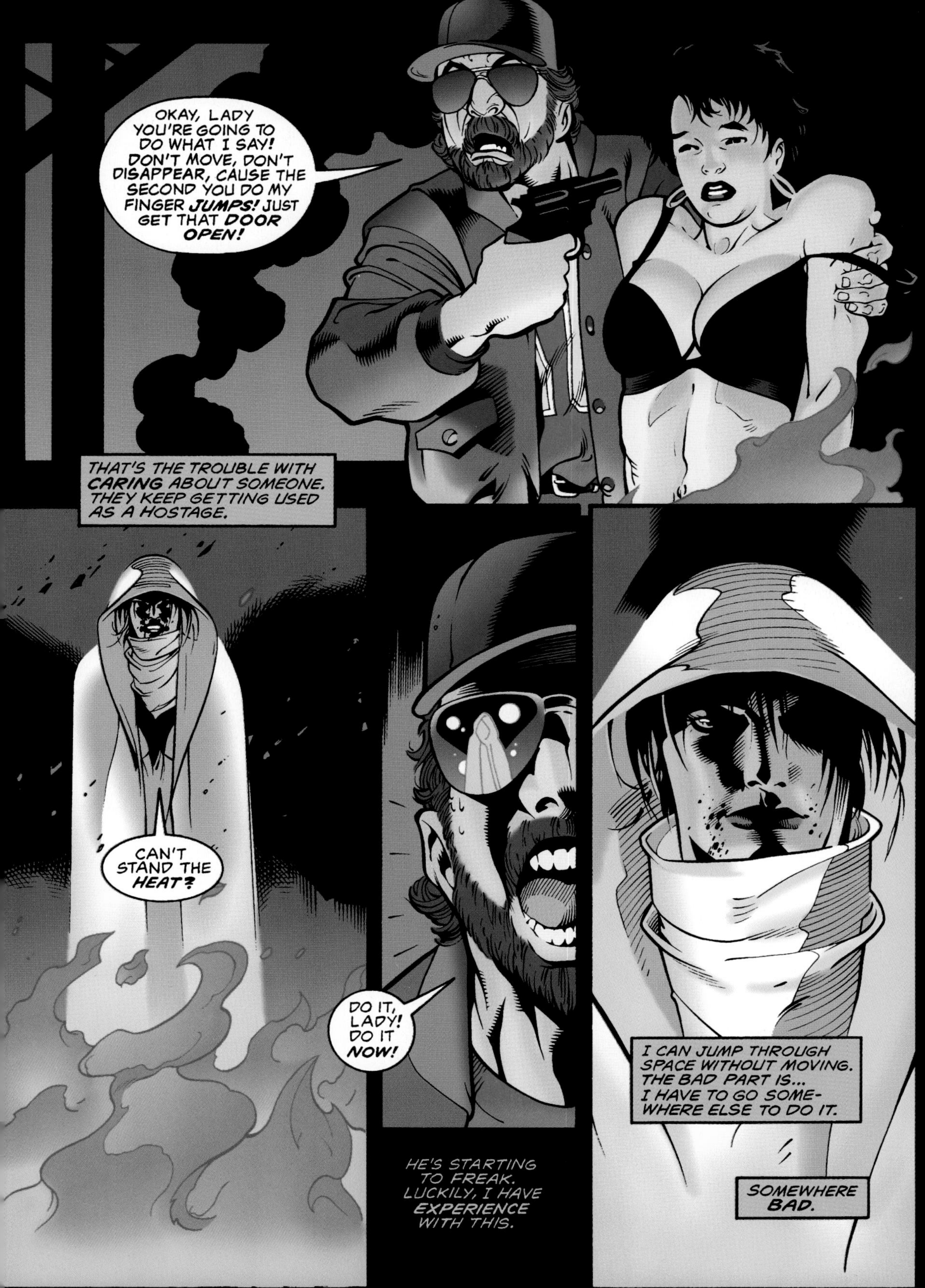

OKAY, LADY YOU'RE GOING TO DO WHAT I SAY! DON'T MOVE, DON'T DISAPPEAR, CAUSE THE SECOND YOU DO MY FINGER JUMPS! JUST GET THAT DOOR OPEN!
THAT'S THE TROUBLE WITH CARING ABOUT SOMEONE. THEY KEEP GETTING USED AS A HOSTAGE.
CAN'T STAND THE HEAT?
DO IT, LADY! DO IT NOW!
HE'S STARTING TO FREAK. LUCKILY, I HAVE EXPERIENCE WITH THIS.
I CAN JUMP THROUGH SPACE WITHOUT MOVING. THE BAD PART IS... I HAVE TO GO SOME-WHERE ELSE TO DO IT.
SOMEWHERE BAD.

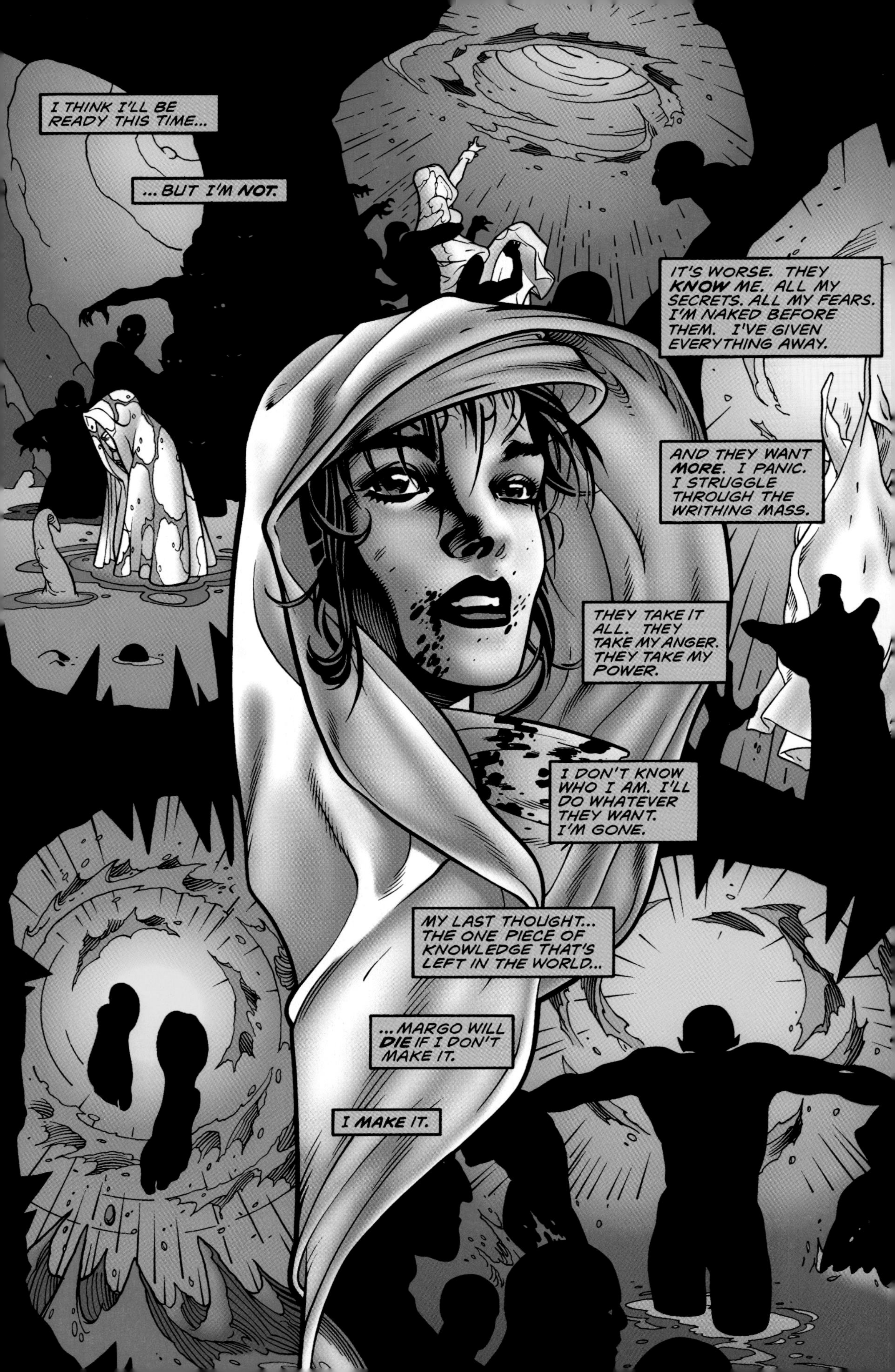

I THINK I'LL BE READY THIS TIME...
...BUT I'M **NOT.**
IT'S WORSE. THEY **KNOW ME**. ALL MY SECRETS. ALL MY FEARS. I'M NAKED BEFORE THEM. I'VE GIVEN EVERYTHING AWAY.
AND THEY WANT **MORE**. I PANIC. I STRUGGLE THROUGH THE WRITHING MASS.
THEY TAKE IT ALL. THEY TAKE MY ANGER. THEY TAKE MY POWER.
I DON'T KNOW WHO I AM. I'LL DO WHATEVER THEY WANT. I'M GONE.
MY LAST THOUGHT... THE ONE PIECE OF KNOWLEDGE THAT'S LEFT IN THE WORLD...
...MARGO WILL **DIE** IF I DON'T MAKE IT.
I **MAKE** IT.

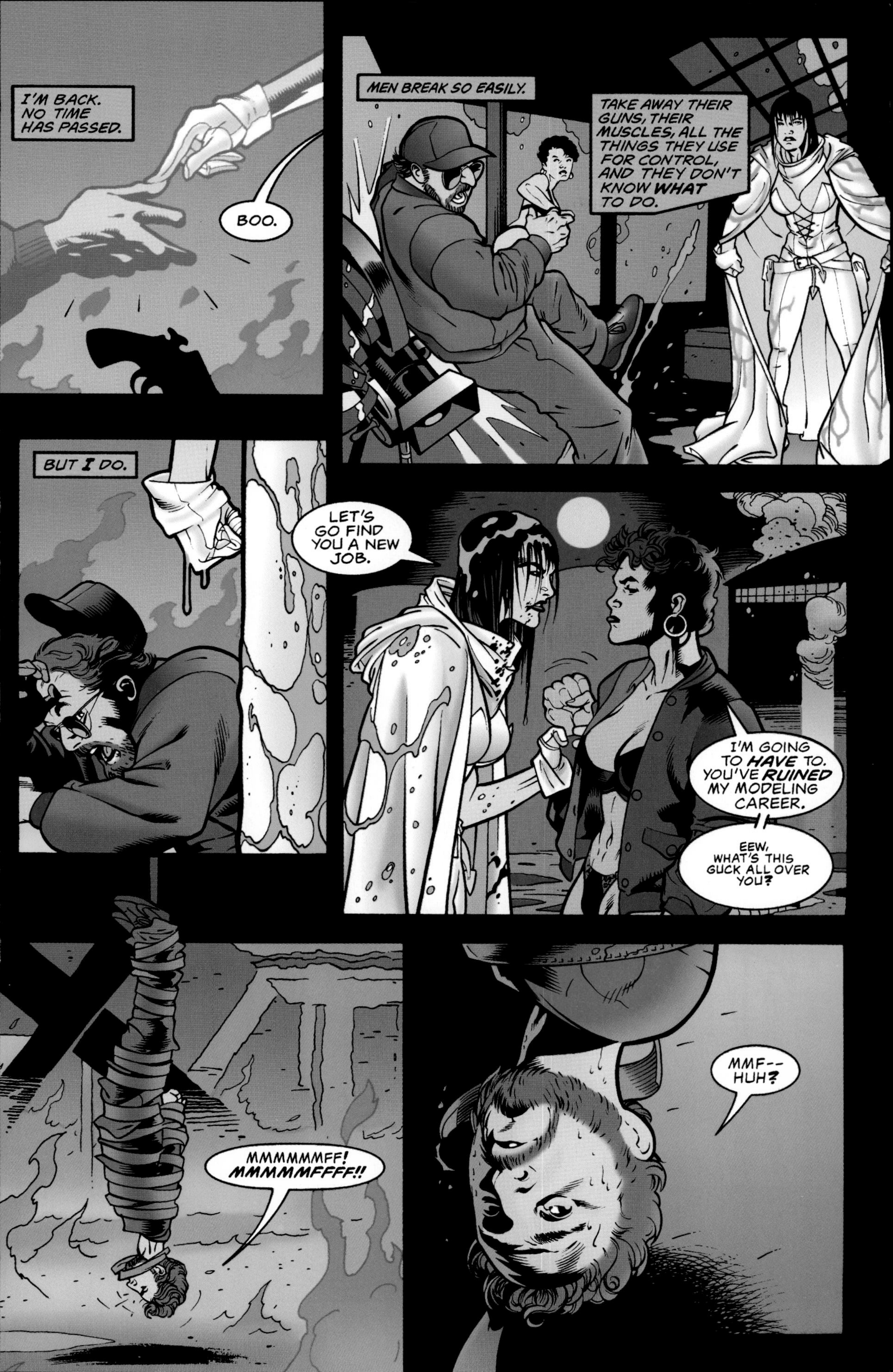
I'M BACK. NO TIME HAS PASSED.
BOO.
MEN BREAK SO EASILY.
TAKE AWAY THEIR GUNS, THEIR MUSCLES, ALL THE THINGS THEY USE FOR CONTROL, AND THEY DON'T KNOW **WHAT** TO DO.
BUT **I** DO.
LET'S GO FIND YOU A NEW JOB.
I'M GOING TO **HAVE** TO. YOU'VE **RUINED** MY MODELING CAREER.
EEW, WHAT'S THIS GUCK ALL OVER YOU?
MMMMMMFF! **MMMMMFFFF!!**
MMF-- HUH?

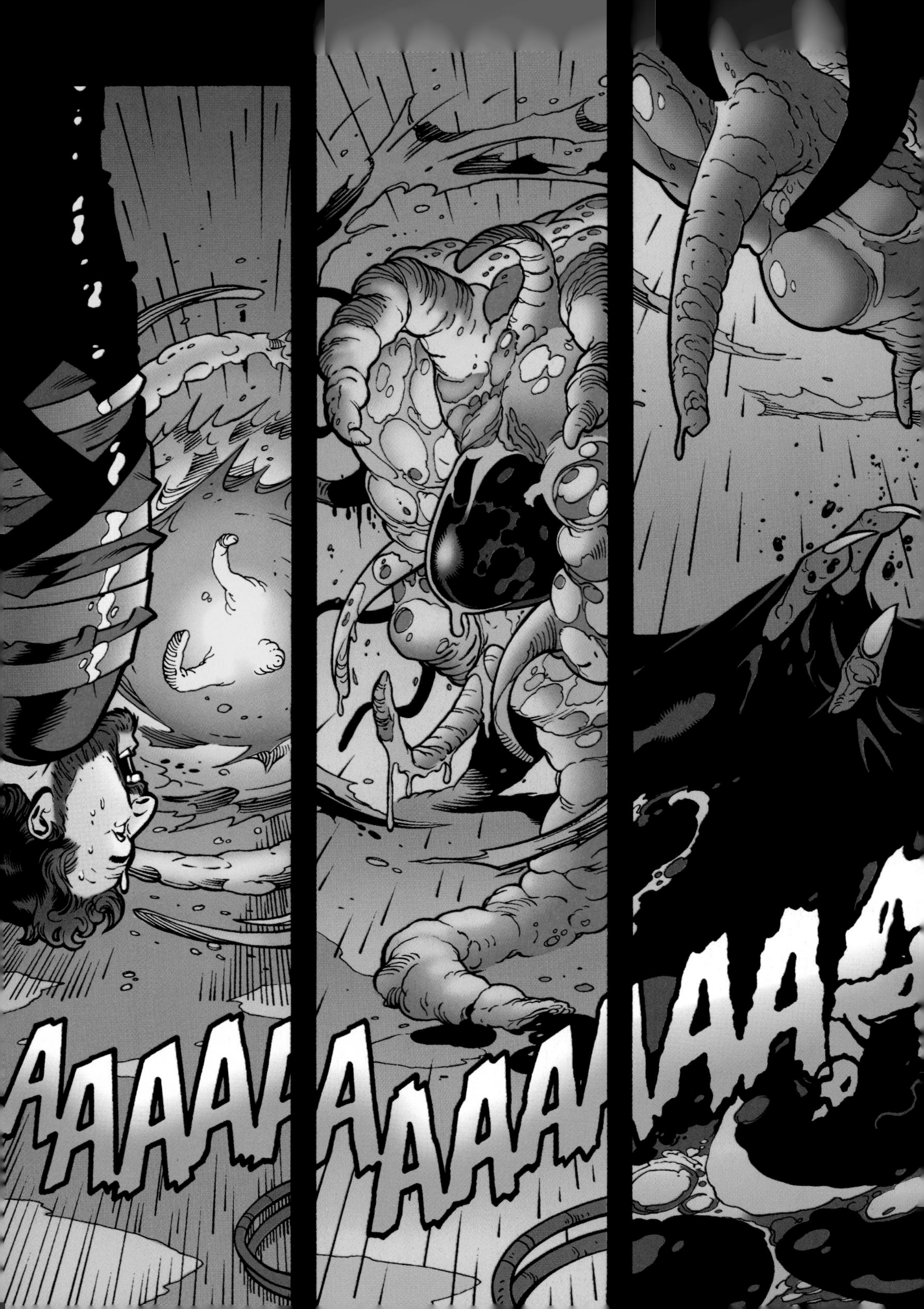
AAAAAAAAAAAA

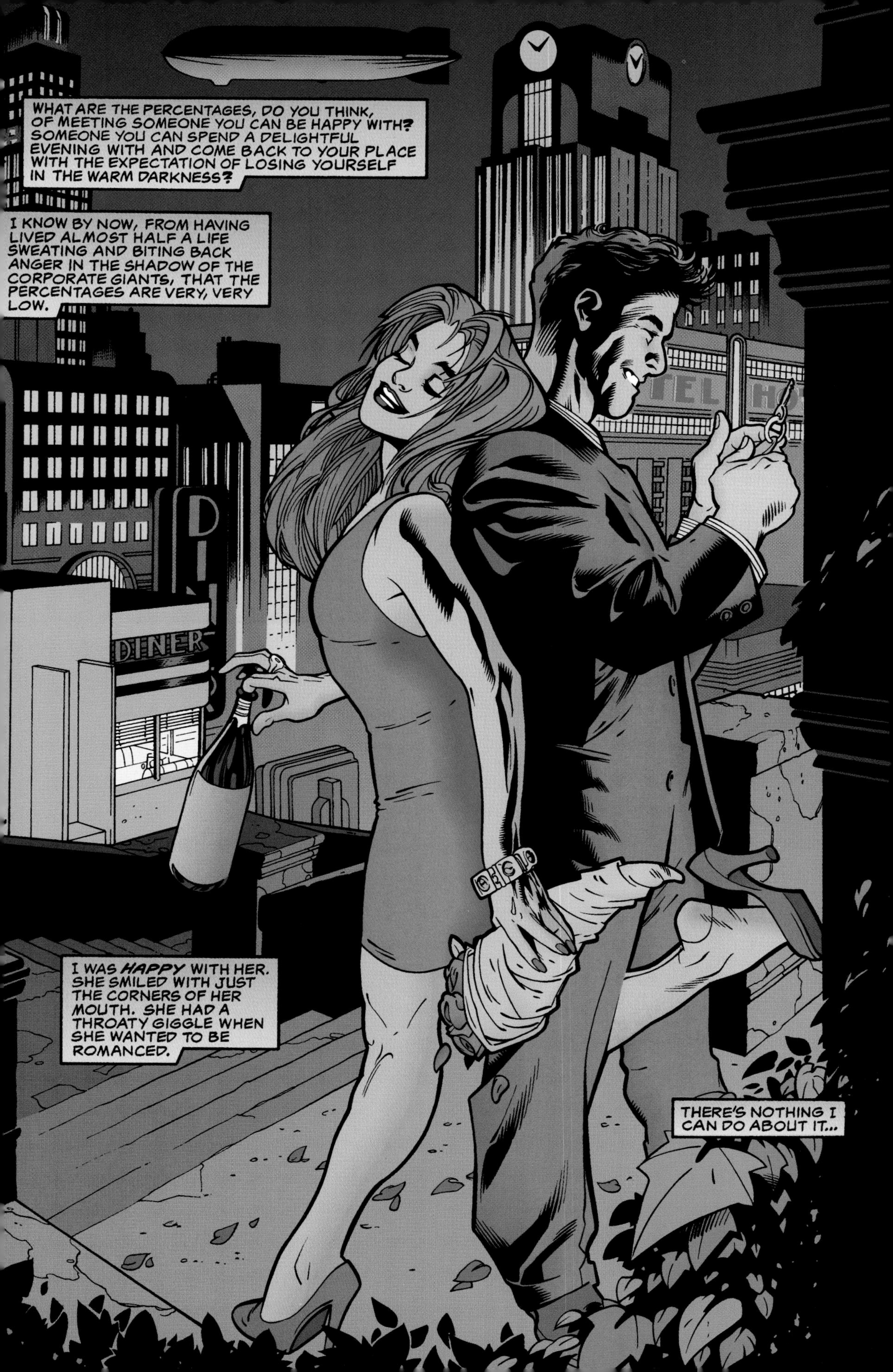
WHAT ARE THE PERCENTAGES, DO YOU THINK, OF MEETING SOMEONE YOU CAN BE HAPPY WITH? SOMEONE YOU CAN SPEND A DELIGHTFUL EVENING WITH AND COME BACK TO YOUR PLACE WITH THE EXPECTATION OF LOSING YOURSELF IN THE WARM DARKNESS?
I KNOW BY NOW, FROM HAVING LIVED ALMOST HALF A LIFE SWEATING AND BITING BACK ANGER IN THE SHADOW OF THE CORPORATE GIANTS, THAT THE PERCENTAGES ARE VERY, VERY LOW.
DINER
I WAS *HAPPY* WITH HER. SHE SMILED WITH JUST THE CORNERS OF HER MOUTH. SHE HAD A THROATY GIGGLE WHEN SHE WANTED TO BE ROMANCED.
THERE'S NOTHING I CAN DO ABOUT IT...

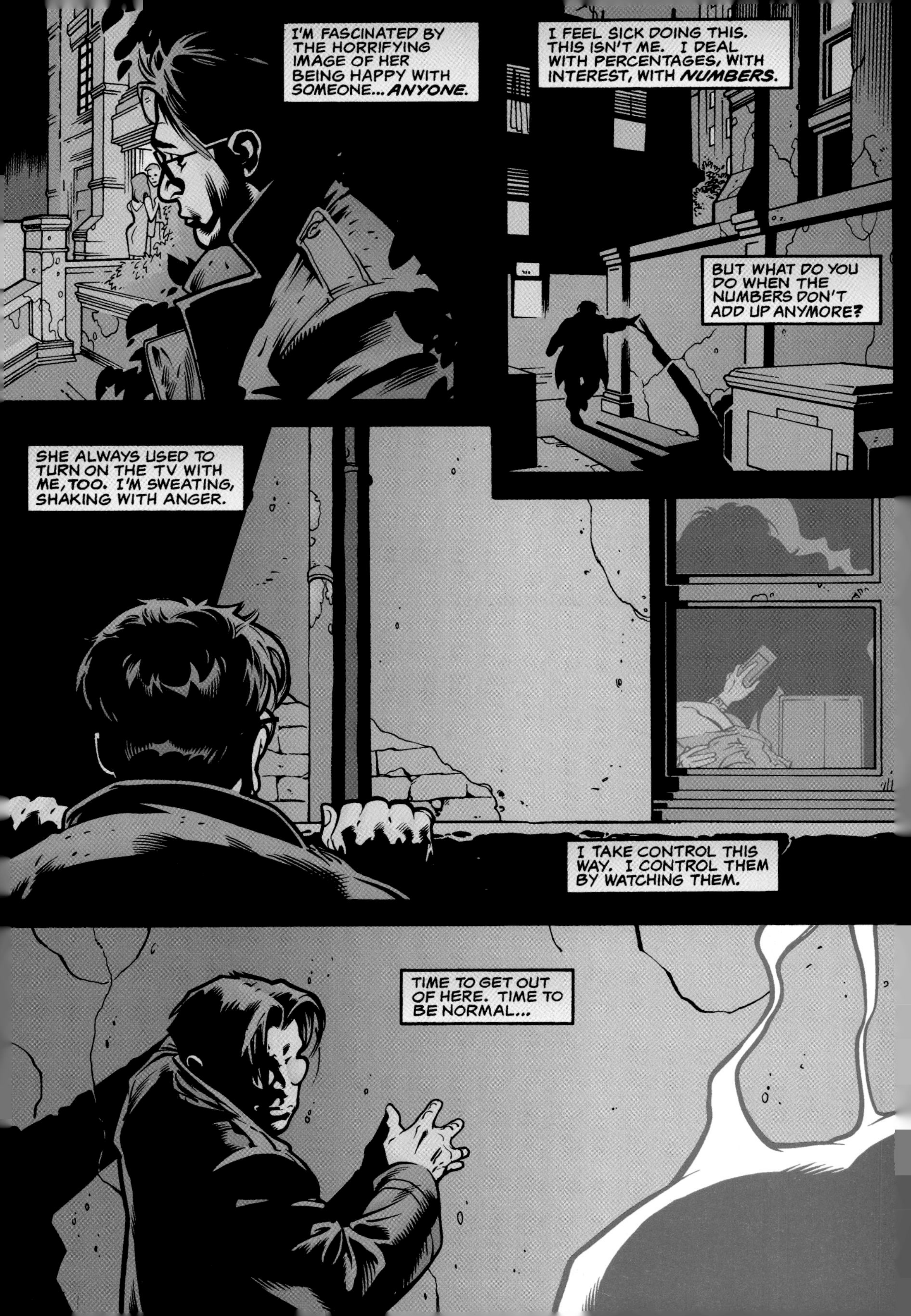
I'M FASCINATED BY THE HORRIFYING IMAGE OF HER BEING HAPPY WITH SOMEONE... ANYONE.
I FEEL SICK DOING THIS. THIS ISN'T ME. I DEAL WITH PERCENTAGES, WITH INTEREST, WITH NUMBERS.
BUT WHAT DO YOU DO WHEN THE NUMBERS DON'T ADD UP ANYMORE?
SHE ALWAYS USED TO TURN ON THE TV WITH ME, TOO. I'M SWEATING, SHAKING WITH ANGER.
I TAKE CONTROL THIS WAY. I CONTROL THEM BY WATCHING THEM.
TIME TO GET OUT OF HERE. TIME TO BE NORMAL...

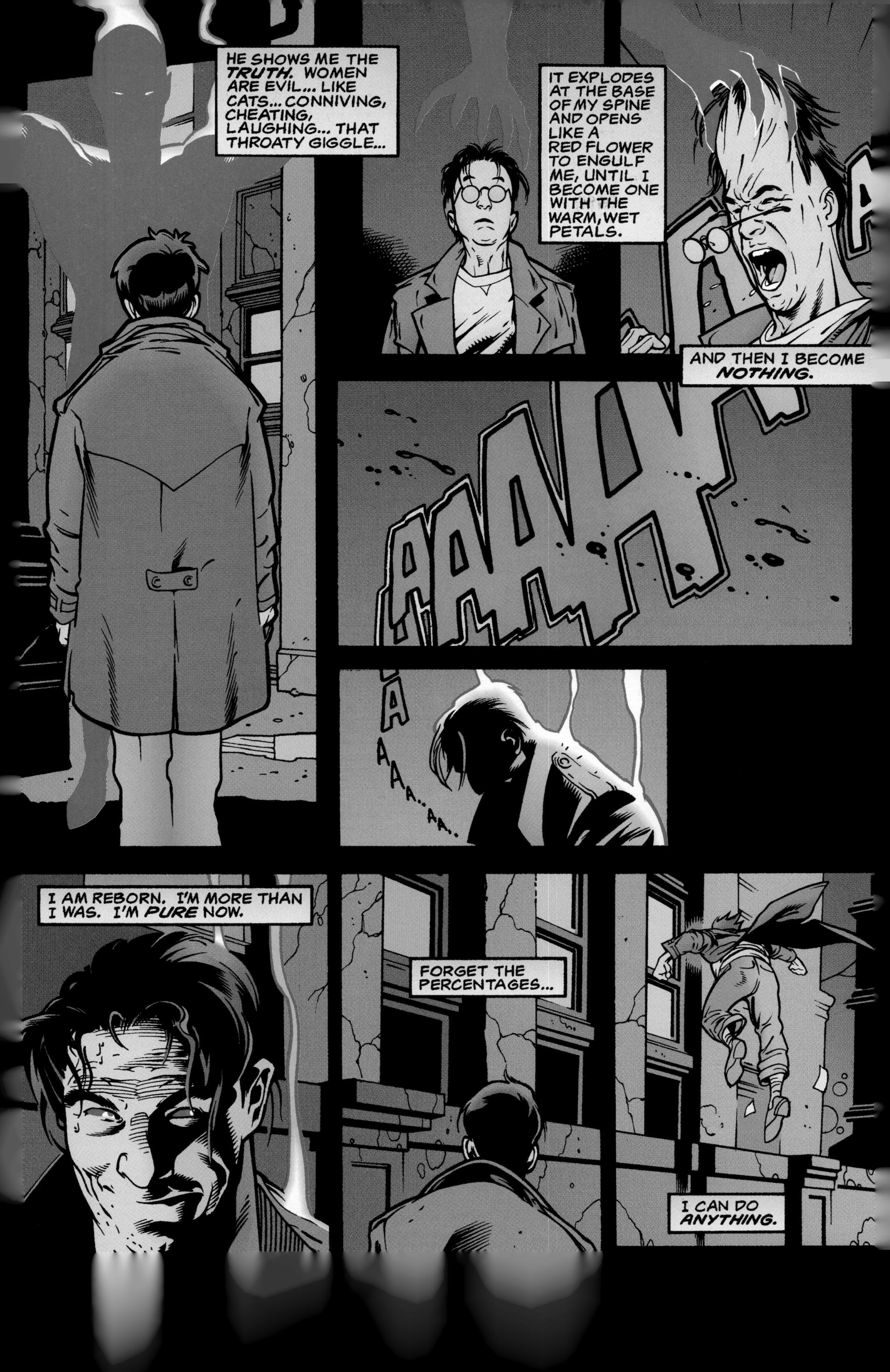
HE SHOWS ME THE TRUTH. WOMEN ARE EVIL... LIKE CATS... CONNIVING, CHEATING, LAUGHING... THAT THROATY GIGGLE...
IT EXPLODES AT THE BASE OF MY SPINE AND OPENS LIKE A RED FLOWER TO ENGULF ME, UNTIL I BECOME ONE WITH THE WARM, WET PETALS.
AND THEN I BECOME NOTHING.
AAAAH
AAAA...AA...
I AM REBORN. I'M MORE THAN I WAS. I'M PURE NOW.
FORGET THE PERCENTAGES...
I CAN DO ANYTHING.

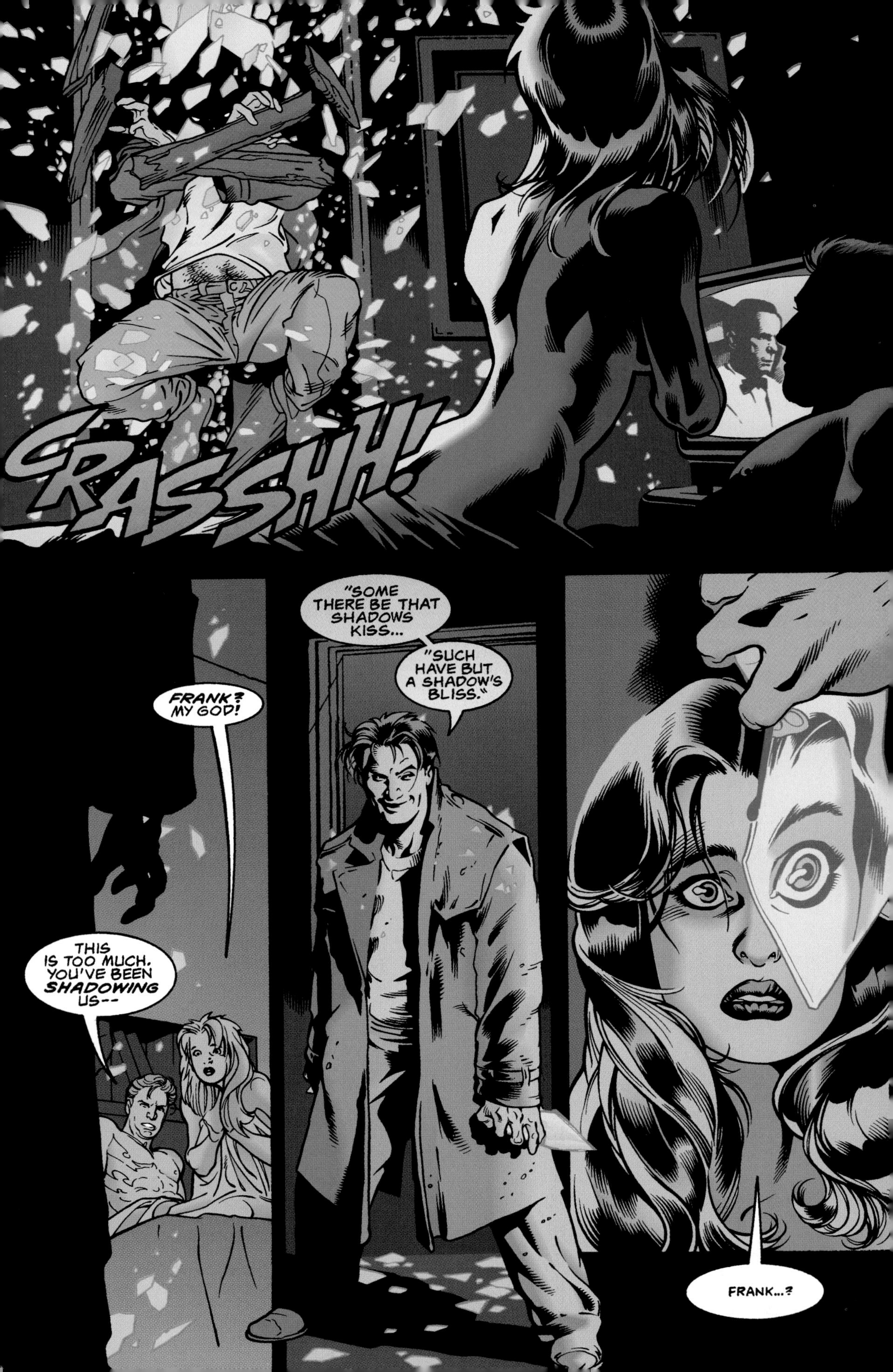
CRASSHH!
"SOME THERE BE THAT SHADOWS KISS...
"SUCH HAVE BUT A SHADOW'S BLISS."
FRANK? MY GOD!
THIS IS TOO MUCH. YOU'VE BEEN SHADOWING US--
FRANK...?

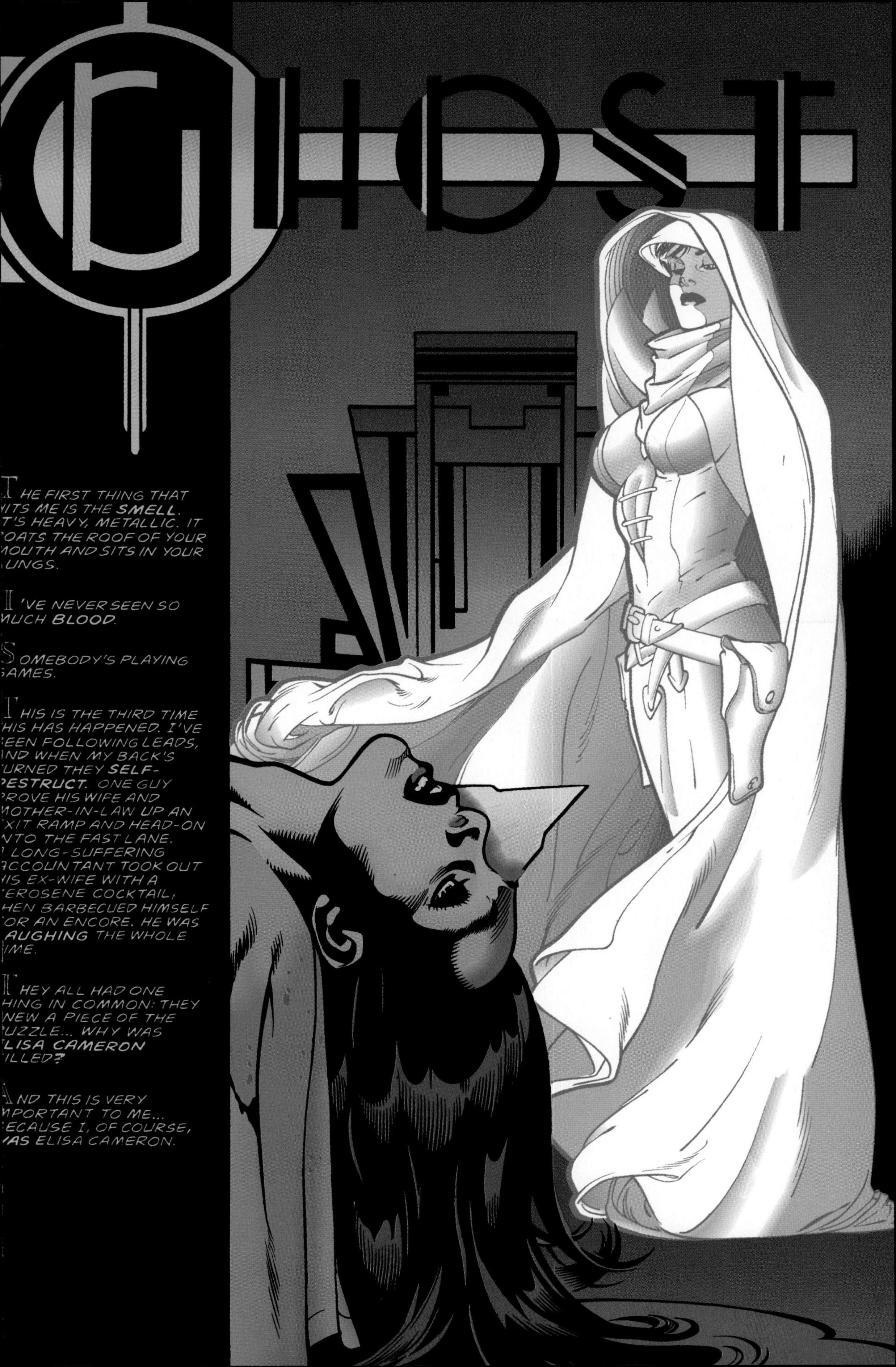
GHOST
THE FIRST THING THAT HITS ME IS THE SMELL. IT'S HEAVY, METALLIC. IT COATS THE ROOF OF YOUR MOUTH AND SITS IN YOUR LUNGS.
I'VE NEVER SEEN SO MUCH BLOOD.
SOMEBODY'S PLAYING GAMES.
THIS IS THE THIRD TIME THIS HAS HAPPENED. I'VE BEEN FOLLOWING LEADS, AND WHEN MY BACK'S TURNED THEY SELF-DESTRUCT. ONE GUY DROVE HIS WIFE AND MOTHER-IN-LAW UP AN EXIT RAMP AND HEAD-ON INTO THE FAST LANE. A LONG-SUFFERING ACCOUNTANT TOOK OUT HIS EX-WIFE WITH A KEROSENE COCKTAIL, THEN BARBECUED HIMSELF FOR AN ENCORE. HE WAS LAUGHING THE WHOLE TIME.
THEY ALL HAD ONE THING IN COMMON: THEY KNEW A PIECE OF THE PUZZLE... WHY WAS ELISA CAMERON KILLED?
AND THIS IS VERY IMPORTANT TO ME... BECAUSE I, OF COURSE, WAS ELISA CAMERON.

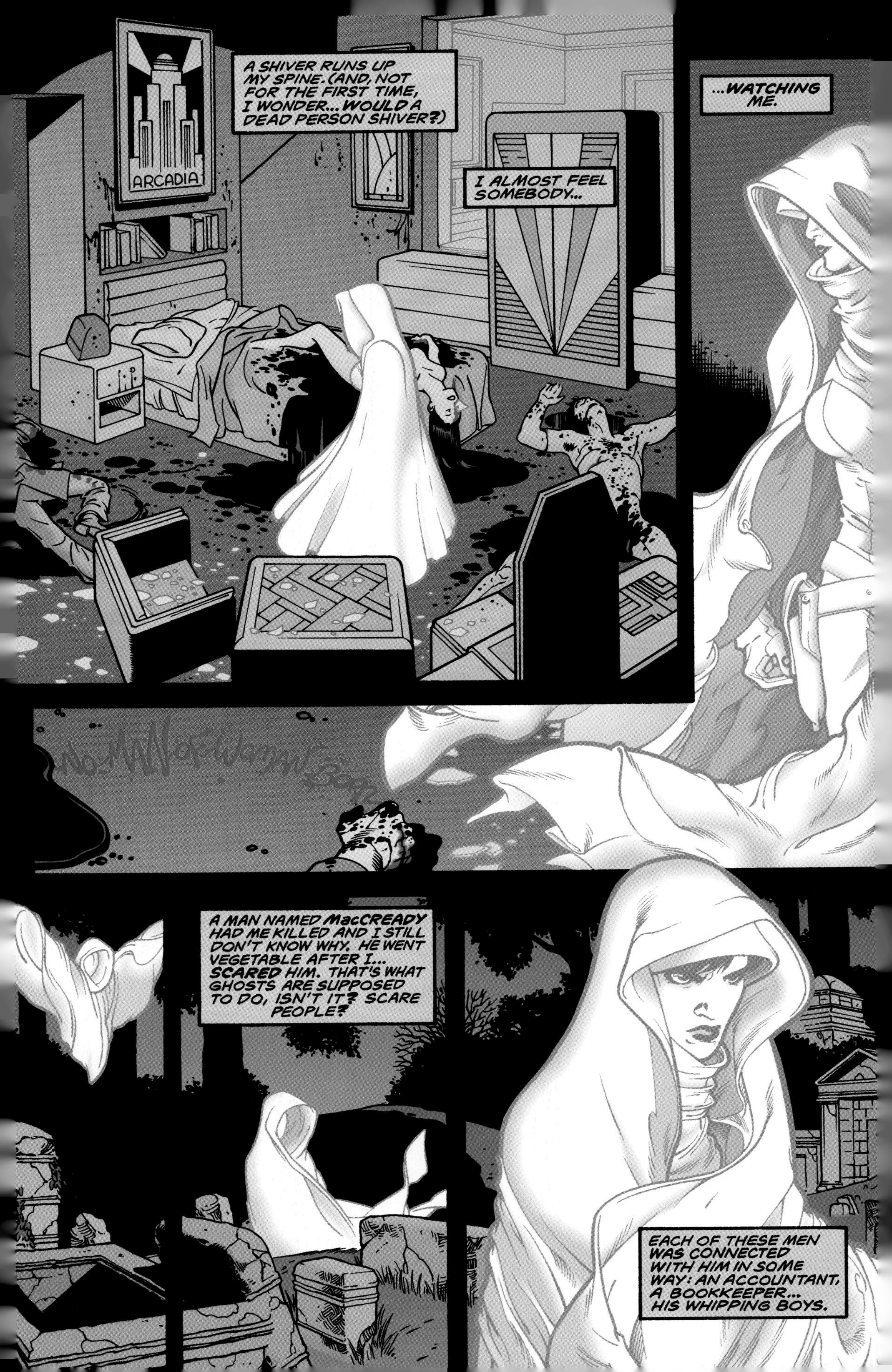
A SHIVER RUNS UP MY SPINE. (AND, NOT FOR THE FIRST TIME, I WONDER... WOULD A DEAD PERSON SHIVER?)
ARCADIA
I ALMOST FEEL SOMEBODY...
...WATCHING ME.
NO MAN OF WOMAN BORN
A MAN NAMED MacCREADY HAD ME KILLED AND I STILL DON'T KNOW WHY. HE WENT VEGETABLE AFTER I... SCARED HIM. THAT'S WHAT GHOSTS ARE SUPPOSED TO DO, ISN'T IT? SCARE PEOPLE?
EACH OF THESE MEN WAS CONNECTED WITH HIM IN SOME WAY: AN ACCOUNTANT, A BOOKKEEPER... HIS WHIPPING BOYS.

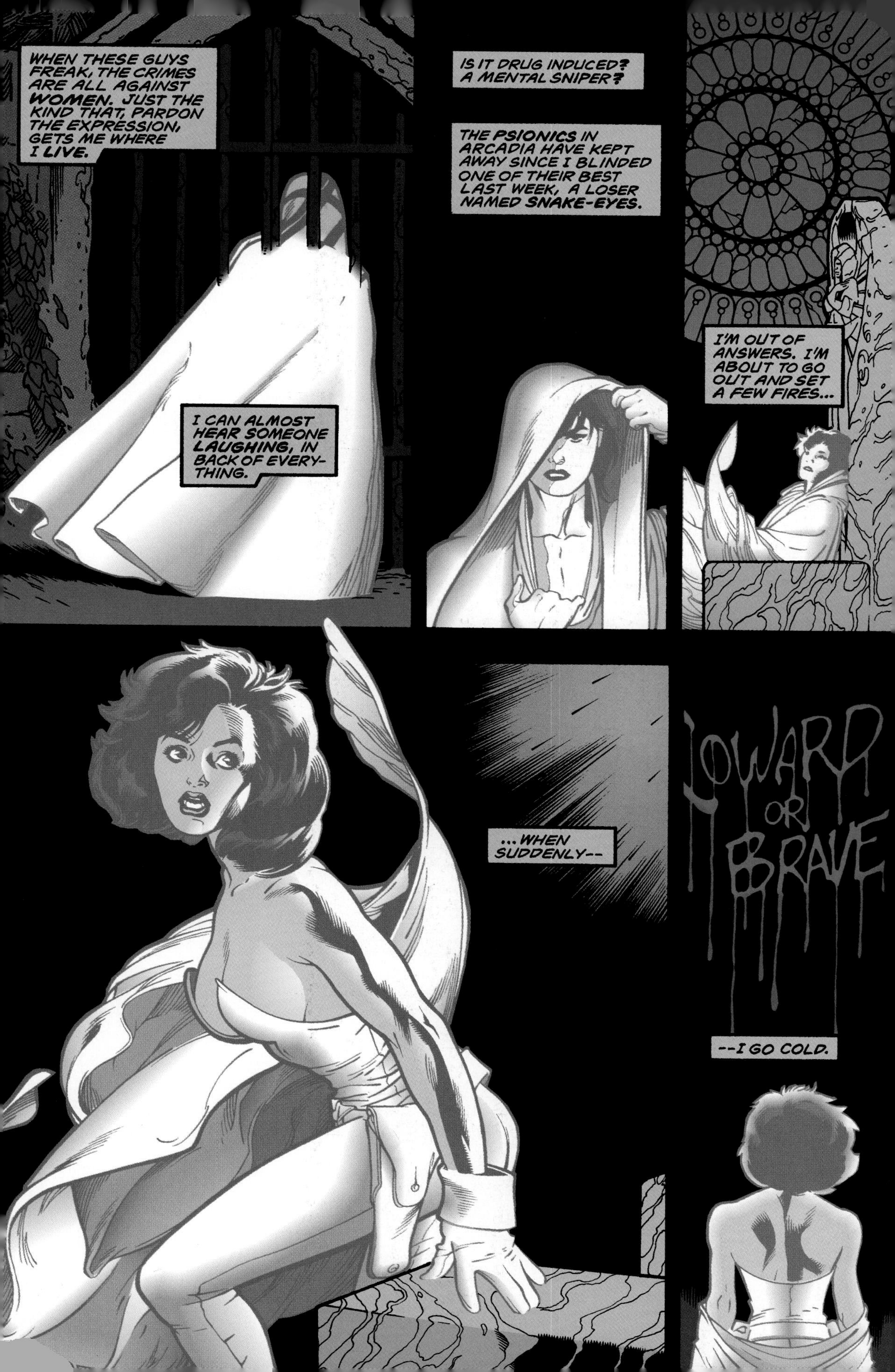

WHEN THESE GUYS FREAK, THE CRIMES ARE ALL AGAINST WOMEN. JUST THE KIND THAT, PARDON THE EXPRESSION, GETS ME WHERE I LIVE.
I CAN ALMOST HEAR SOMEONE LAUGHING, IN BACK OF EVERY-THING.
IS IT DRUG INDUCED? A MENTAL SNIPER?
THE PSIONICS IN ARCADIA HAVE KEPT AWAY SINCE I BLINDED ONE OF THEIR BEST LAST WEEK, A LOSER NAMED SNAKE-EYES.
I'M OUT OF ANSWERS. I'M ABOUT TO GO OUT AND SET A FEW FIRES...
...WHEN SUDDENLY--
COWARD OR BRAVE
--I GO COLD.

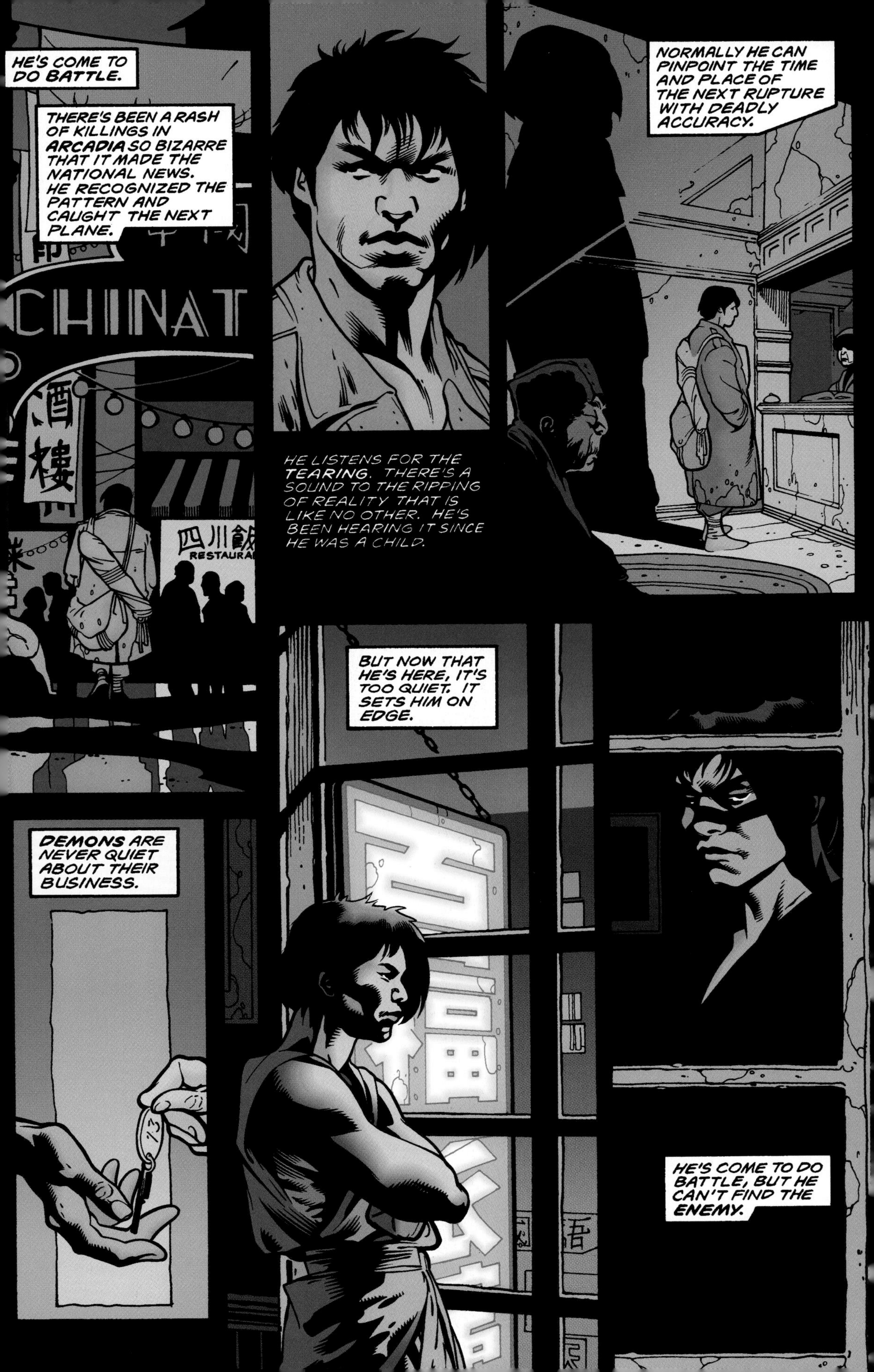
HE'S COME TO DO BATTLE.
THERE'S BEEN A RASH OF KILLINGS IN ARCADIA SO BIZARRE THAT IT MADE THE NATIONAL NEWS. HE RECOGNIZED THE PATTERN AND CAUGHT THE NEXT PLANE.
CHINAT
RESTAURA
HE LISTENS FOR THE TEARING. THERE'S A SOUND TO THE RIPPING OF REALITY THAT IS LIKE NO OTHER. HE'S BEEN HEARING IT SINCE HE WAS A CHILD.
NORMALLY HE CAN PINPOINT THE TIME AND PLACE OF THE NEXT RUPTURE WITH DEADLY ACCURACY.
BUT NOW THAT HE'S HERE, IT'S TOO QUIET. IT SETS HIM ON EDGE.
DEMONS ARE NEVER QUIET ABOUT THEIR BUSINESS.
HE'S COME TO DO BATTLE, BUT HE CAN'T FIND THE ENEMY.

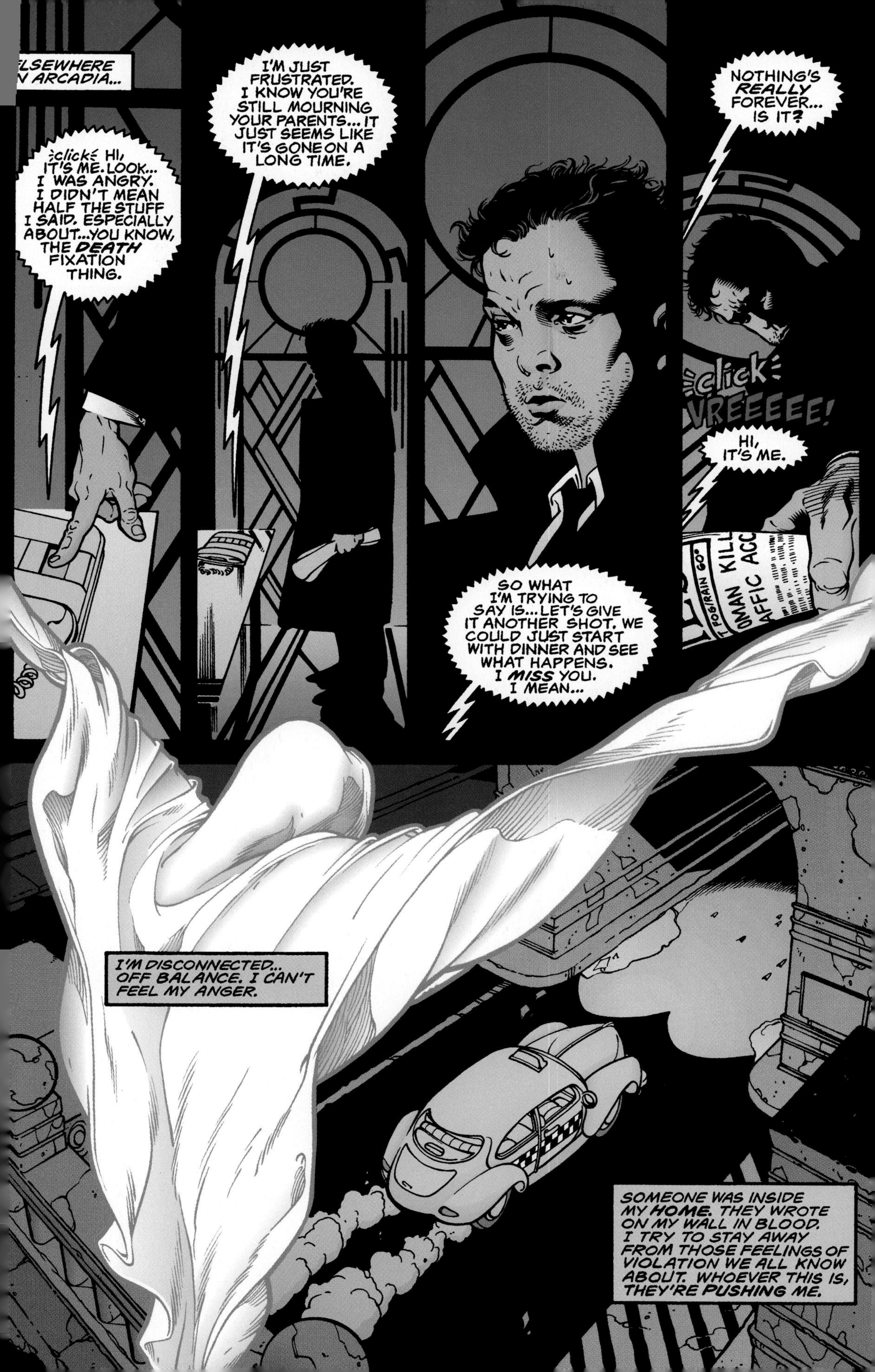
ELSEWHERE IN ARCADIA...
<click> HI, IT'S ME. LOOK... I WAS ANGRY. I DIDN'T MEAN HALF THE STUFF I SAID. ESPECIALLY ABOUT...YOU KNOW, THE DEATH FIXATION THING.
I'M JUST FRUSTRATED. I KNOW YOU'RE STILL MOURNING YOUR PARENTS... IT JUST SEEMS LIKE IT'S GONE ON A LONG TIME.
NOTHING'S REALLY FOREVER... IS IT?
click
VREEEEE!
HI, IT'S ME.
SO WHAT I'M TRYING TO SAY IS... LET'S GIVE IT ANOTHER SHOT. WE COULD JUST START WITH DINNER AND SEE WHAT HAPPENS. I MISS YOU. I MEAN...
I'M DISCONNECTED... OFF BALANCE. I CAN'T FEEL MY ANGER.
SOMEONE WAS INSIDE MY HOME. THEY WROTE ON MY WALL IN BLOOD. I TRY TO STAY AWAY FROM THOSE FEELINGS OF VIOLATION WE ALL KNOW ABOUT. WHOEVER THIS IS, THEY'RE PUSHING ME.

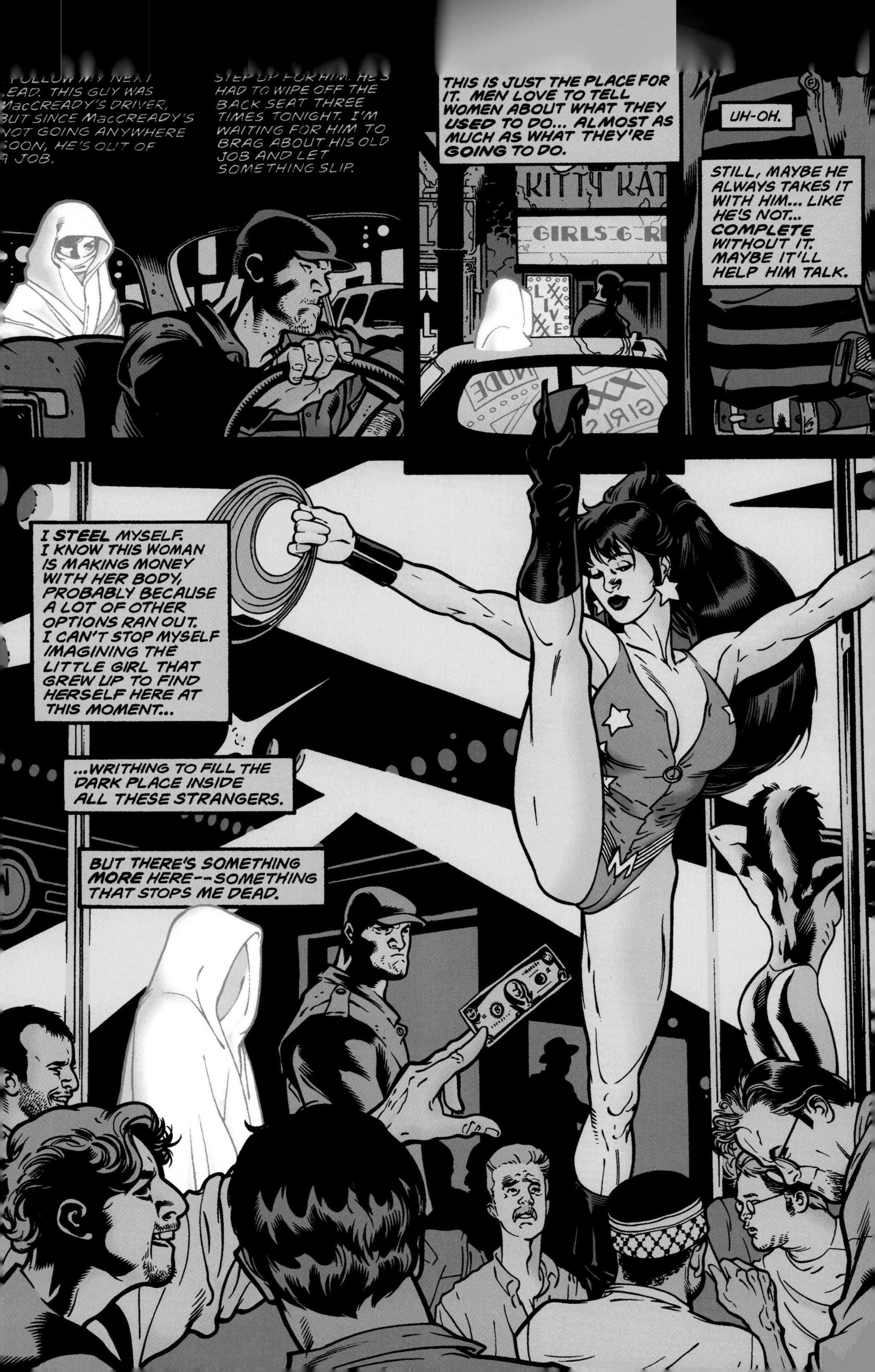

FOLLOW MY NEXT
EAD. THIS GUY WAS
MacCREADY'S DRIVER,
BUT SINCE MacCREADY'S
NOT GOING ANYWHERE
SOON, HE'S OUT OF
A JOB.
STEP UP FOR HIM. HE'S
HAD TO WIPE OFF THE
BACK SEAT THREE
TIMES TONIGHT. I'M
WAITING FOR HIM TO
BRAG ABOUT HIS OLD
JOB AND LET
SOMETHING SLIP.
THIS IS JUST THE PLACE FOR IT. MEN LOVE TO TELL WOMEN ABOUT WHAT THEY USED TO DO... ALMOST AS MUCH AS WHAT THEY'RE GOING TO DO.
KITTY KAT
GIRLS G
LIVE XXX
NUDE
XXX GIRLS
UH-OH.
STILL, MAYBE HE ALWAYS TAKES IT WITH HIM... LIKE HE'S NOT... COMPLETE WITHOUT IT. MAYBE IT'LL HELP HIM TALK.
I STEEL MYSELF. I KNOW THIS WOMAN IS MAKING MONEY WITH HER BODY, PROBABLY BECAUSE A LOT OF OTHER OPTIONS RAN OUT. I CAN'T STOP MYSELF IMAGINING THE LITTLE GIRL THAT GREW UP TO FIND HERSELF HERE AT THIS MOMENT...
...WRITHING TO FILL THE DARK PLACE INSIDE ALL THESE STRANGERS.
BUT THERE'S SOMETHING MORE HERE--SOMETHING THAT STOPS ME DEAD.

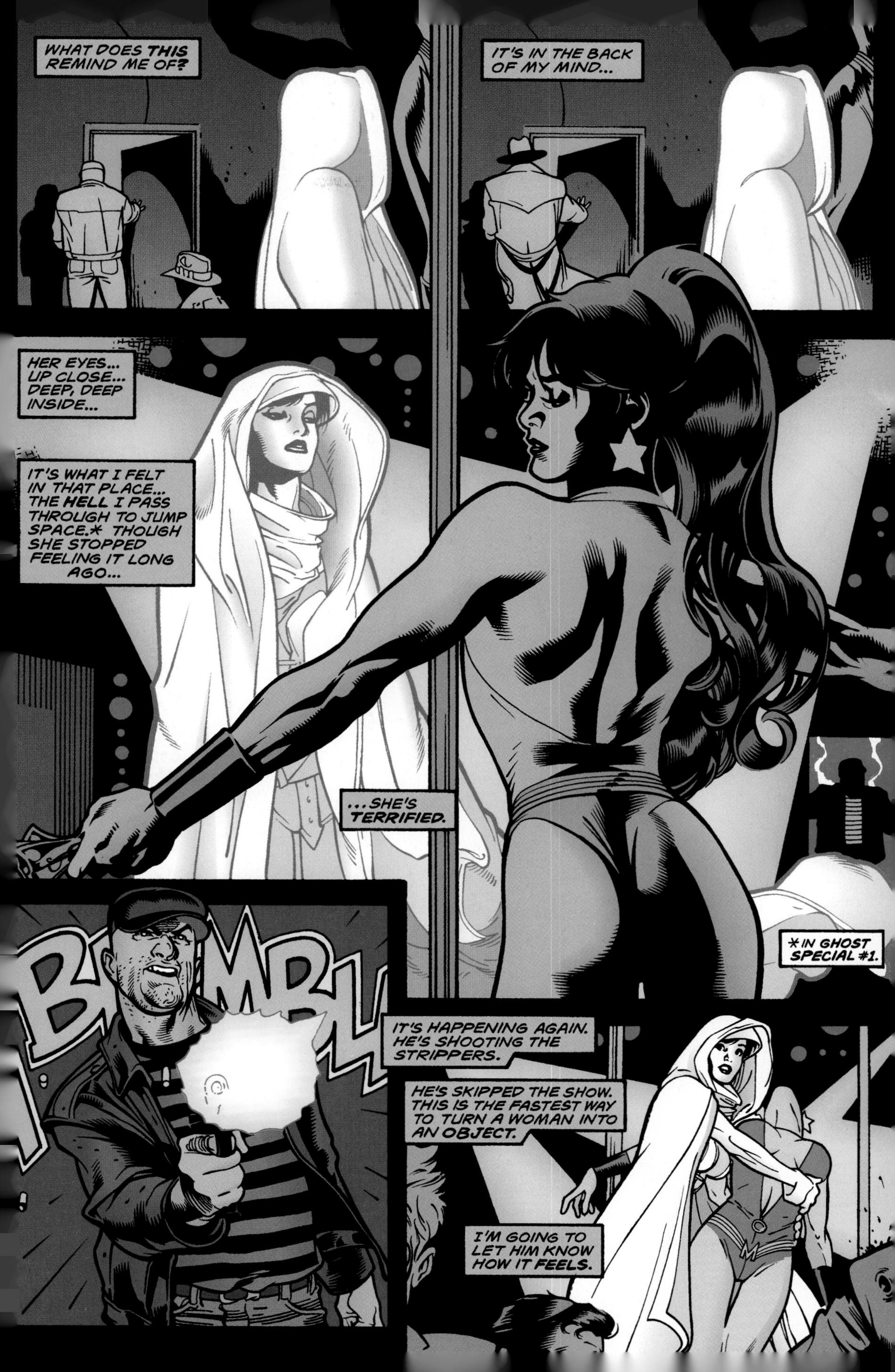
WHAT DOES THIS REMIND ME OF?
IT'S IN THE BACK OF MY MIND...
HER EYES... UP CLOSE... DEEP, DEEP INSIDE...
IT'S WHAT I FELT IN THAT PLACE... THE HELL I PASS THROUGH TO JUMP SPACE.* THOUGH SHE STOPPED FEELING IT LONG AGO...
...SHE'S TERRIFIED.
*IN GHOST SPECIAL #1.
BLAM
IT'S HAPPENING AGAIN. HE'S SHOOTING THE STRIPPERS.
HE'S SKIPPED THE SHOW. THIS IS THE FASTEST WAY TO TURN A WOMAN INTO AN OBJECT.
I'M GOING TO LET HIM KNOW HOW IT FEELS.

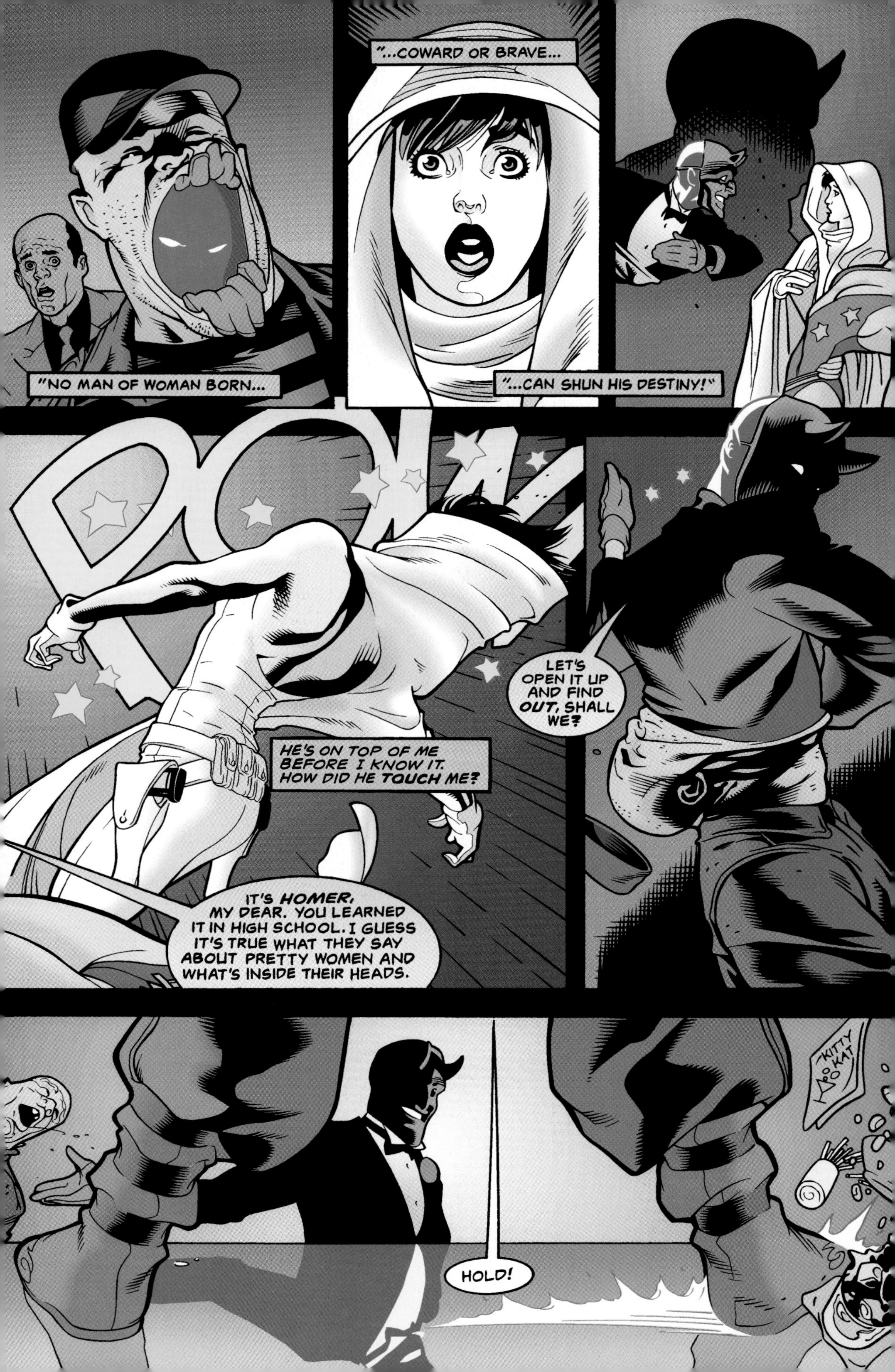
"NO MAN OF WOMAN BORN...
"...COWARD OR BRAVE...
"...CAN SHUN HIS DESTINY!"
HE'S ON TOP OF ME BEFORE I KNOW IT. HOW DID HE TOUCH ME?
IT'S HOMER, MY DEAR. YOU LEARNED IT IN HIGH SCHOOL. I GUESS IT'S TRUE WHAT THEY SAY ABOUT PRETTY WOMEN AND WHAT'S INSIDE THEIR HEADS.
LET'S OPEN IT UP AND FIND OUT, SHALL WE?
KITTY KAT
HOLD!

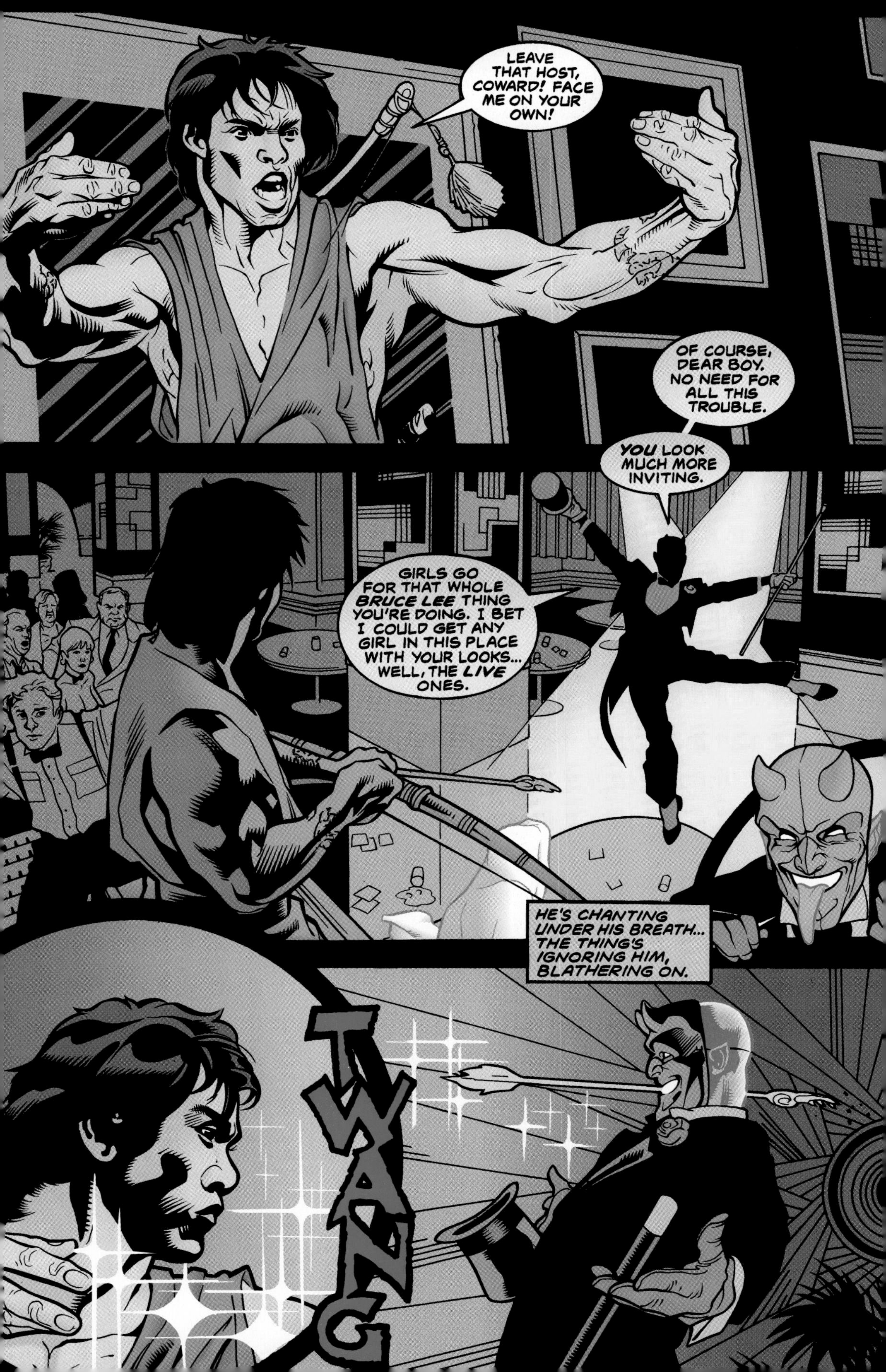
LEAVE THAT HOST, COWARD! FACE ME ON YOUR OWN!
OF COURSE, DEAR BOY. NO NEED FOR ALL THIS TROUBLE.
YOU LOOK MUCH MORE INVITING.
GIRLS GO FOR THAT WHOLE BRUCE LEE THING YOU'RE DOING. I BET I COULD GET ANY GIRL IN THIS PLACE WITH YOUR LOOKS... WELL, THE LIVE ONES.
HE'S CHANTING UNDER HIS BREATH... THE THING'S IGNORING HIM, BLATHERING ON.
TWANG

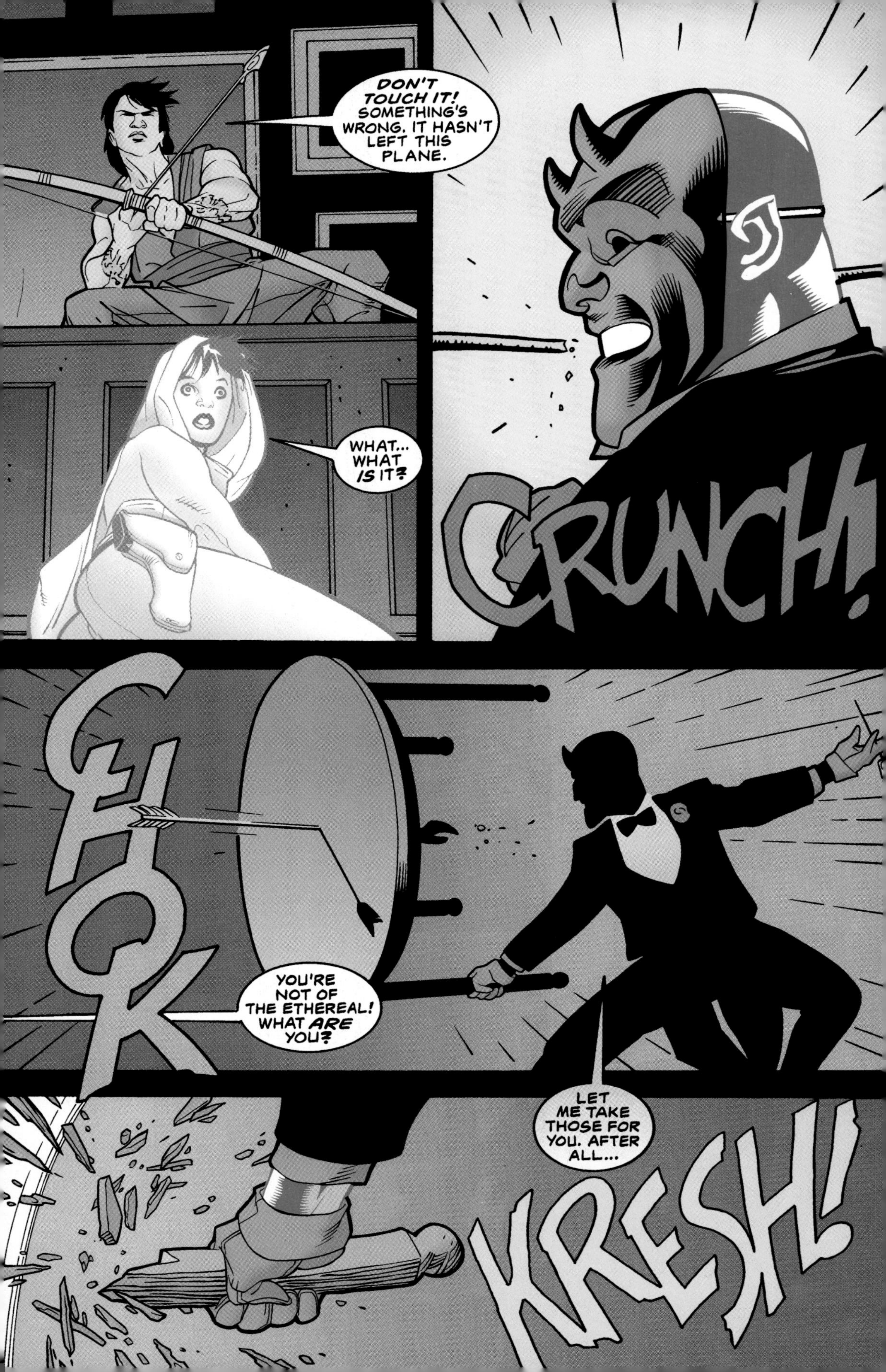
DON'T TOUCH IT! SOMETHING'S WRONG. IT HASN'T LEFT THIS PLANE.
WHAT... WHAT IS IT?
CRUNCH!
YOU'RE NOT OF THE ETHEREAL! WHAT ARE YOU?
LET ME TAKE THOSE FOR YOU. AFTER ALL...
KRESH!

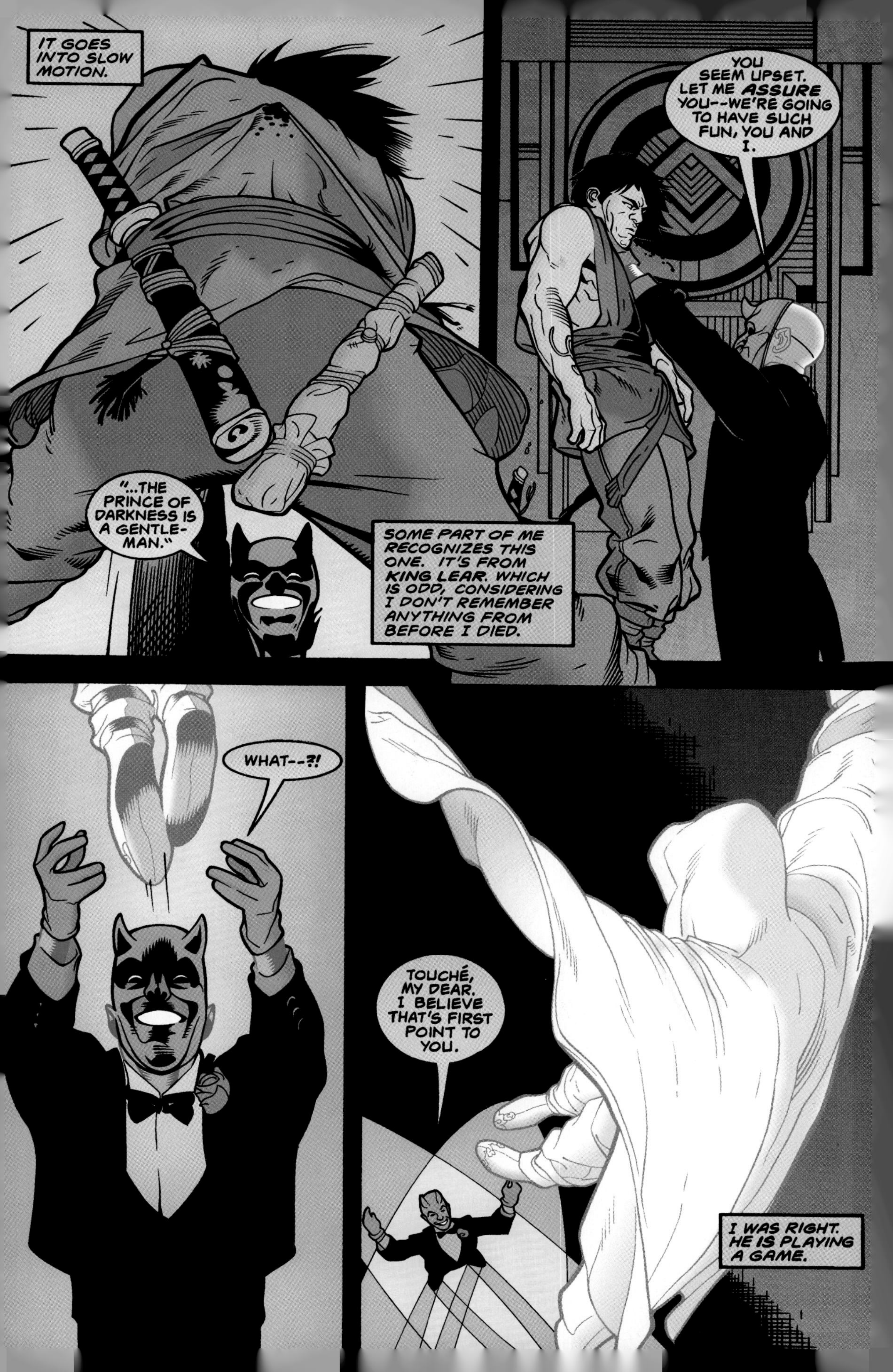
IT GOES INTO SLOW MOTION.
"...THE PRINCE OF DARKNESS IS A GENTLE-MAN."
YOU SEEM UPSET. LET ME ASSURE YOU--WE'RE GOING TO HAVE SUCH FUN, YOU AND I.
SOME PART OF ME RECOGNIZES THIS ONE. IT'S FROM KING LEAR. WHICH IS ODD, CONSIDERING I DON'T REMEMBER ANYTHING FROM BEFORE I DIED.
WHAT--?!
TOUCHÉ, MY DEAR. I BELIEVE THAT'S FIRST POINT TO YOU.
I WAS RIGHT. HE IS PLAYING A GAME.

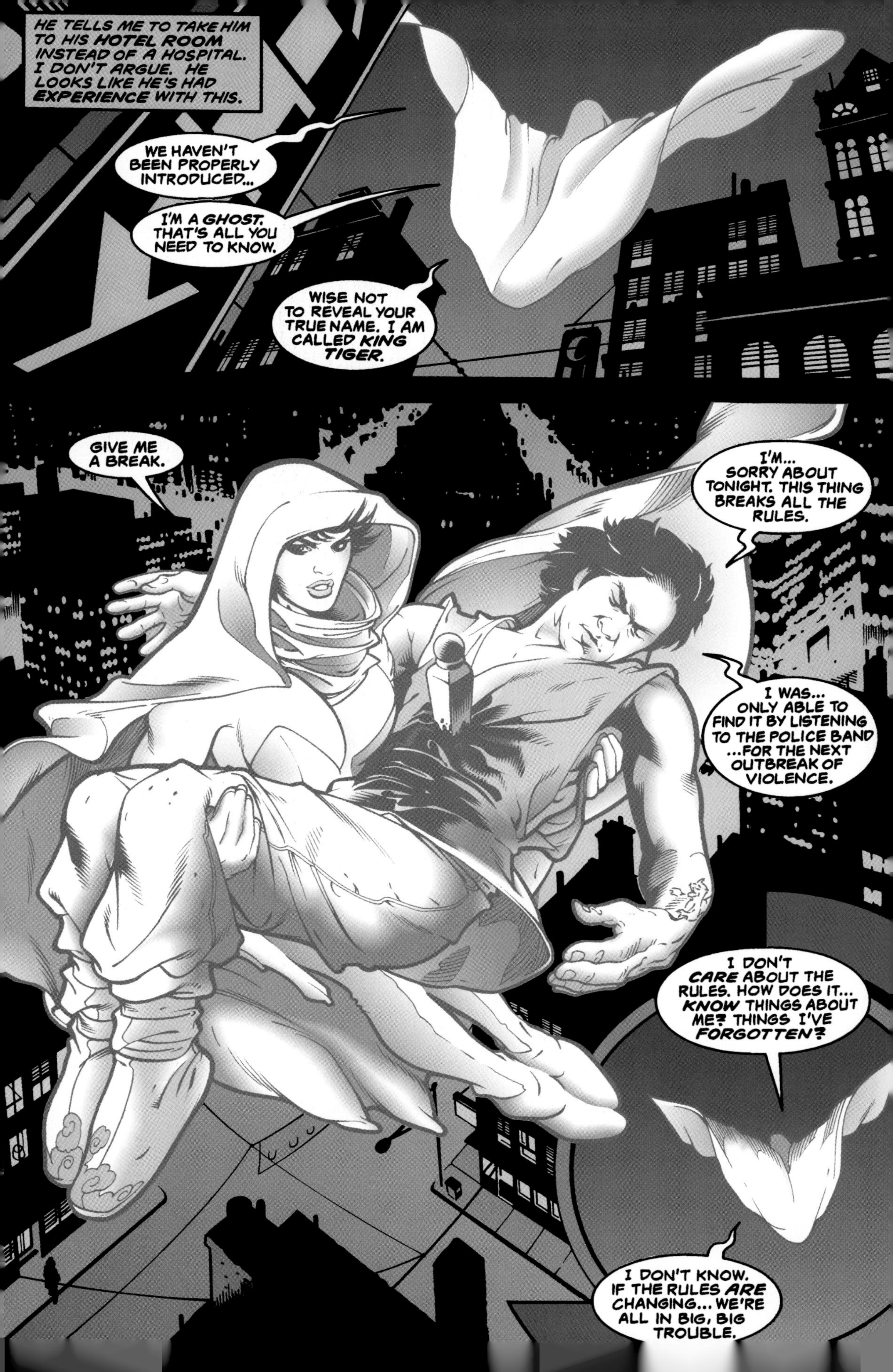
HE TELLS ME TO TAKE HIM TO HIS HOTEL ROOM INSTEAD OF A HOSPITAL. I DON'T ARGUE. HE LOOKS LIKE HE'S HAD EXPERIENCE WITH THIS.
WE HAVEN'T BEEN PROPERLY INTRODUCED...
I'M A GHOST. THAT'S ALL YOU NEED TO KNOW.
WISE NOT TO REVEAL YOUR TRUE NAME. I AM CALLED KING TIGER.
GIVE ME A BREAK.
I'M... SORRY ABOUT TONIGHT. THIS THING BREAKS ALL THE RULES.
I WAS... ONLY ABLE TO FIND IT BY LISTENING TO THE POLICE BAND ...FOR THE NEXT OUTBREAK OF VIOLENCE.
I DON'T CARE ABOUT THE RULES. HOW DOES IT... KNOW THINGS ABOUT ME? THINGS I'VE FORGOTTEN?
I DON'T KNOW. IF THE RULES ARE CHANGING... WE'RE ALL IN BIG, BIG TROUBLE.

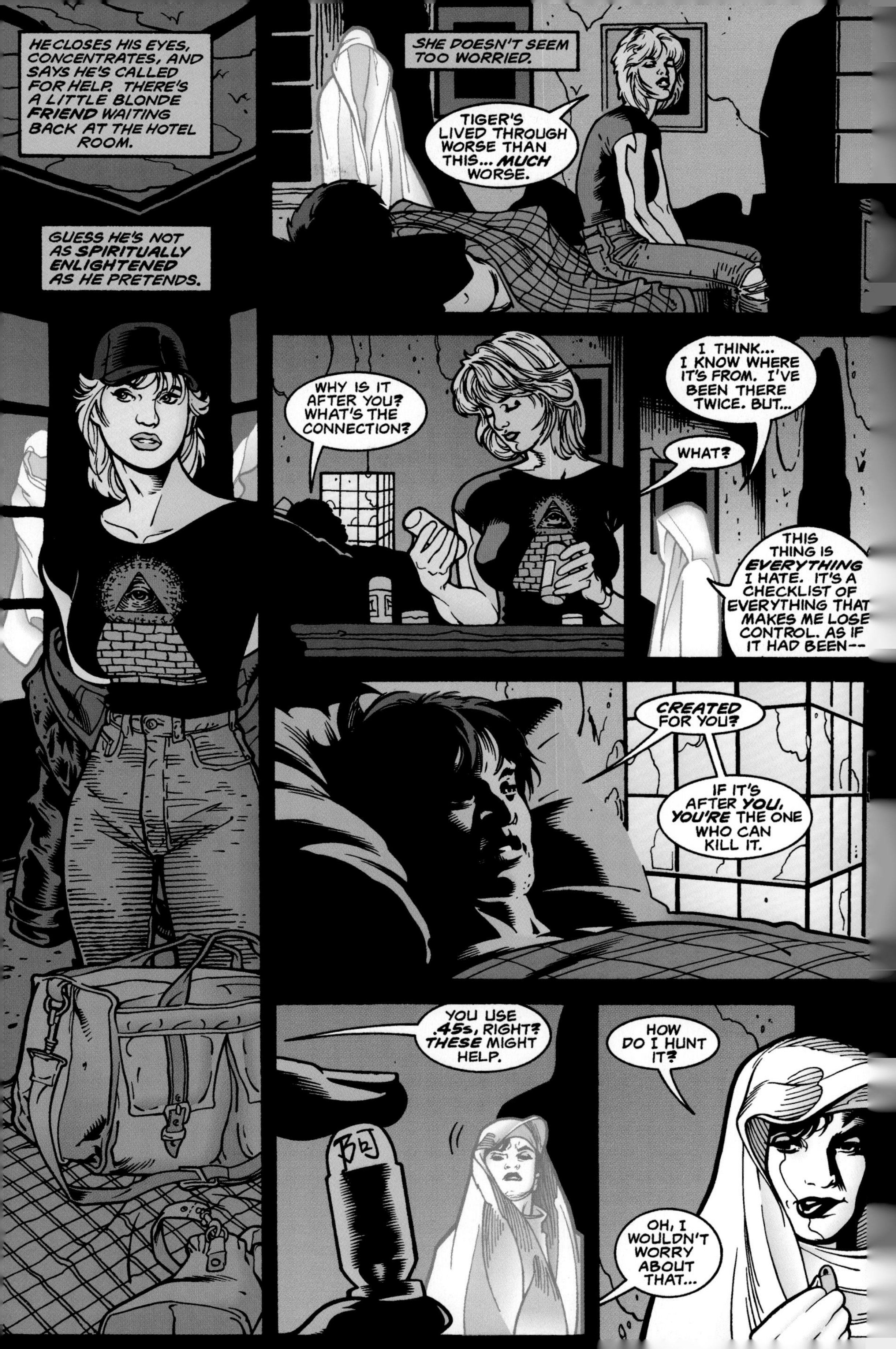
HE CLOSES HIS EYES, CONCENTRATES, AND SAYS HE'S CALLED FOR HELP. THERE'S A LITTLE BLONDE FRIEND WAITING BACK AT THE HOTEL ROOM.
GUESS HE'S NOT AS SPIRITUALLY ENLIGHTENED AS HE PRETENDS.
SHE DOESN'T SEEM TOO WORRIED.
TIGER'S LIVED THROUGH WORSE THAN THIS... MUCH WORSE.
WHY IS IT AFTER YOU? WHAT'S THE CONNECTION?
I THINK... I KNOW WHERE IT'S FROM. I'VE BEEN THERE TWICE. BUT...
WHAT?
THIS THING IS EVERYTHING I HATE. IT'S A CHECKLIST OF EVERYTHING THAT MAKES ME LOSE CONTROL. AS IF IT HAD BEEN--
CREATED FOR YOU?
IF IT'S AFTER YOU, YOU'RE THE ONE WHO CAN KILL IT.
YOU USE .45s, RIGHT? THESE MIGHT HELP.
HOW DO I HUNT IT?
OH, I WOULDN'T WORRY ABOUT THAT...

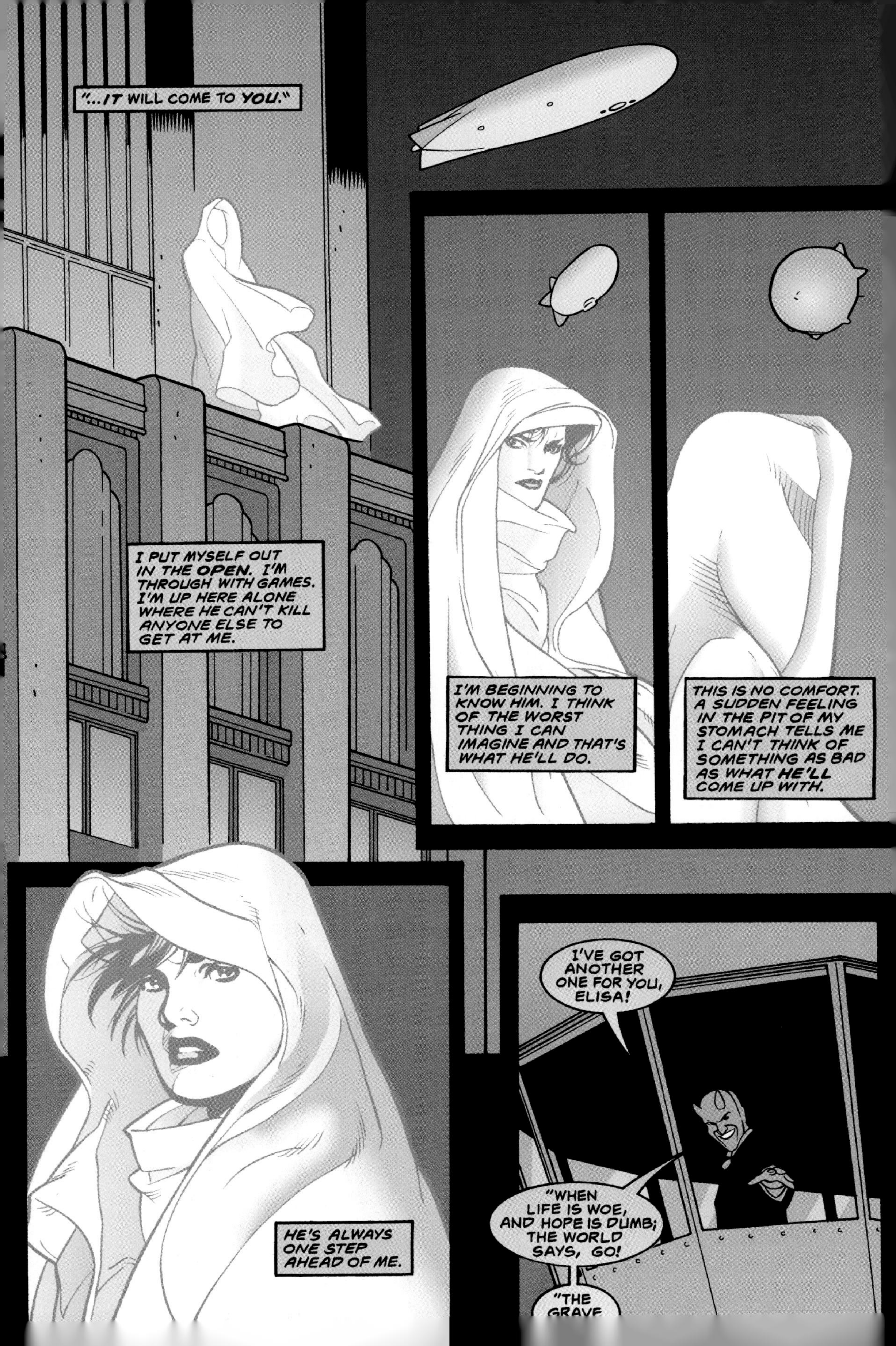
"...IT WILL COME TO YOU."
I PUT MYSELF OUT IN THE OPEN. I'M THROUGH WITH GAMES. I'M UP HERE ALONE WHERE HE CAN'T KILL ANYONE ELSE TO GET AT ME.
I'M BEGINNING TO KNOW HIM. I THINK OF THE WORST THING I CAN IMAGINE AND THAT'S WHAT HE'LL DO.
THIS IS NO COMFORT. A SUDDEN FEELING IN THE PIT OF MY STOMACH TELLS ME I CAN'T THINK OF SOMETHING AS BAD AS WHAT HE'LL COME UP WITH.
HE'S ALWAYS ONE STEP AHEAD OF ME.
I'VE GOT ANOTHER ONE FOR YOU, ELISA!
"WHEN LIFE IS WOE, AND HOPE IS DUMB; THE WORLD SAYS, GO!
"THE GRAVE

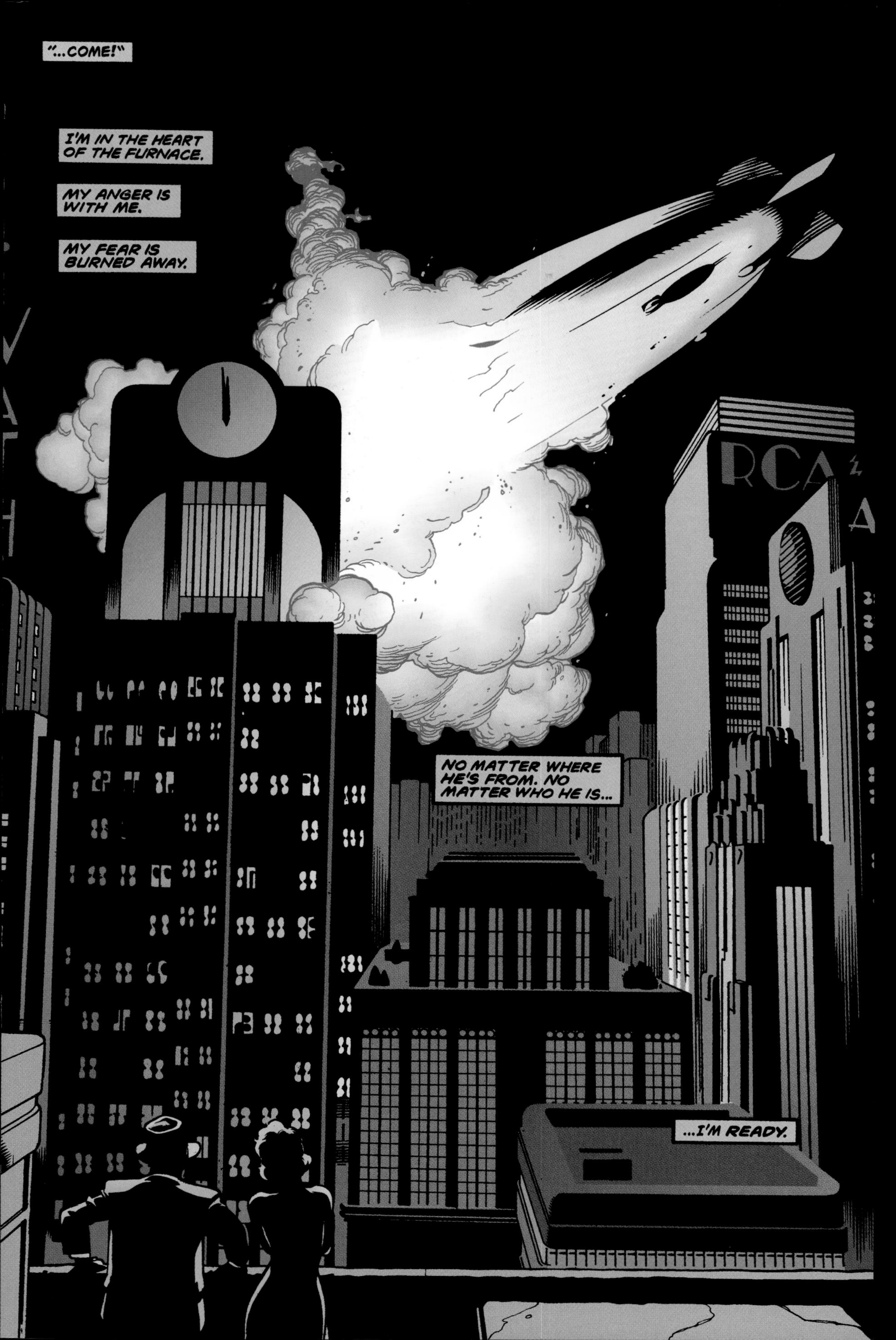
"...COME!"
I'M IN THE HEART OF THE FURNACE.
MY ANGER IS WITH ME.
MY FEAR IS BURNED AWAY.
RCA
NO MATTER WHERE HE'S FROM. NO MATTER WHO HE IS...
...I'M READY.

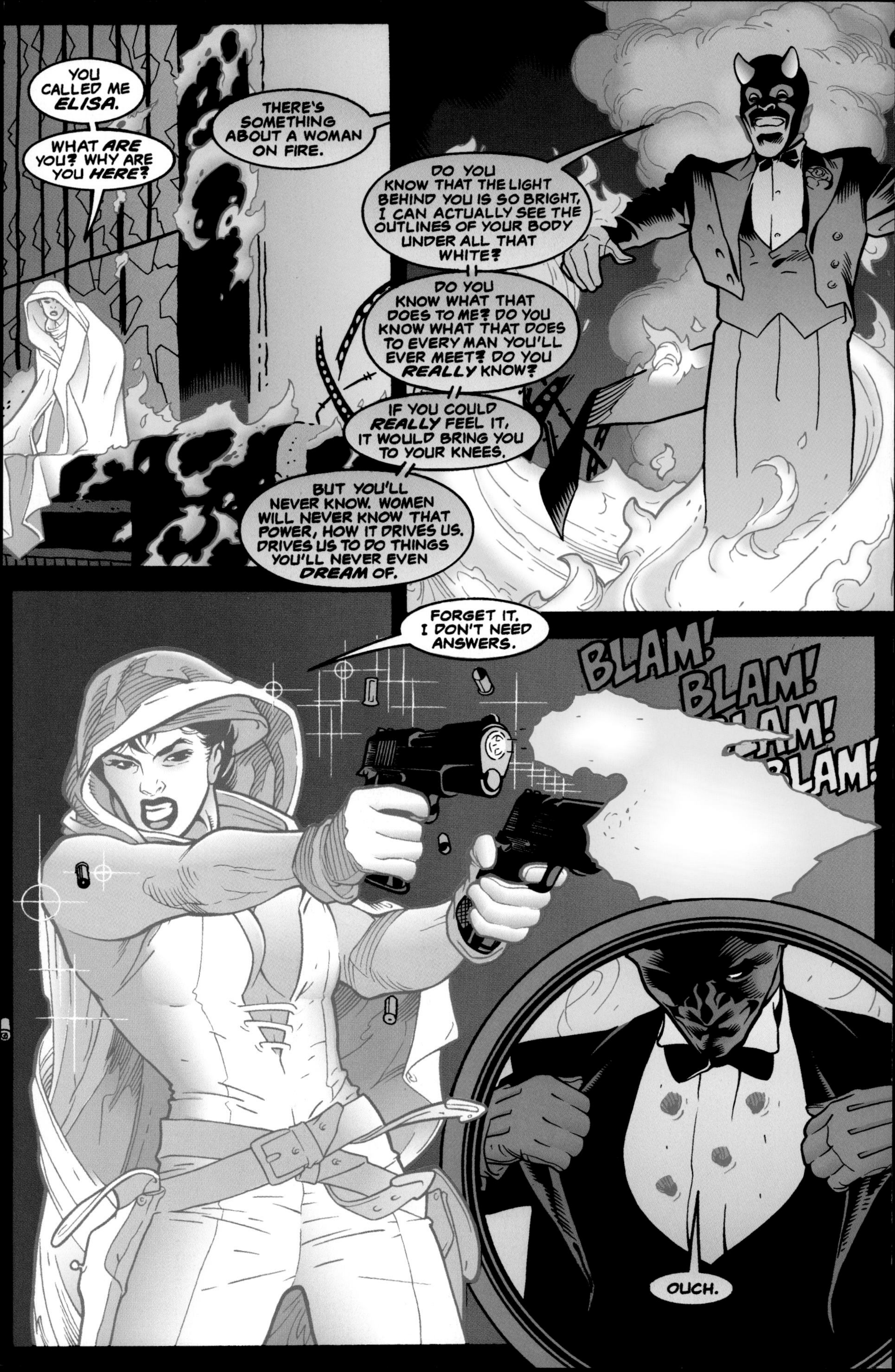
YOU CALLED ME *ELISA*.
WHAT *ARE* YOU? WHY ARE YOU *HERE*?
THERE'S SOMETHING ABOUT A WOMAN ON FIRE.
DO YOU KNOW THAT THE LIGHT BEHIND YOU IS SO BRIGHT, I CAN ACTUALLY SEE THE OUTLINES OF YOUR BODY UNDER ALL THAT WHITE?
DO YOU KNOW WHAT THAT DOES TO ME? DO YOU KNOW WHAT THAT DOES TO EVERY MAN YOU'LL EVER MEET? DO YOU *REALLY* KNOW?
IF YOU COULD *REALLY* FEEL IT, IT WOULD BRING YOU TO YOUR KNEES.
BUT YOU'LL NEVER KNOW. WOMEN WILL NEVER KNOW THAT POWER, HOW IT DRIVES US. DRIVES US TO DO THINGS YOU'LL NEVER EVEN *DREAM* OF.
FORGET IT. I DON'T NEED ANSWERS.
BLAM!
BLAM!
AM!
LAM!
OUCH.

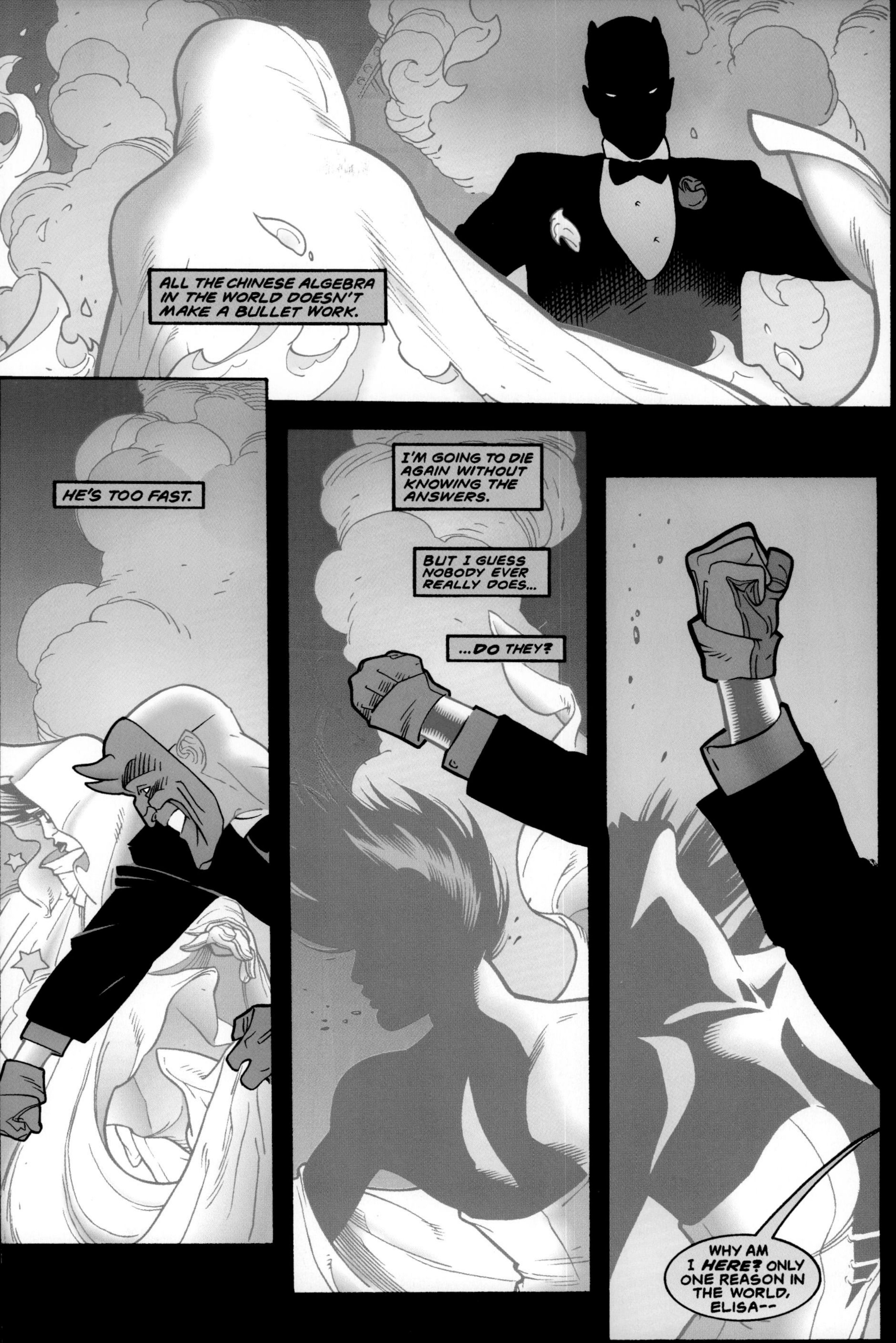
ALL THE CHINESE ALGEBRA IN THE WORLD DOESN'T MAKE A BULLET WORK.
HE'S TOO FAST.
I'M GOING TO DIE AGAIN WITHOUT KNOWING THE ANSWERS.
BUT I GUESS NOBODY EVER REALLY DOES...
...DO THEY?
WHY AM I **HERE?** ONLY ONE REASON IN THE WORLD, ELISA--

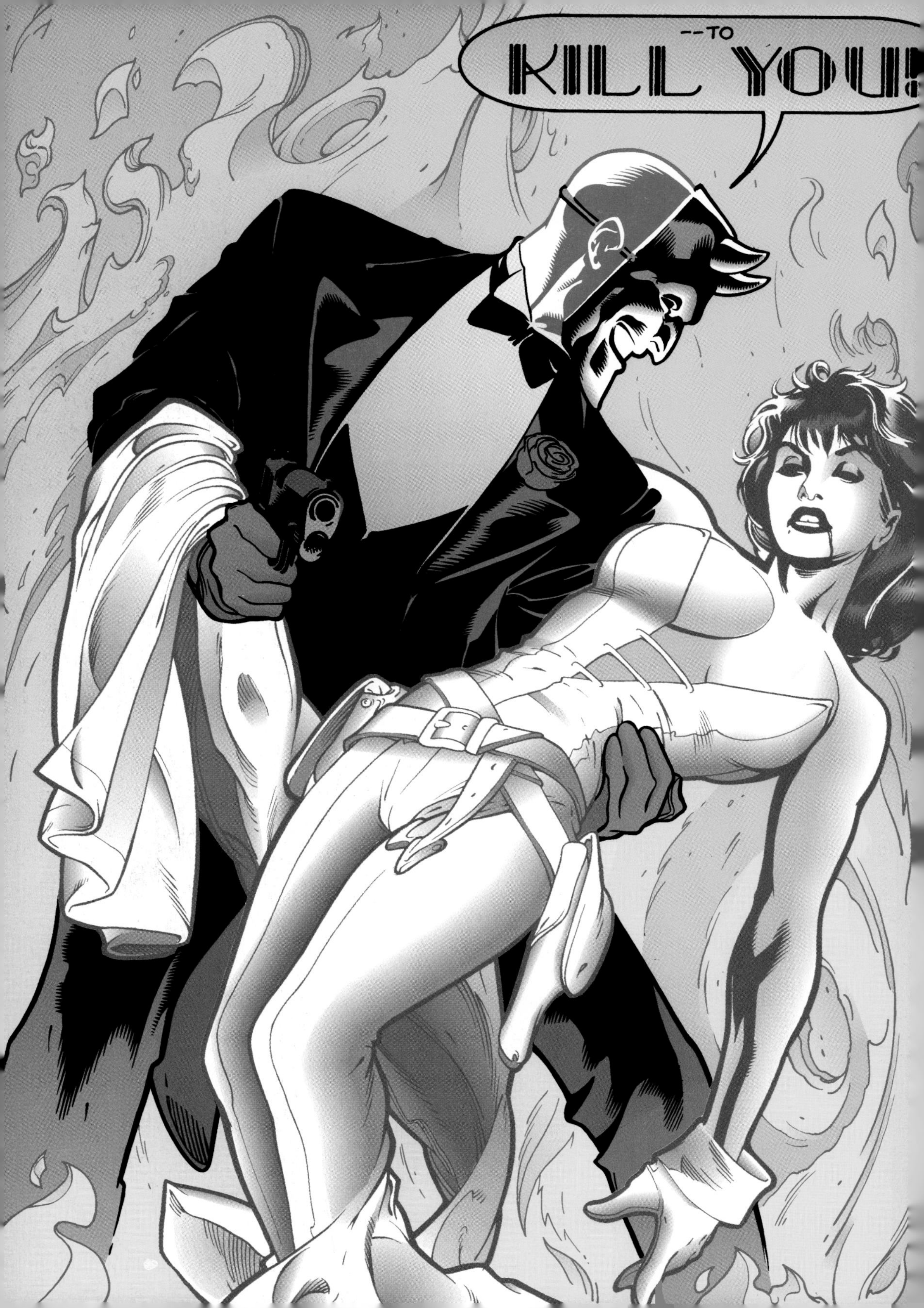
--TO KILL YOU!!

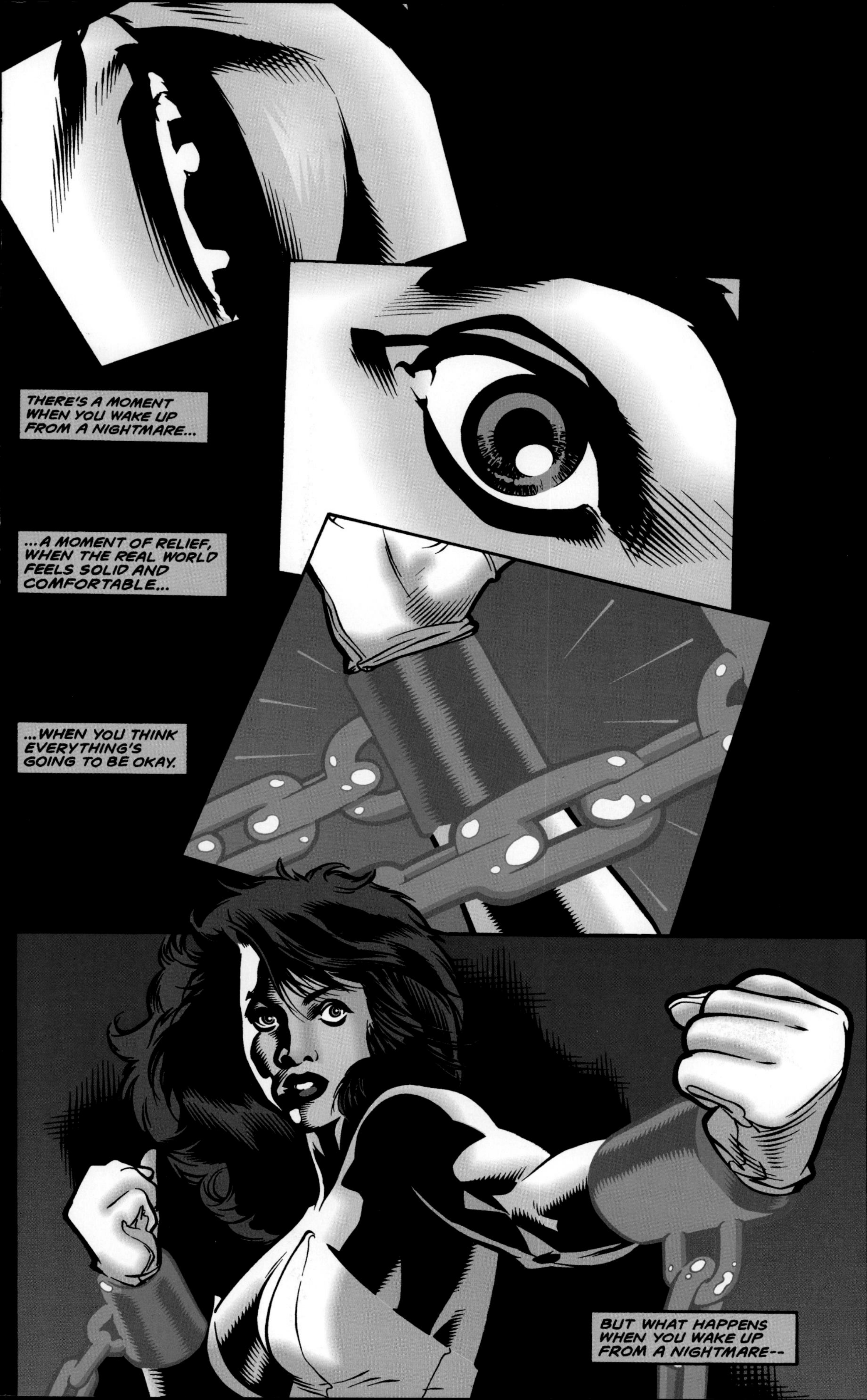

THERE'S A MOMENT WHEN YOU WAKE UP FROM A NIGHTMARE...
...A MOMENT OF RELIEF, WHEN THE REAL WORLD FEELS SOLID AND COMFORTABLE...
...WHEN YOU THINK EVERYTHING'S GOING TO BE OKAY.
BUT WHAT HAPPENS WHEN YOU WAKE UP FROM A NIGHTMARE--

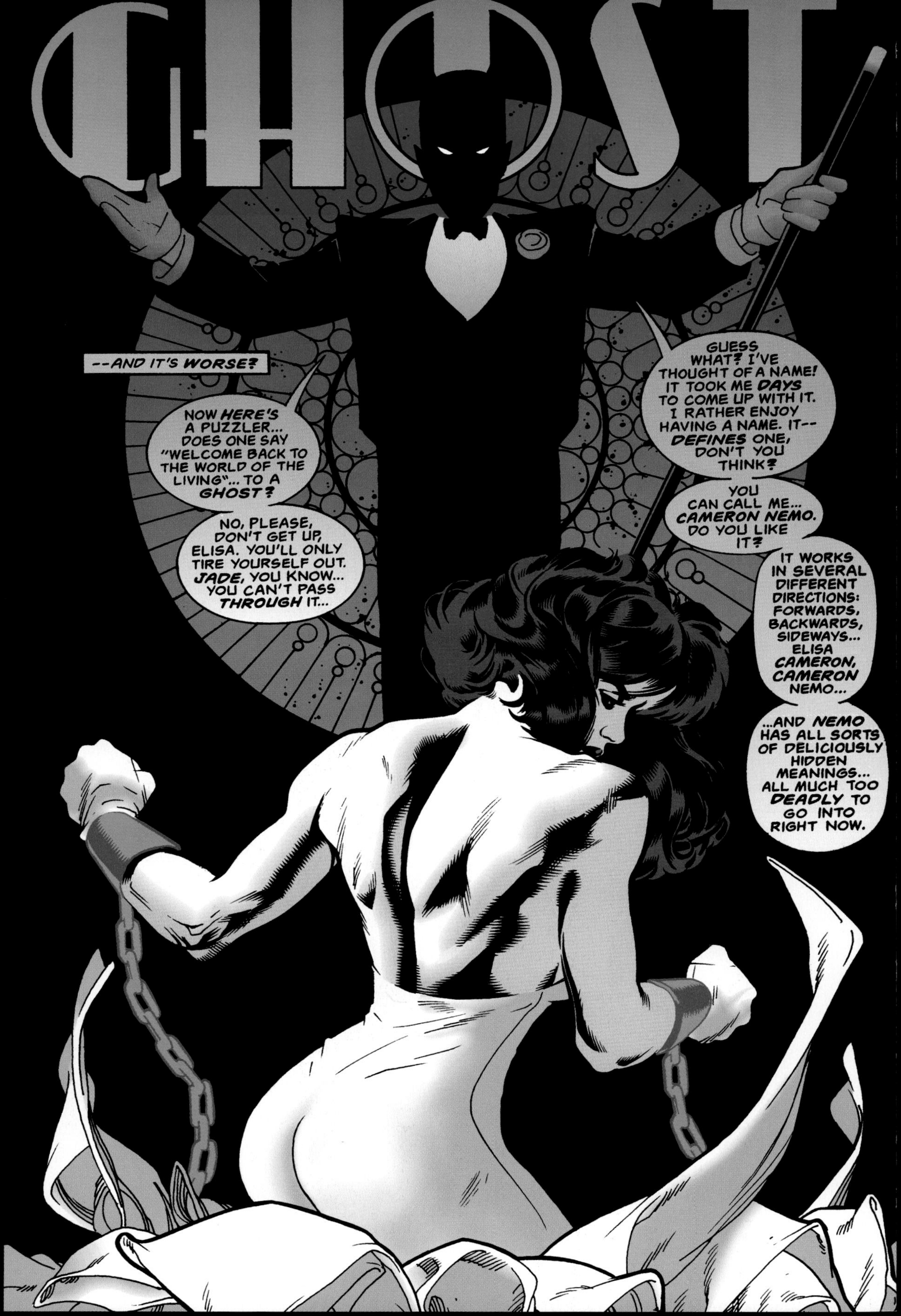
GHOST
--AND IT'S WORSE?
NOW HERE'S A PUZZLER... DOES ONE SAY "WELCOME BACK TO THE WORLD OF THE LIVING"... TO A GHOST?
NO, PLEASE, DON'T GET UP, ELISA. YOU'LL ONLY TIRE YOURSELF OUT. JADE, YOU KNOW... YOU CAN'T PASS THROUGH IT...
GUESS WHAT? I'VE THOUGHT OF A NAME! IT TOOK ME DAYS TO COME UP WITH IT. I RATHER ENJOY HAVING A NAME. IT--DEFINES ONE, DON'T YOU THINK?
YOU CAN CALL ME... CAMERON NEMO. DO YOU LIKE IT?
IT WORKS IN SEVERAL DIFFERENT DIRECTIONS: FORWARDS, BACKWARDS, SIDEWAYS... ELISA CAMERON, CAMERON NEMO...
...AND NEMO HAS ALL SORTS OF DELICIOUSLY HIDDEN MEANINGS... ALL MUCH TOO DEADLY TO GO INTO RIGHT NOW.

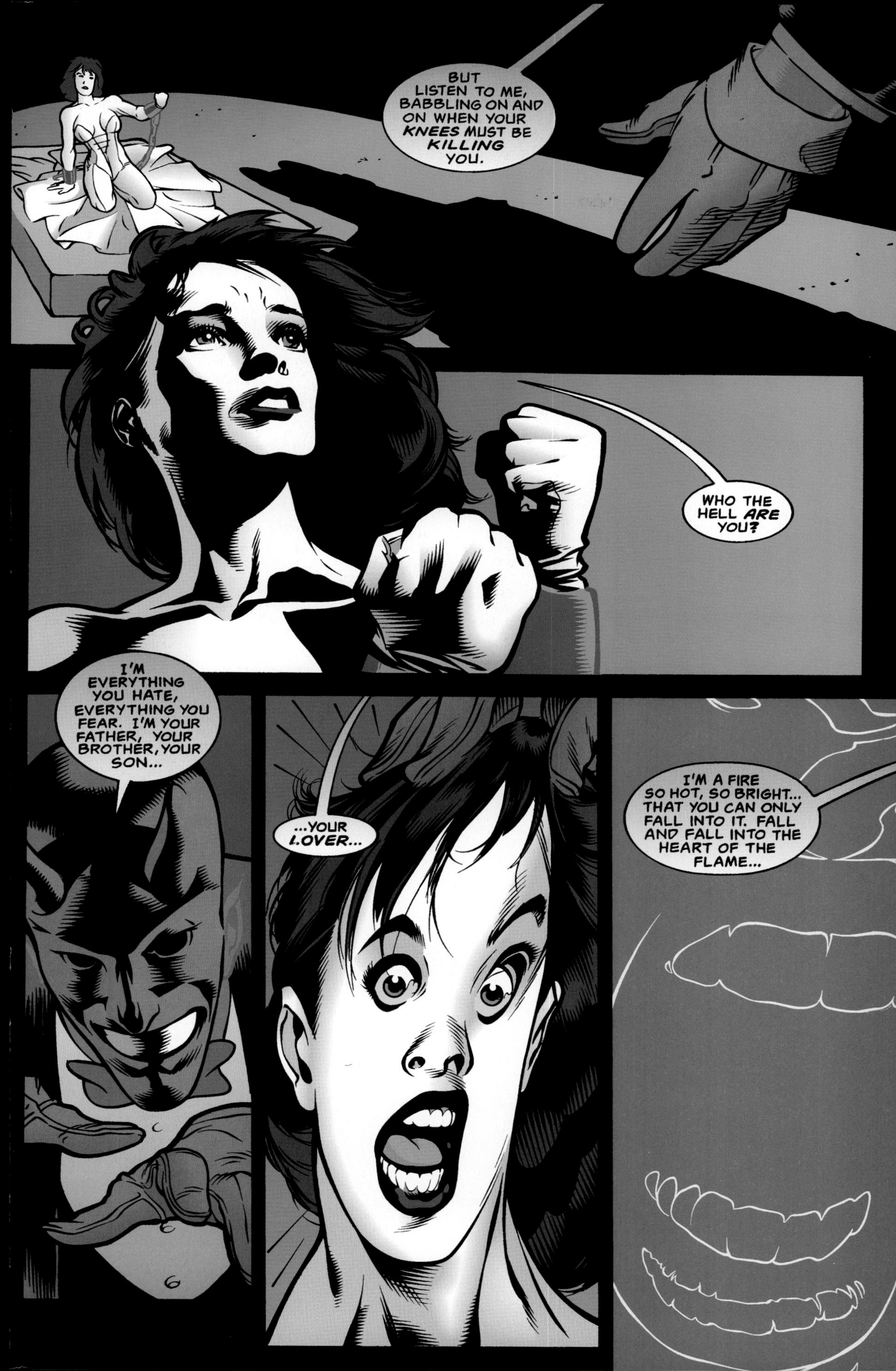
BUT LISTEN TO ME, BABBLING ON AND ON WHEN YOUR KNEES MUST BE KILLING YOU.
WHO THE HELL ARE YOU?
I'M EVERYTHING YOU HATE, EVERYTHING YOU FEAR. I'M YOUR FATHER, YOUR BROTHER, YOUR SON...
...YOUR LOVER...
I'M A FIRE SO HOT, SO BRIGHT... THAT YOU CAN ONLY FALL INTO IT. FALL AND FALL INTO THE HEART OF THE FLAME...

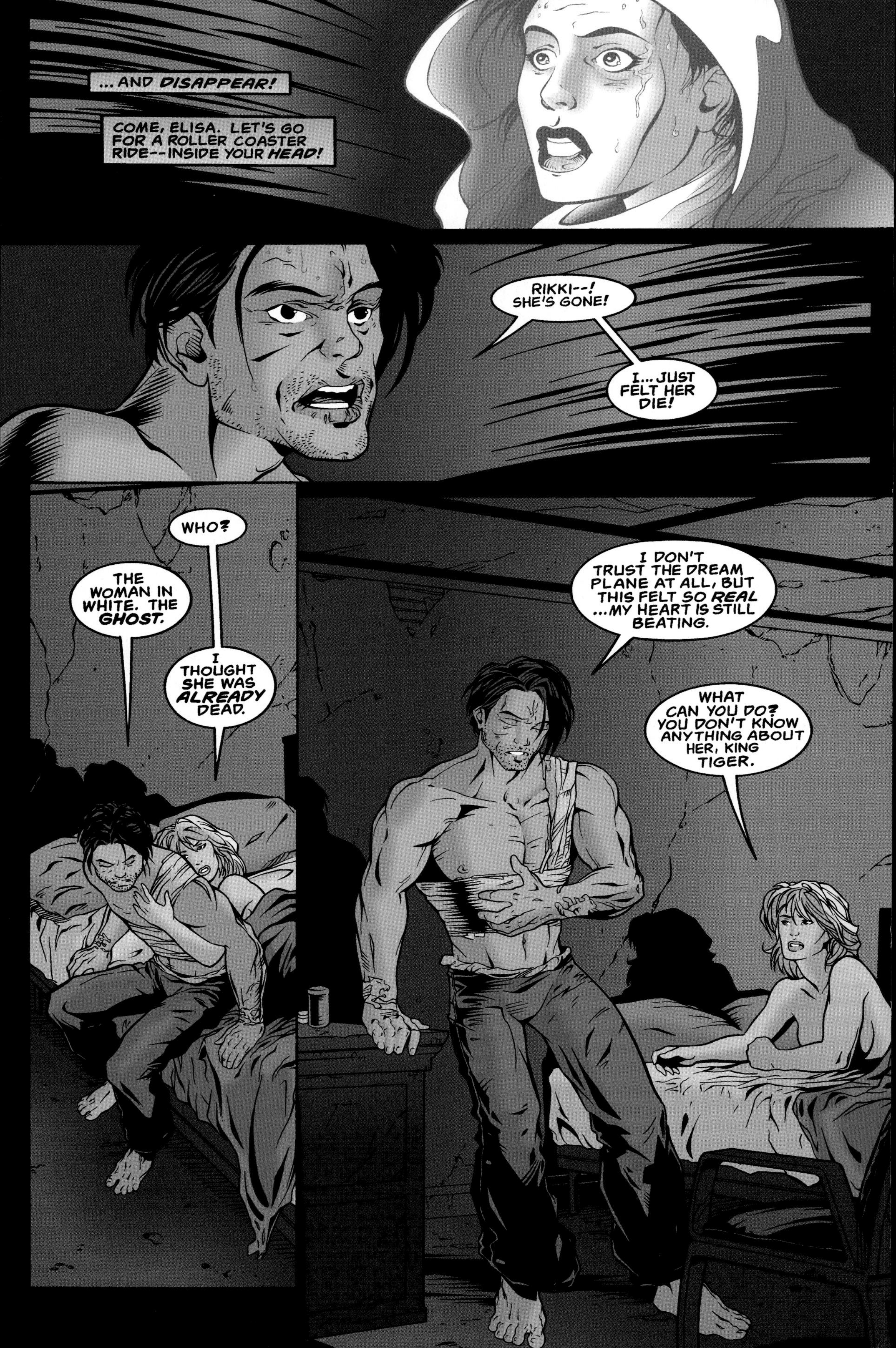
...AND DISAPPEAR!
COME, ELISA. LET'S GO FOR A ROLLER COASTER RIDE--INSIDE YOUR HEAD!
RIKKI--! SHE'S GONE!
I... JUST FELT HER DIE!
WHO?
THE WOMAN IN WHITE. THE GHOST.
I THOUGHT SHE WAS ALREADY DEAD.
I DON'T TRUST THE DREAM PLANE AT ALL, BUT THIS FELT SO REAL ...MY HEART IS STILL BEATING.
WHAT CAN YOU DO? YOU DON'T KNOW ANYTHING ABOUT HER, KING TIGER.

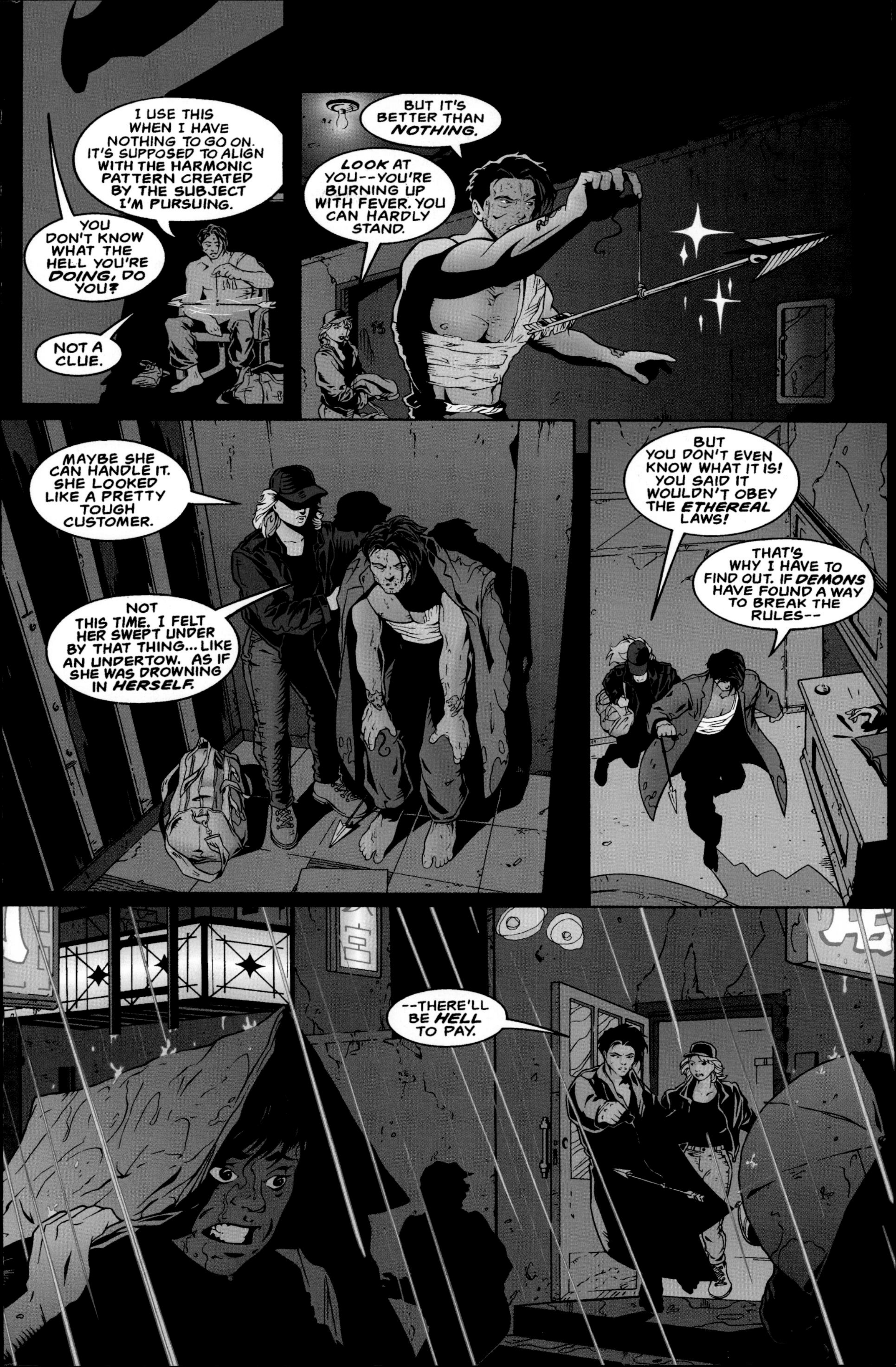
I USE THIS WHEN I HAVE NOTHING TO GO ON. IT'S SUPPOSED TO ALIGN WITH THE HARMONIC PATTERN CREATED BY THE SUBJECT I'M PURSUING.
YOU DON'T KNOW WHAT THE HELL YOU'RE DOING, DO YOU?
NOT A CLUE.
BUT IT'S BETTER THAN NOTHING.
LOOK AT YOU--YOU'RE BURNING UP WITH FEVER. YOU CAN HARDLY STAND.
MAYBE SHE CAN HANDLE IT. SHE LOOKED LIKE A PRETTY TOUGH CUSTOMER.
NOT THIS TIME. I FELT HER SWEPT UNDER BY THAT THING... LIKE AN UNDERTOW. AS IF SHE WAS DROWNING IN HERSELF.
BUT YOU DON'T EVEN KNOW WHAT IT IS! YOU SAID IT WOULDN'T OBEY THE ETHEREAL LAWS!
THAT'S WHY I HAVE TO FIND OUT. IF DEMONS HAVE FOUND A WAY TO BREAK THE RULES--
--THERE'LL BE HELL TO PAY.

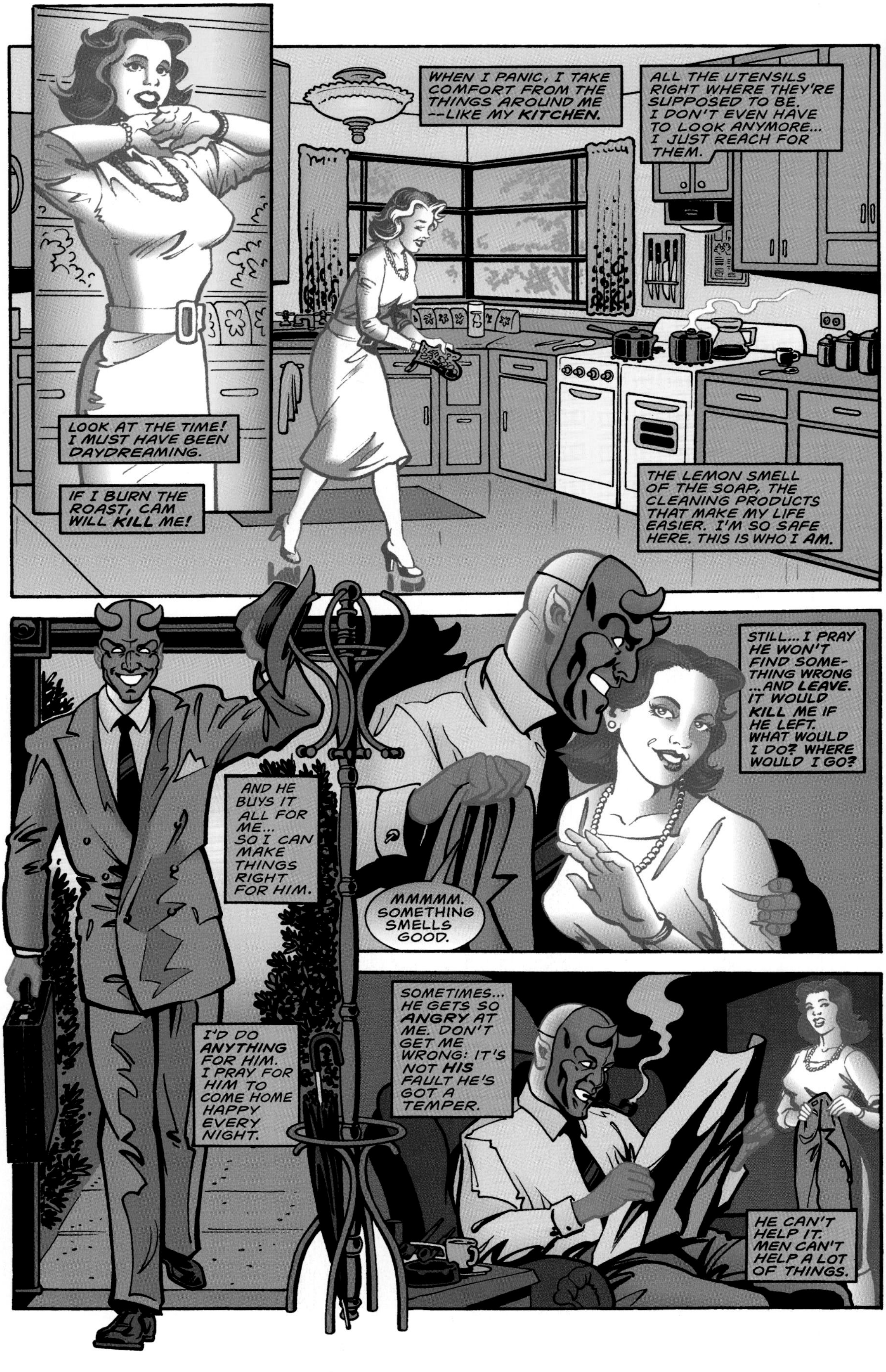

LOOK AT THE TIME! I MUST HAVE BEEN DAYDREAMING.
IF I BURN THE ROAST, CAM WILL KILL ME!
WHEN I PANIC, I TAKE COMFORT FROM THE THINGS AROUND ME --LIKE MY KITCHEN.
ALL THE UTENSILS RIGHT WHERE THEY'RE SUPPOSED TO BE. I DON'T EVEN HAVE TO LOOK ANYMORE... I JUST REACH FOR THEM.
THE LEMON SMELL OF THE SOAP, THE CLEANING PRODUCTS THAT MAKE MY LIFE EASIER. I'M SO SAFE HERE. THIS IS WHO I AM.
AND HE BUYS IT ALL FOR ME... SO I CAN MAKE THINGS RIGHT FOR HIM.
MMMMM. SOMETHING SMELLS GOOD.
STILL... I PRAY HE WON'T FIND SOMETHING WRONG ...AND LEAVE. IT WOULD KILL ME IF HE LEFT. WHAT WOULD I DO? WHERE WOULD I GO?
I'D DO ANYTHING FOR HIM. I PRAY FOR HIM TO COME HOME HAPPY EVERY NIGHT.
SOMETIMES... HE GETS SO ANGRY AT ME. DON'T GET ME WRONG: IT'S NOT HIS FAULT HE'S GOT A TEMPER.
HE CAN'T HELP IT. MEN CAN'T HELP A LOT OF THINGS.

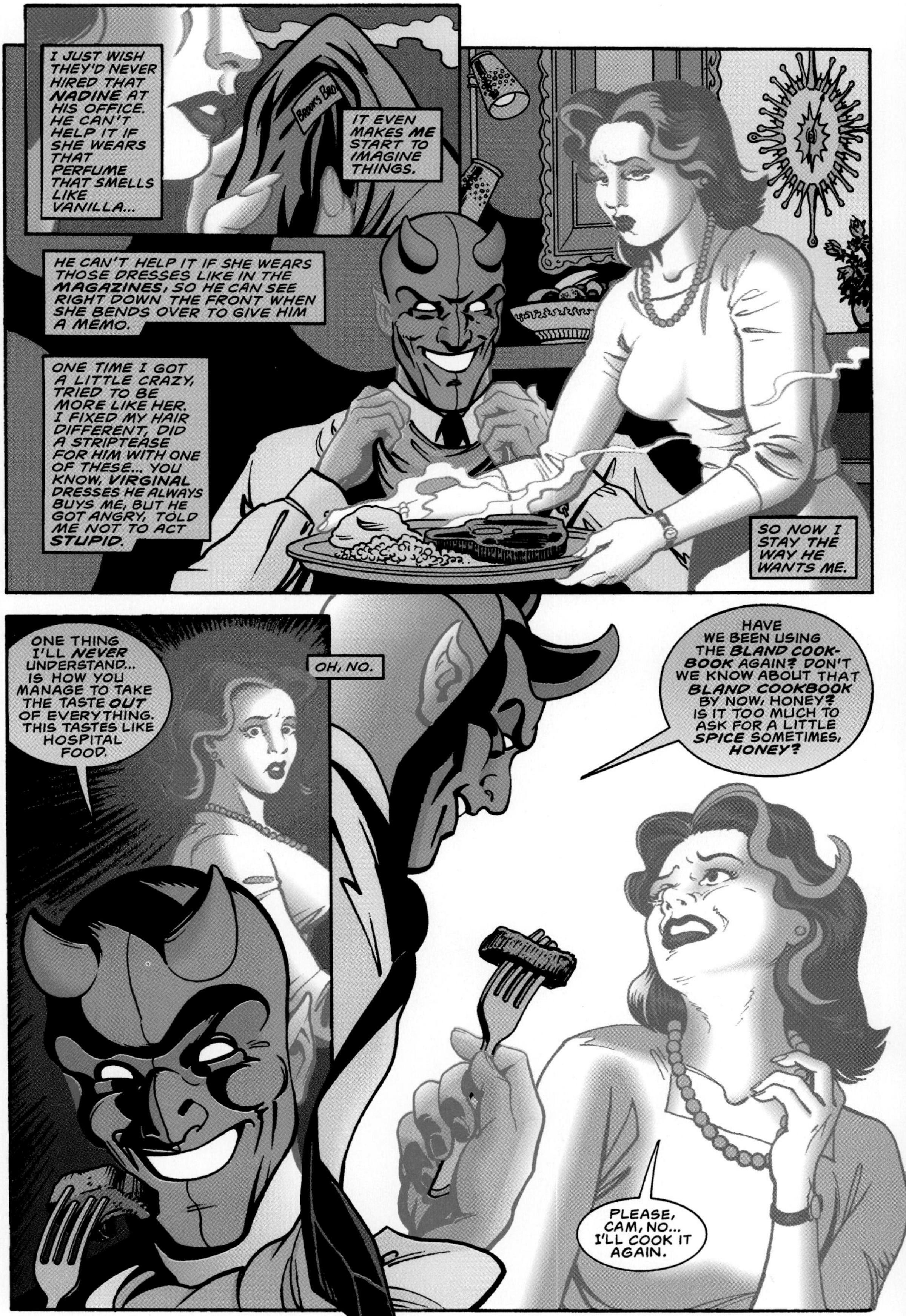

I JUST WISH THEY'D NEVER HIRED THAT NADINE AT HIS OFFICE. HE CAN'T HELP IT IF SHE WEARS THAT PERFUME THAT SMELLS LIKE VANILLA...
IT EVEN MAKES ME START TO IMAGINE THINGS.
HE CAN'T HELP IT IF SHE WEARS THOSE DRESSES LIKE IN THE MAGAZINES, SO HE CAN SEE RIGHT DOWN THE FRONT WHEN SHE BENDS OVER TO GIVE HIM A MEMO.
ONE TIME I GOT A LITTLE CRAZY, TRIED TO BE MORE LIKE HER. I FIXED MY HAIR DIFFERENT, DID A STRIPTEASE FOR HIM WITH ONE OF THESE... YOU KNOW, VIRGINAL DRESSES HE ALWAYS BUYS ME, BUT HE GOT ANGRY, TOLD ME NOT TO ACT STUPID.
SO NOW I STAY THE WAY HE WANTS ME.
ONE THING I'LL NEVER UNDERSTAND... IS HOW YOU MANAGE TO TAKE THE TASTE OUT OF EVERYTHING. THIS TASTES LIKE HOSPITAL FOOD.
OH, NO.
HAVE WE BEEN USING THE BLAND COOK-BOOK AGAIN? DON'T WE KNOW ABOUT THAT BLAND COOKBOOK BY NOW, HONEY? IS IT TOO MUCH TO ASK FOR A LITTLE SPICE SOMETIMES, HONEY?
PLEASE, CAM, NO... I'LL COOK IT AGAIN.

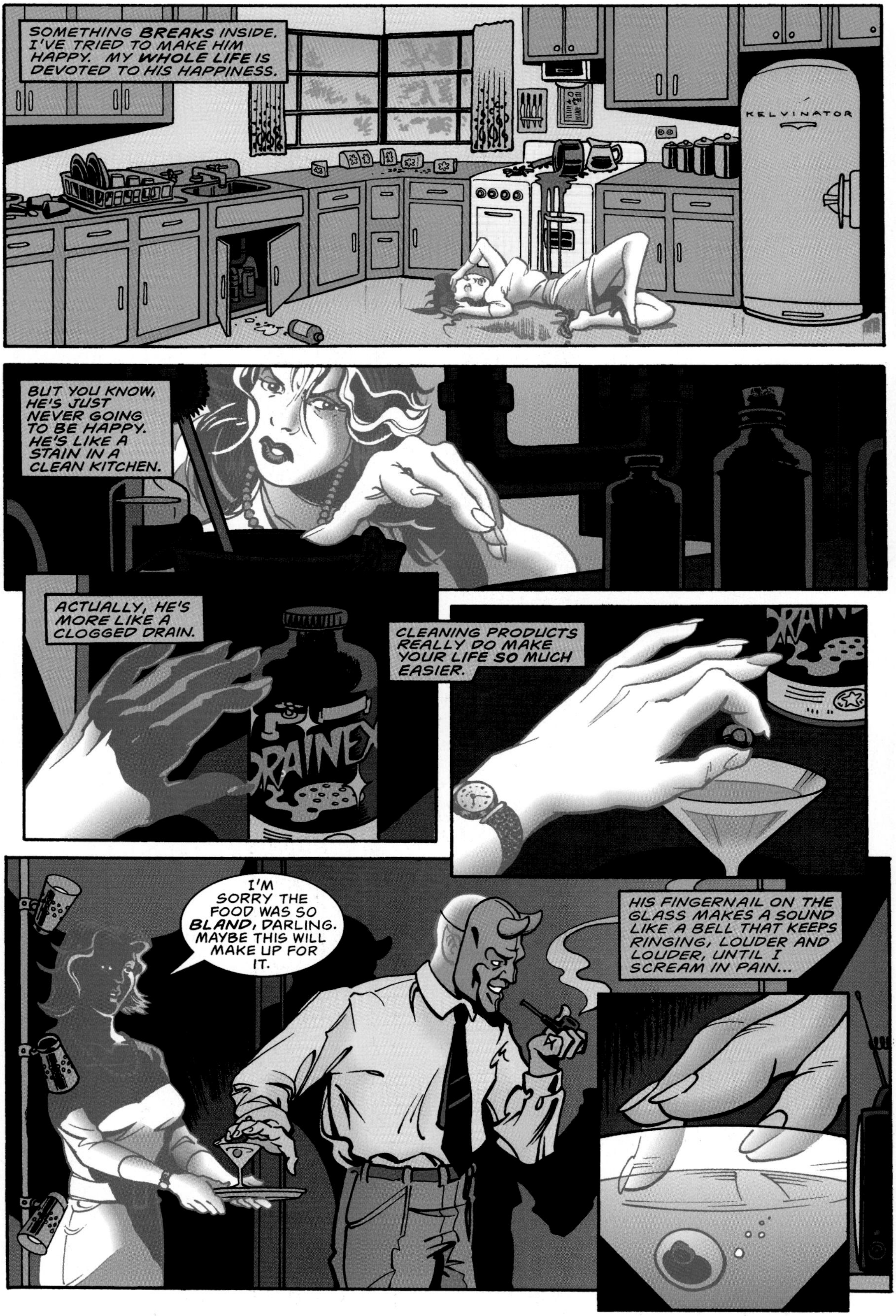
SOMETHING BREAKS INSIDE. I'VE TRIED TO MAKE HIM HAPPY. MY WHOLE LIFE IS DEVOTED TO HIS HAPPINESS.
KELVINATOR
BUT YOU KNOW, HE'S JUST NEVER GOING TO BE HAPPY. HE'S LIKE A STAIN IN A CLEAN KITCHEN.
ACTUALLY, HE'S MORE LIKE A CLOGGED DRAIN.
DRAINEX
CLEANING PRODUCTS REALLY DO MAKE YOUR LIFE SO MUCH EASIER.
I'M SORRY THE FOOD WAS SO BLAND, DARLING. MAYBE THIS WILL MAKE UP FOR IT.
HIS FINGERNAIL ON THE GLASS MAKES A SOUND LIKE A BELL THAT KEEPS RINGING, LOUDER AND LOUDER, UNTIL I SCREAM IN PAIN...

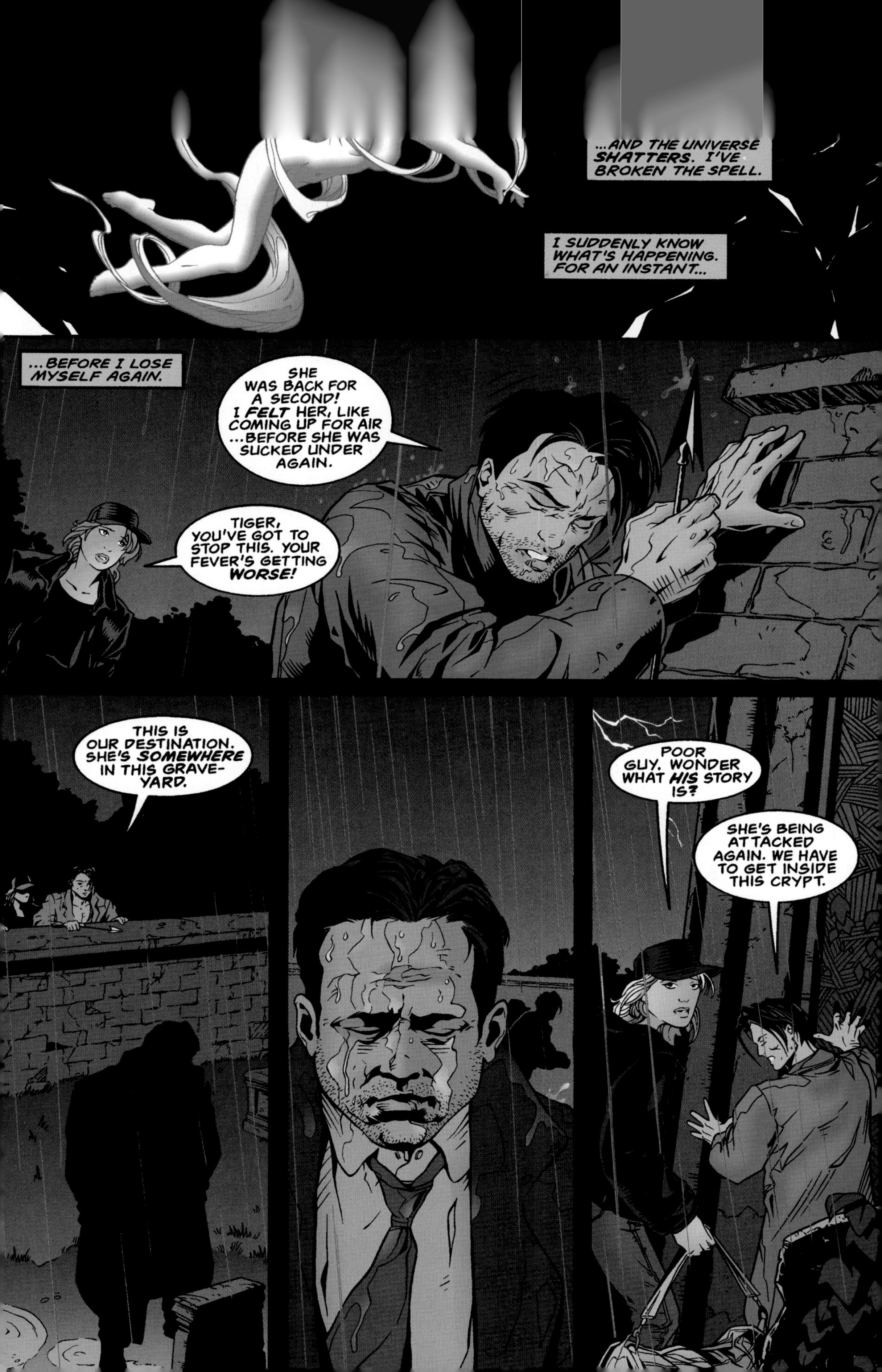
...AND THE UNIVERSE SHATTERS. I'VE BROKEN THE SPELL.
I SUDDENLY KNOW WHAT'S HAPPENING. FOR AN INSTANT...
...BEFORE I LOSE MYSELF AGAIN.
SHE WAS BACK FOR A SECOND! I FELT HER, LIKE COMING UP FOR AIR ...BEFORE SHE WAS SUCKED UNDER AGAIN.
TIGER, YOU'VE GOT TO STOP THIS. YOUR FEVER'S GETTING WORSE!
THIS IS OUR DESTINATION. SHE'S SOMEWHERE IN THIS GRAVE-YARD.
POOR GUY. WONDER WHAT HIS STORY IS?
SHE'S BEING ATTACKED AGAIN. WE HAVE TO GET INSIDE THIS CRYPT.

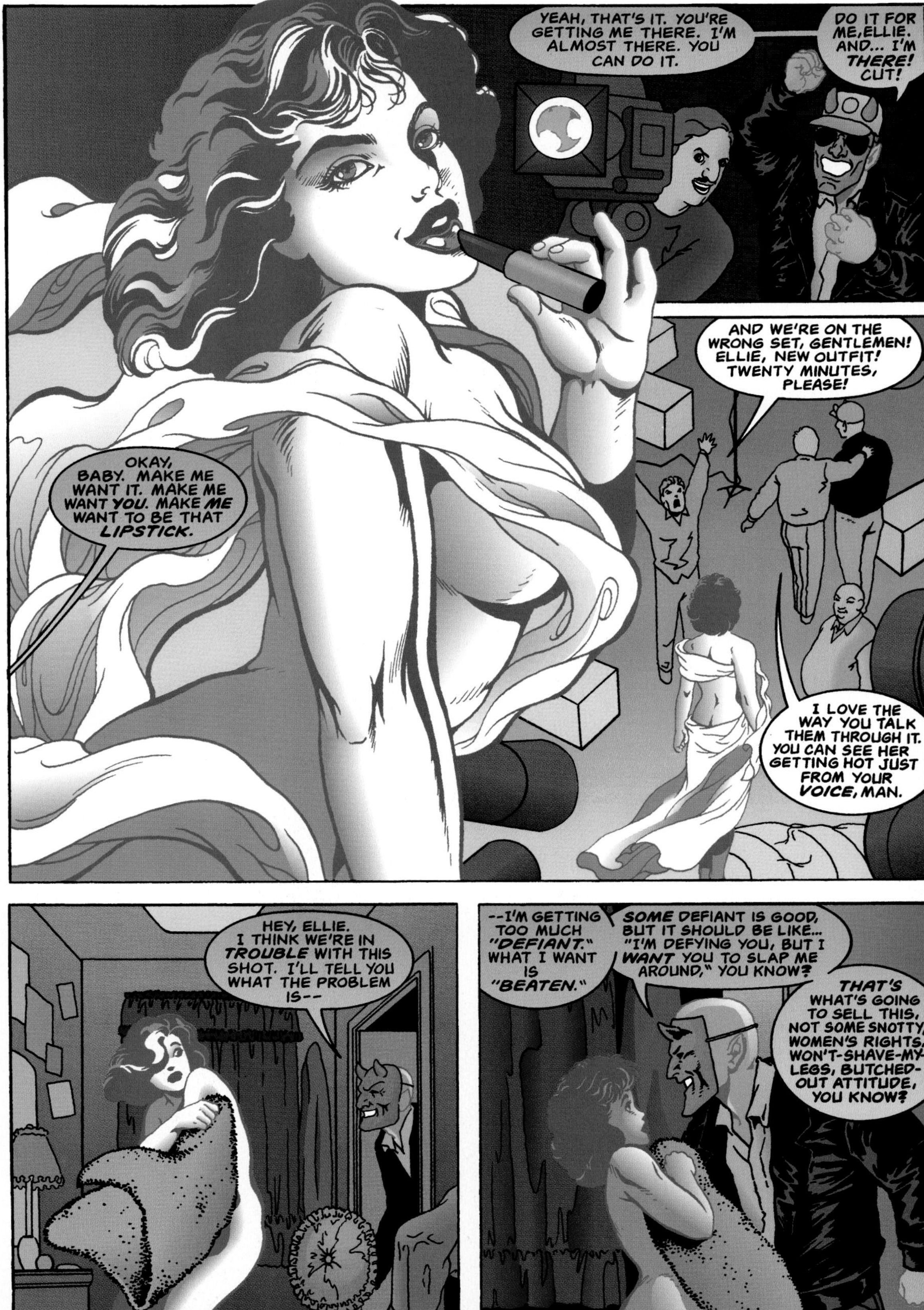
OKAY, BABY. MAKE ME WANT IT. MAKE ME WANT YOU. MAKE ME WANT TO BE THAT LIPSTICK.
YEAH, THAT'S IT. YOU'RE GETTING ME THERE. I'M ALMOST THERE. YOU CAN DO IT.
DO IT FOR ME, ELLIE. AND... I'M THERE! CUT!
AND WE'RE ON THE WRONG SET, GENTLEMEN! ELLIE, NEW OUTFIT! TWENTY MINUTES, PLEASE!
I LOVE THE WAY YOU TALK THEM THROUGH IT. YOU CAN SEE HER GETTING HOT JUST FROM YOUR VOICE, MAN.
HEY, ELLIE. I THINK WE'RE IN TROUBLE WITH THIS SHOT. I'LL TELL YOU WHAT THE PROBLEM IS--
--I'M GETTING TOO MUCH "DEFIANT." WHAT I WANT IS "BEATEN."
SOME DEFIANT IS GOOD, BUT IT SHOULD BE LIKE... "I'M DEFYING YOU, BUT I WANT YOU TO SLAP ME AROUND," YOU KNOW?
THAT'S WHAT'S GOING TO SELL THIS, NOT SOME SNOTTY, WOMEN'S RIGHTS, WON'T-SHAVE-MY-LEGS, BUTCHED-OUT ATTITUDE, YOU KNOW?

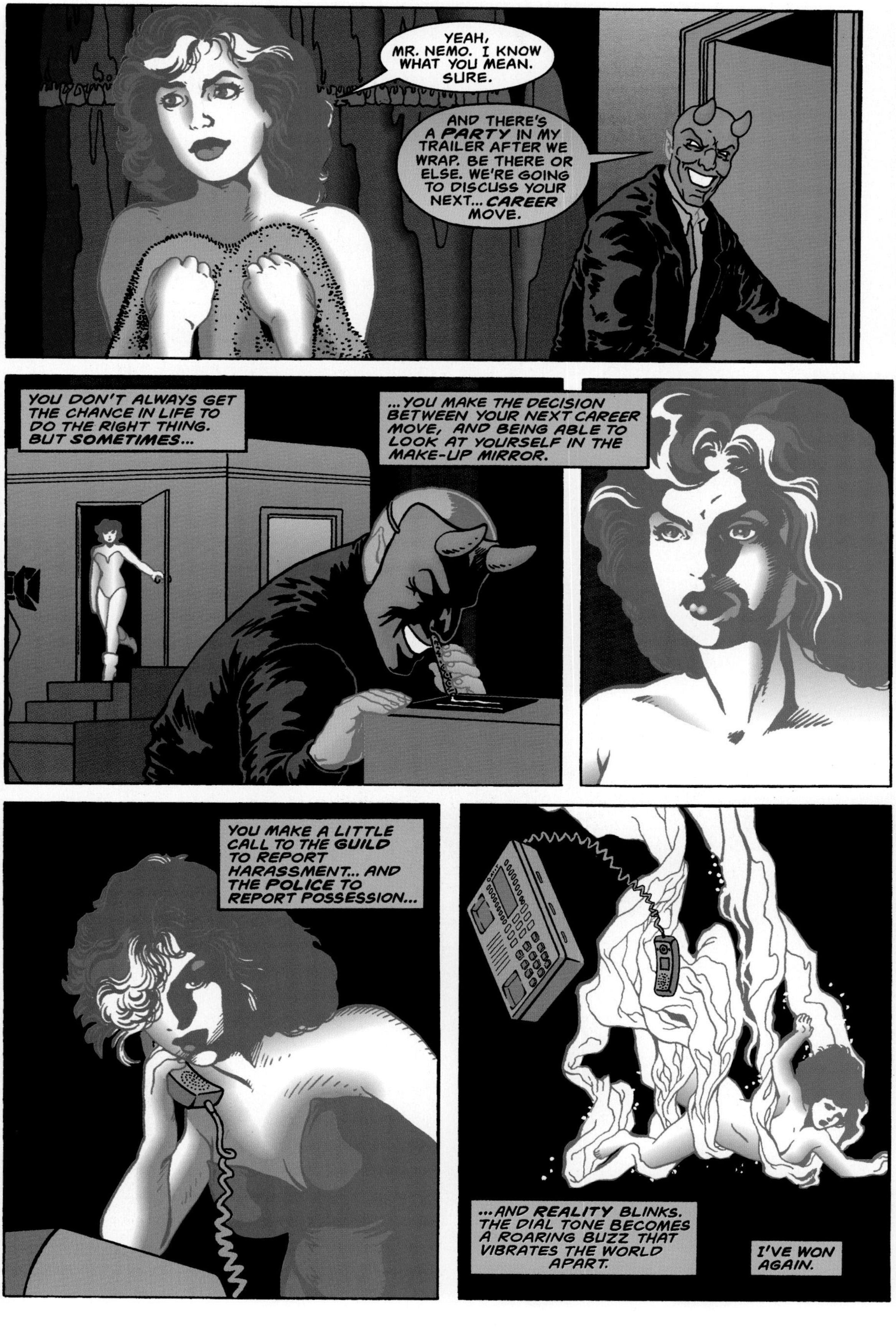
YEAH, MR. NEMO. I KNOW WHAT YOU MEAN. SURE.
AND THERE'S A PARTY IN MY TRAILER AFTER WE WRAP. BE THERE OR ELSE. WE'RE GOING TO DISCUSS YOUR NEXT... CAREER MOVE.
YOU DON'T ALWAYS GET THE CHANCE IN LIFE TO DO THE RIGHT THING. BUT SOMETIMES...
...YOU MAKE THE DECISION BETWEEN YOUR NEXT CAREER MOVE, AND BEING ABLE TO LOOK AT YOURSELF IN THE MAKE-UP MIRROR.
YOU MAKE A LITTLE CALL TO THE GUILD TO REPORT HARASSMENT... AND THE POLICE TO REPORT POSSESSION...
...AND REALITY BLINKS. THE DIAL TONE BECOMES A ROARING BUZZ THAT VIBRATES THE WORLD APART.
I'VE WON AGAIN.

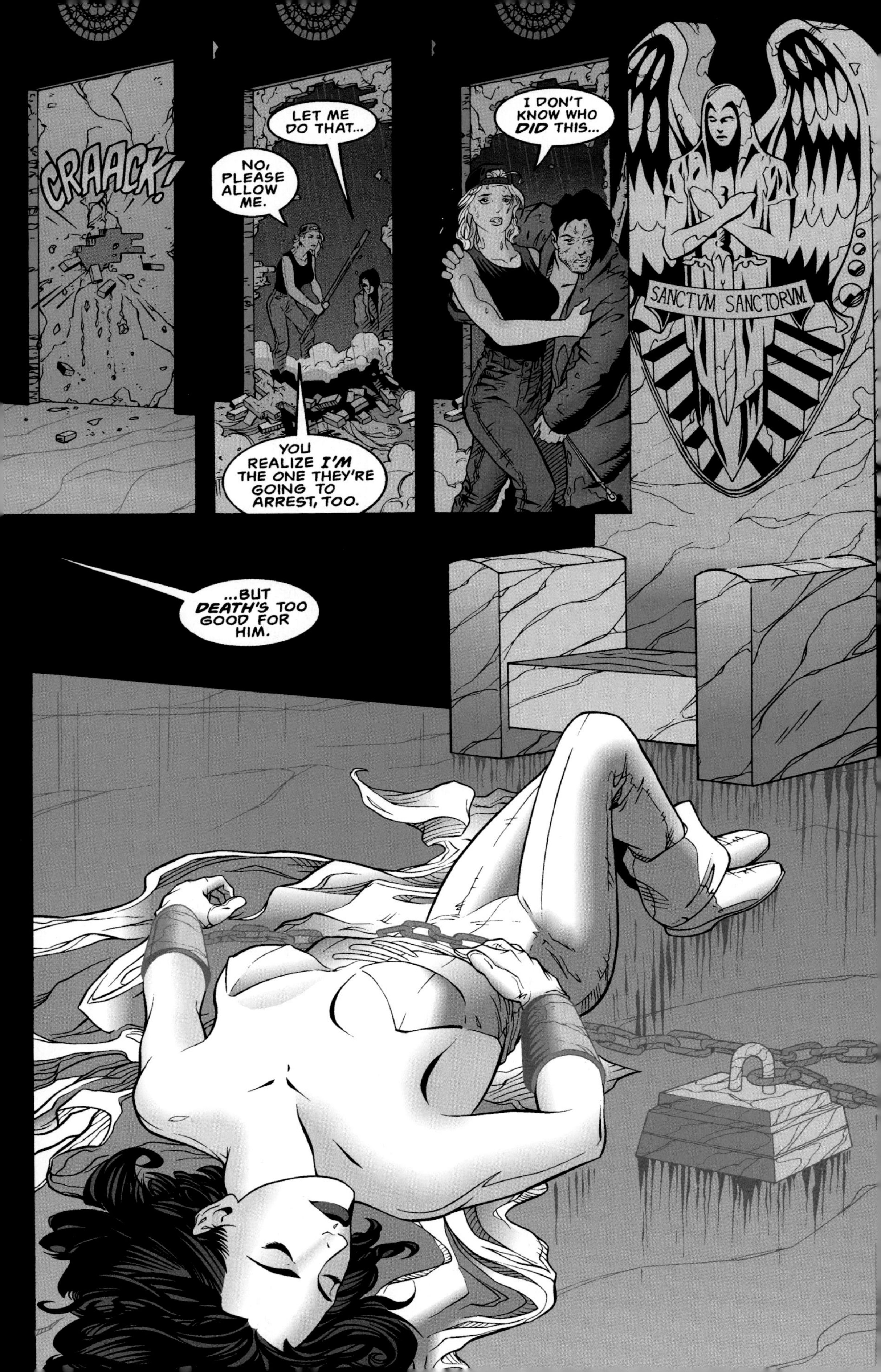
CRAACK!
LET ME DO THAT...
NO, PLEASE ALLOW ME.
YOU REALIZE I'M THE ONE THEY'RE GOING TO ARREST, TOO.
I DON'T KNOW WHO DID THIS...
SANCTVM SANCTORVM
...BUT DEATH'S TOO GOOD FOR HIM.

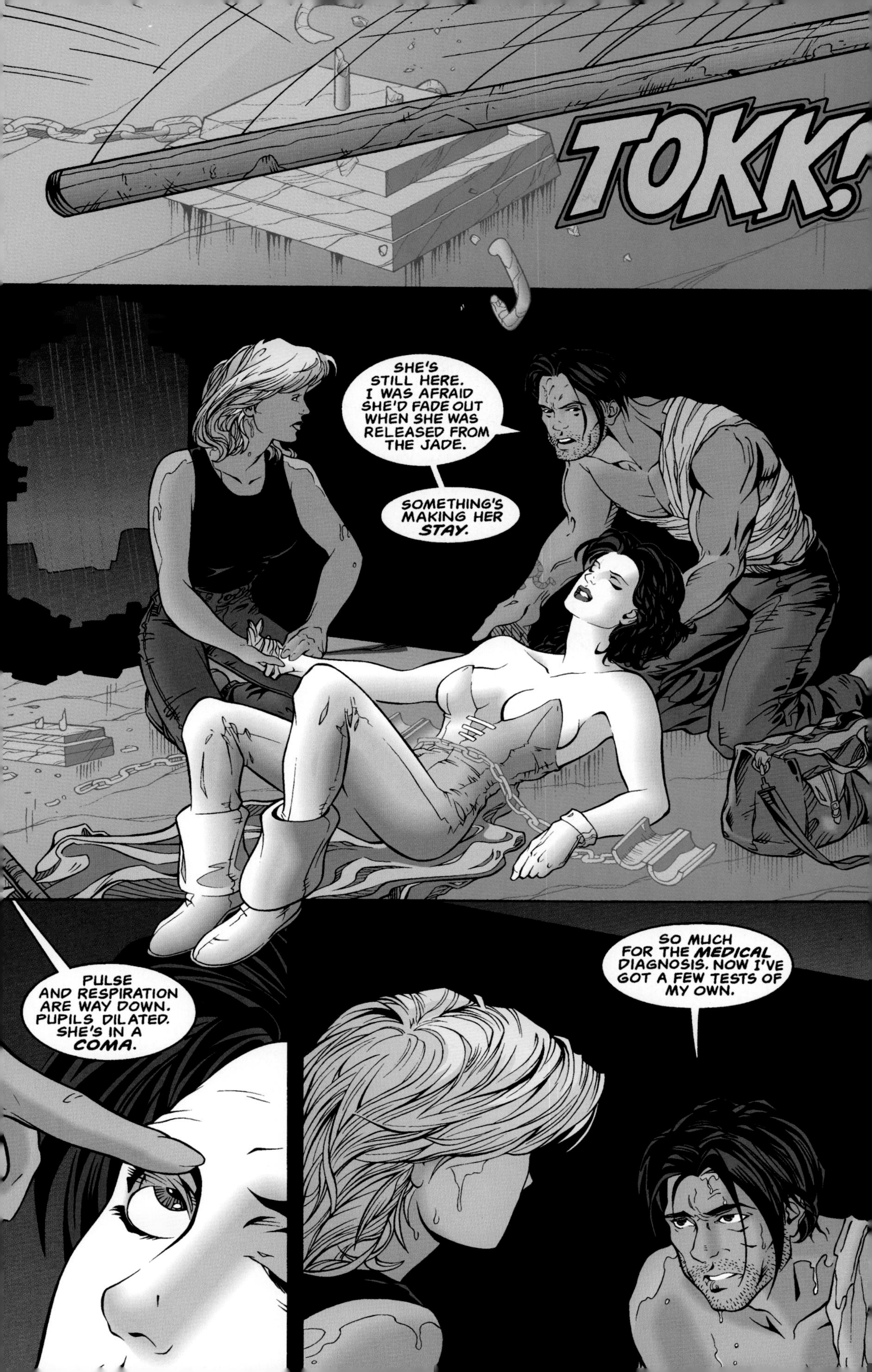
TOKK!
SHE'S STILL HERE. I WAS AFRAID SHE'D FADE OUT WHEN SHE WAS RELEASED FROM THE JADE.
SOMETHING'S MAKING HER STAY.
PULSE AND RESPIRATION ARE WAY DOWN. PUPILS DILATED. SHE'S IN A COMA.
SO MUCH FOR THE MEDICAL DIAGNOSIS. NOW I'VE GOT A FEW TESTS OF MY OWN.

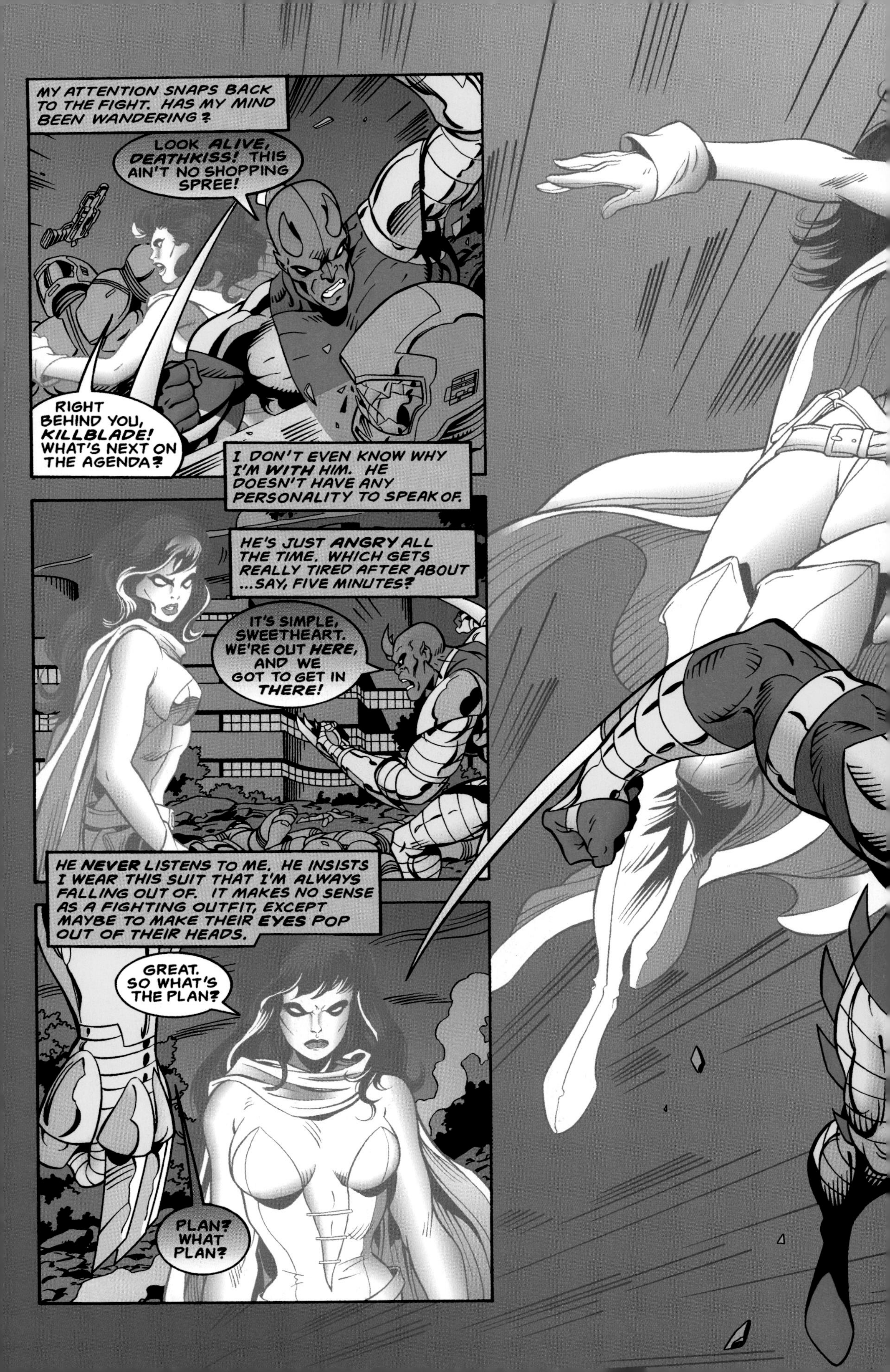
MY ATTENTION SNAPS BACK TO THE FIGHT. HAS MY MIND BEEN WANDERING?
LOOK ALIVE, DEATHKISS! THIS AIN'T NO SHOPPING SPREE!
RIGHT BEHIND YOU, KILLBLADE! WHAT'S NEXT ON THE AGENDA?
I DON'T EVEN KNOW WHY I'M WITH HIM. HE DOESN'T HAVE ANY PERSONALITY TO SPEAK OF.
HE'S JUST ANGRY ALL THE TIME. WHICH GETS REALLY TIRED AFTER ABOUT ...SAY, FIVE MINUTES?
IT'S SIMPLE, SWEETHEART. WE'RE OUT HERE, AND WE GOT TO GET IN THERE!
HE NEVER LISTENS TO ME. HE INSISTS I WEAR THIS SUIT THAT I'M ALWAYS FALLING OUT OF. IT MAKES NO SENSE AS A FIGHTING OUTFIT, EXCEPT MAYBE TO MAKE THEIR EYES POP OUT OF THEIR HEADS.
GREAT. SO WHAT'S THE PLAN?
PLAN? WHAT PLAN?

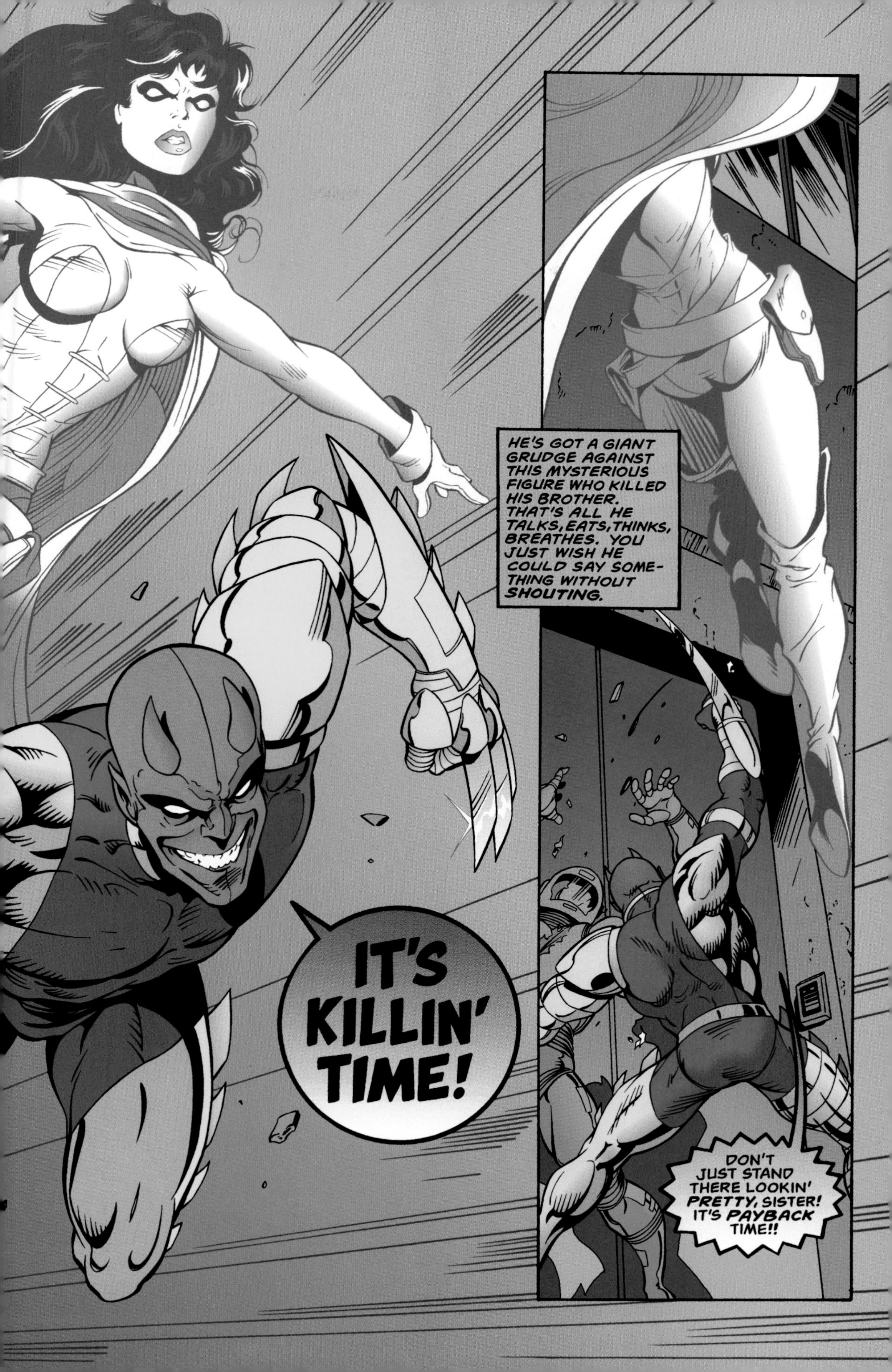
HE'S GOT A GIANT GRUDGE AGAINST THIS MYSTERIOUS FIGURE WHO KILLED HIS BROTHER. THAT'S ALL HE TALKS, EATS, THINKS, BREATHES. YOU JUST WISH HE COULD SAY SOMETHING WITHOUT SHOUTING.
IT'S KILLIN' TIME!
DON'T JUST STAND THERE LOOKIN' PRETTY, SISTER! IT'S PAYBACK TIME!!

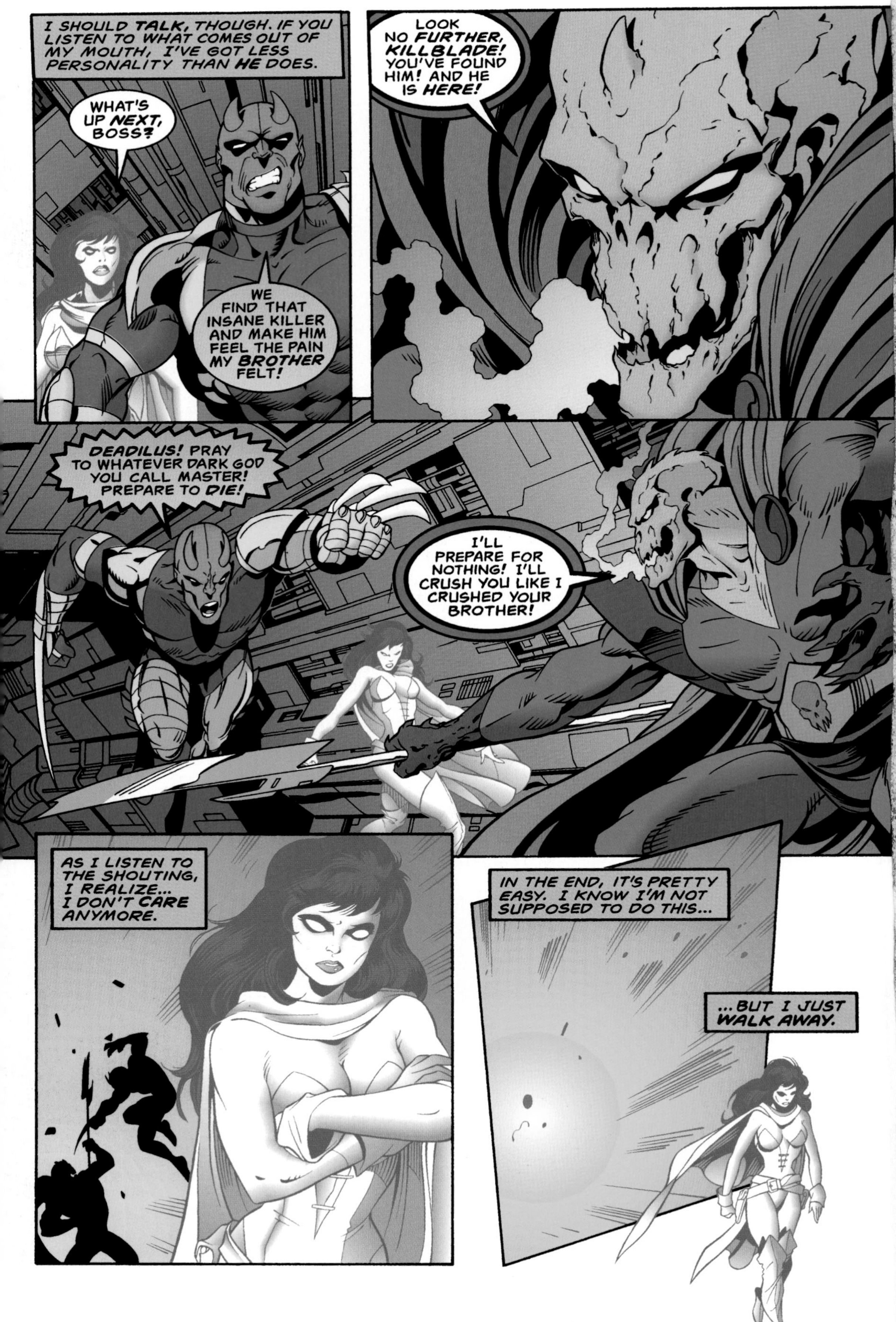
I SHOULD TALK, THOUGH. IF YOU LISTEN TO WHAT COMES OUT OF MY MOUTH, I'VE GOT LESS PERSONALITY THAN HE DOES.
WHAT'S UP NEXT, BOSS?
WE FIND THAT INSANE KILLER AND MAKE HIM FEEL THE PAIN MY BROTHER FELT!
LOOK NO FURTHER, KILLBLADE! YOU'VE FOUND HIM! AND HE IS HERE!
DEADILUS! PRAY TO WHATEVER DARK GOD YOU CALL MASTER! PREPARE TO DIE!
I'LL PREPARE FOR NOTHING! I'LL CRUSH YOU LIKE I CRUSHED YOUR BROTHER!
AS I LISTEN TO THE SHOUTING, I REALIZE... I DON'T CARE ANYMORE.
IN THE END, IT'S PRETTY EASY. I KNOW I'M NOT SUPPOSED TO DO THIS...
...BUT I JUST WALK AWAY.

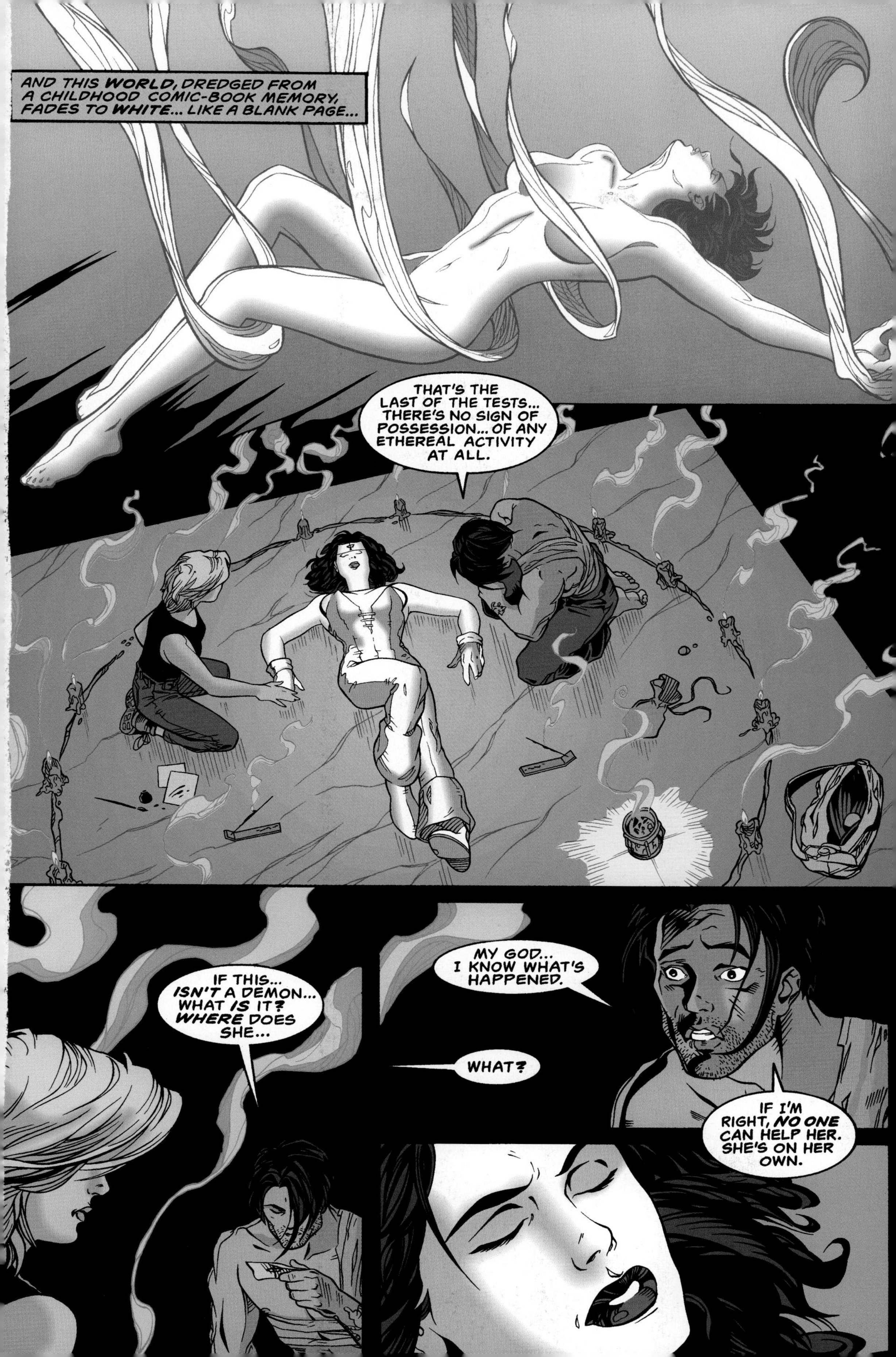
AND THIS WORLD, DREDGED FROM A CHILDHOOD COMIC-BOOK MEMORY, FADES TO WHITE... LIKE A BLANK PAGE...
THAT'S THE LAST OF THE TESTS... THERE'S NO SIGN OF POSSESSION... OF ANY ETHEREAL ACTIVITY AT ALL.
IF THIS... ISN'T A DEMON... WHAT IS IT? WHERE DOES SHE...
MY GOD... I KNOW WHAT'S HAPPENED.
WHAT?
IF I'M RIGHT, NO ONE CAN HELP HER. SHE'S ON HER OWN.

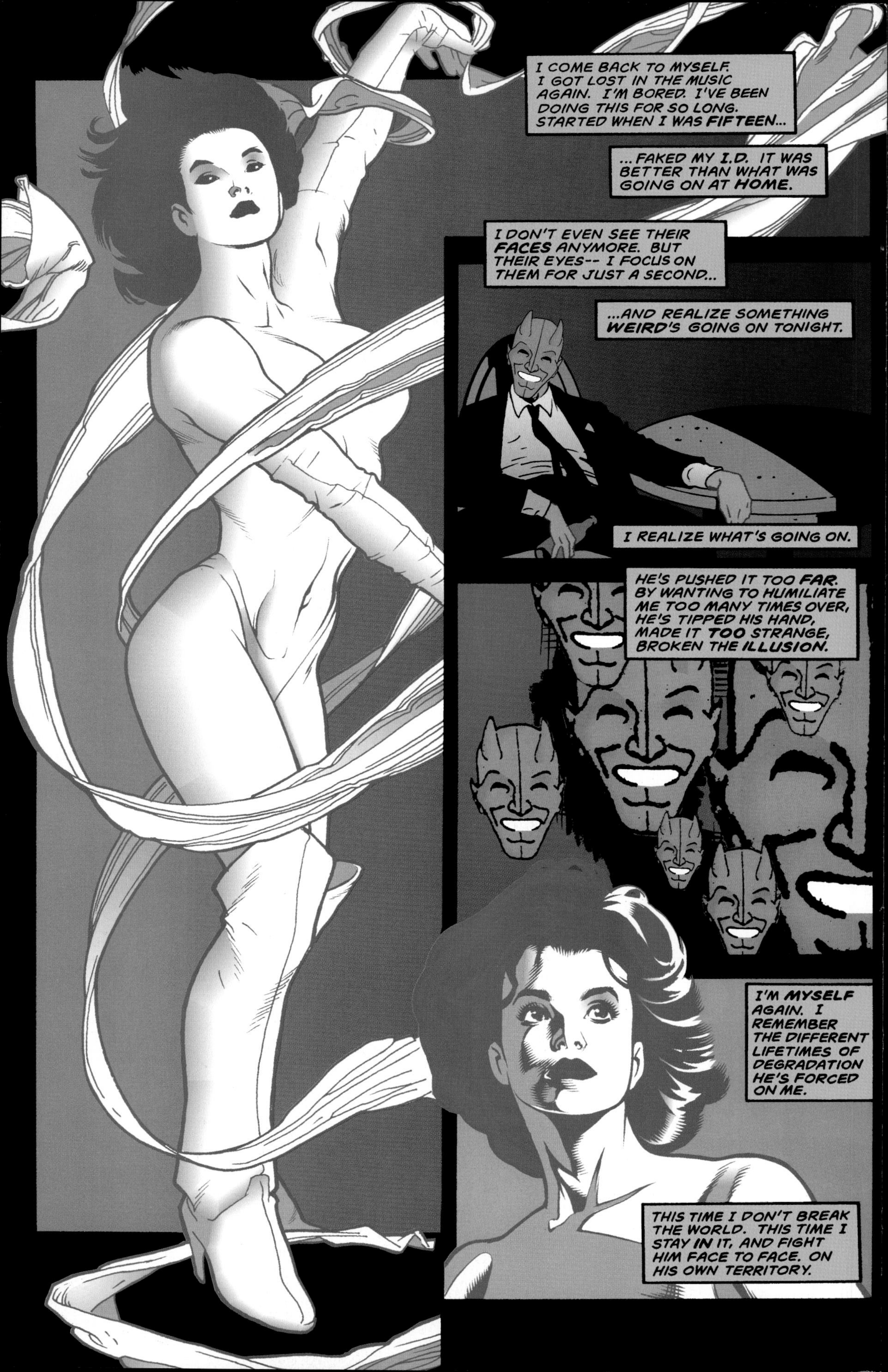
I COME BACK TO MYSELF. I GOT LOST IN THE MUSIC AGAIN. I'M BORED. I'VE BEEN DOING THIS FOR SO LONG. STARTED WHEN I WAS FIFTEEN...
...FAKED MY I.D. IT WAS BETTER THAN WHAT WAS GOING ON AT HOME.
I DON'T EVEN SEE THEIR FACES ANYMORE. BUT THEIR EYES-- I FOCUS ON THEM FOR JUST A SECOND...
...AND REALIZE SOMETHING WEIRD'S GOING ON TONIGHT.
I REALIZE WHAT'S GOING ON.
HE'S PUSHED IT TOO FAR. BY WANTING TO HUMILIATE ME TOO MANY TIMES OVER, HE'S TIPPED HIS HAND, MADE IT TOO STRANGE, BROKEN THE ILLUSION.
I'M MYSELF AGAIN. I REMEMBER THE DIFFERENT LIFETIMES OF DEGRADATION HE'S FORCED ON ME.
THIS TIME I DON'T BREAK THE WORLD. THIS TIME I STAY IN IT, AND FIGHT HIM FACE TO FACE. ON HIS OWN TERRITORY.

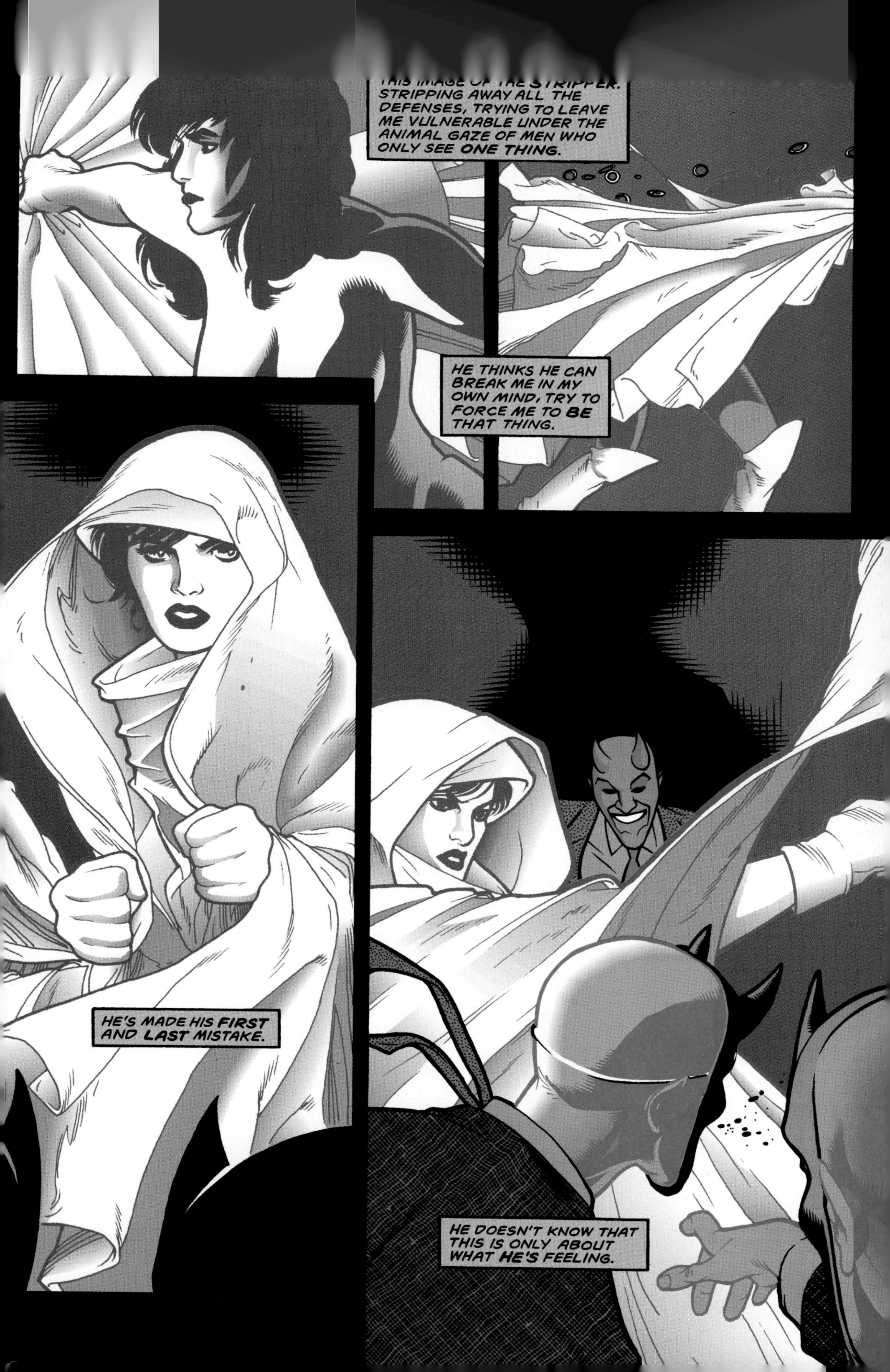
THIS IMAGE OF THE STRIPPER. STRIPPING AWAY ALL THE DEFENSES, TRYING TO LEAVE ME VULNERABLE UNDER THE ANIMAL GAZE OF MEN WHO ONLY SEE ONE THING.
HE THINKS HE CAN BREAK ME IN MY OWN MIND, TRY TO FORCE ME TO BE THAT THING.
HE'S MADE HIS FIRST AND LAST MISTAKE.
HE DOESN'T KNOW THAT THIS IS ONLY ABOUT WHAT HE'S FEELING.

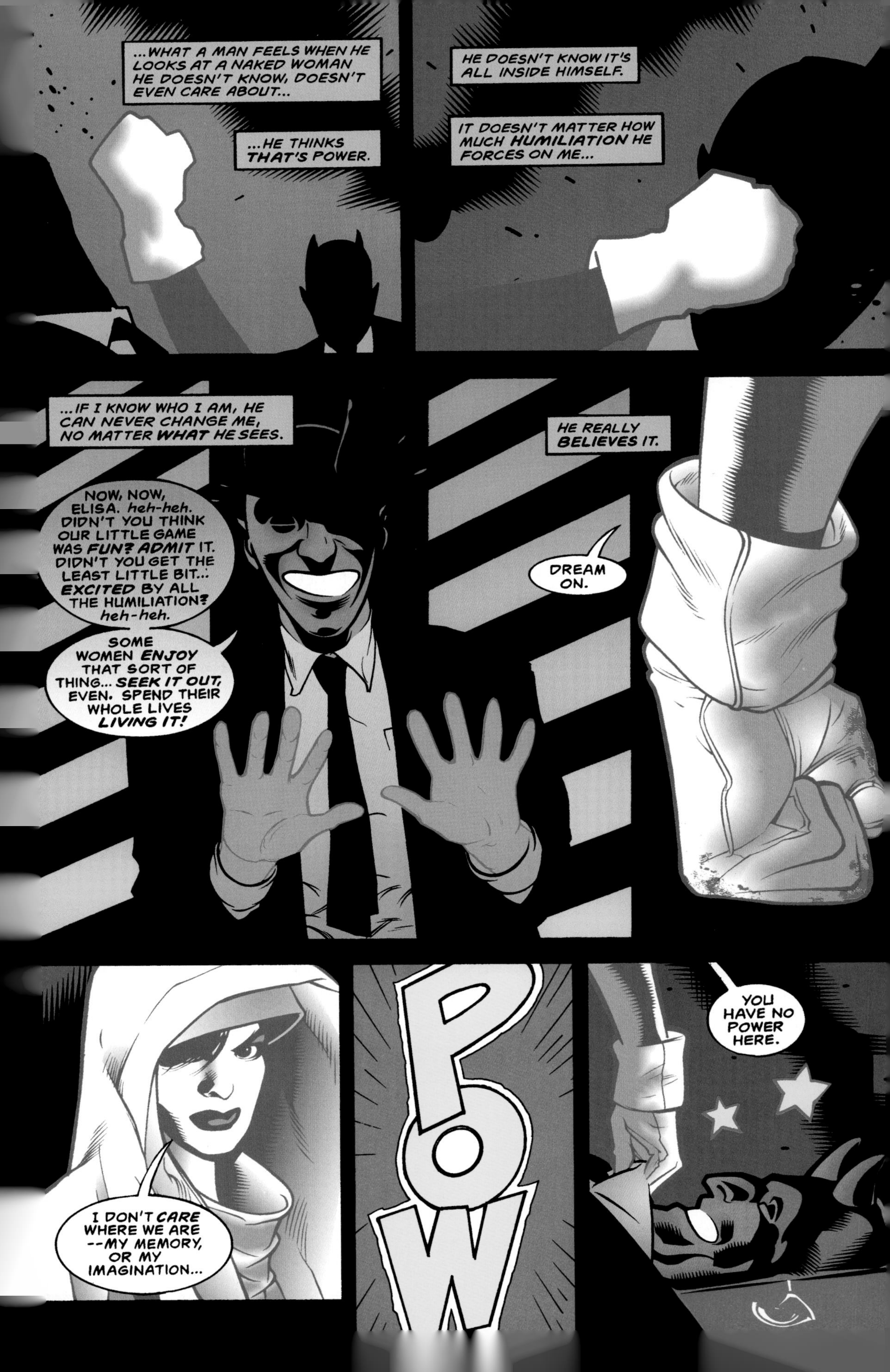
...WHAT A MAN FEELS WHEN HE LOOKS AT A NAKED WOMAN HE DOESN'T KNOW, DOESN'T EVEN CARE ABOUT...
...HE THINKS THAT'S POWER.
HE DOESN'T KNOW IT'S ALL INSIDE HIMSELF.
IT DOESN'T MATTER HOW MUCH HUMILIATION HE FORCES ON ME...
...IF I KNOW WHO I AM, HE CAN NEVER CHANGE ME, NO MATTER WHAT HE SEES.
NOW, NOW, ELISA. heh-heh. DIDN'T YOU THINK OUR LITTLE GAME WAS FUN? ADMIT IT. DIDN'T YOU GET THE LEAST LITTLE BIT... EXCITED BY ALL THE HUMILIATION? heh-heh.
SOME WOMEN ENJOY THAT SORT OF THING... SEEK IT OUT, EVEN. SPEND THEIR WHOLE LIVES LIVING IT!
HE REALLY BELIEVES IT.
DREAM ON.
I DON'T CARE WHERE WE ARE --MY MEMORY, OR MY IMAGINATION...
POW
YOU HAVE NO POWER HERE.

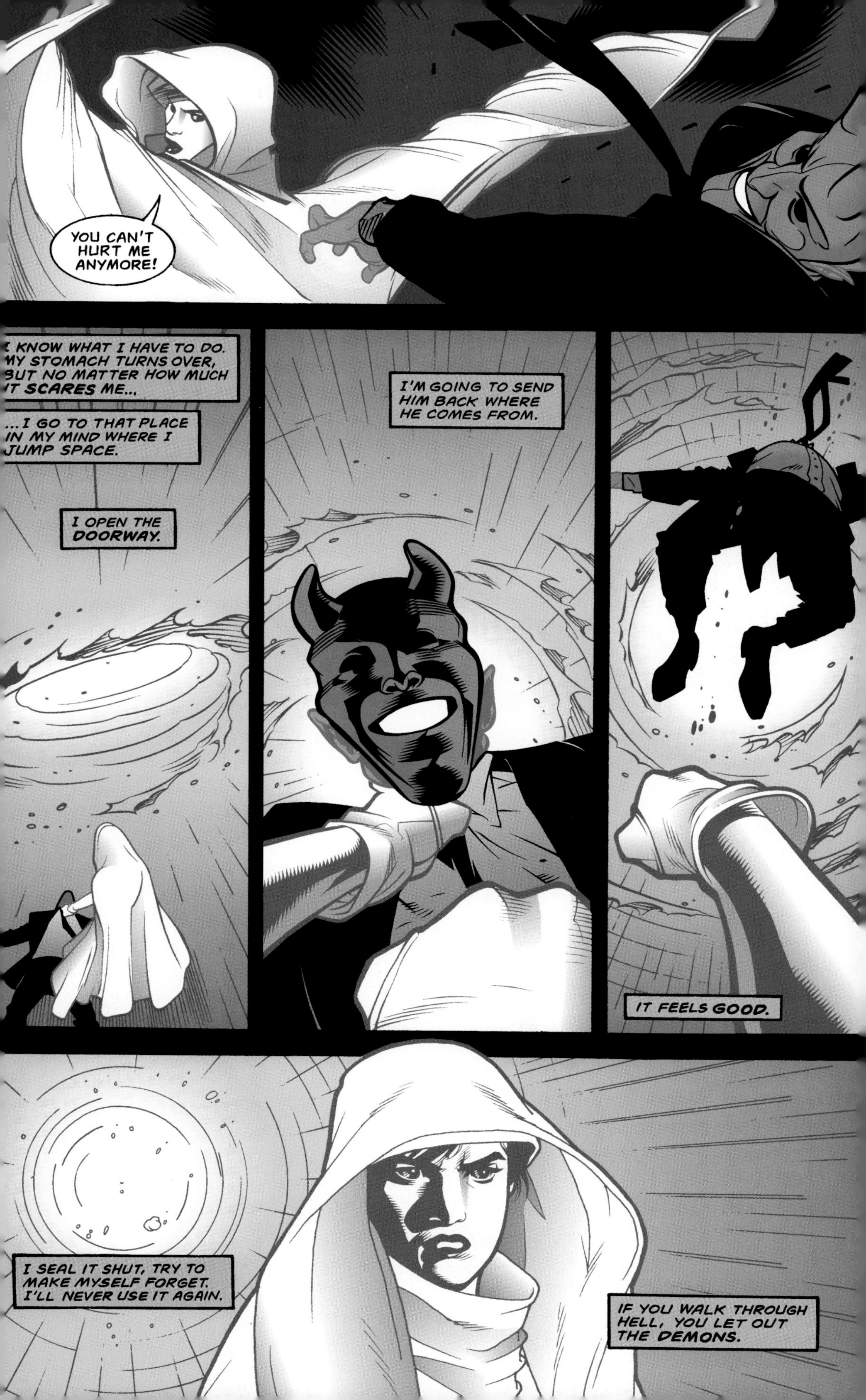
YOU CAN'T HURT ME ANYMORE!
I KNOW WHAT I HAVE TO DO. MY STOMACH TURNS OVER, BUT NO MATTER HOW MUCH IT SCARES ME...
...I GO TO THAT PLACE IN MY MIND WHERE I JUMP SPACE.
I OPEN THE DOORWAY.
I'M GOING TO SEND HIM BACK WHERE HE COMES FROM.
IT FEELS GOOD.
I SEAL IT SHUT, TRY TO MAKE MYSELF FORGET. I'LL NEVER USE IT AGAIN.
IF YOU WALK THROUGH HELL, YOU LET OUT THE DEMONS.

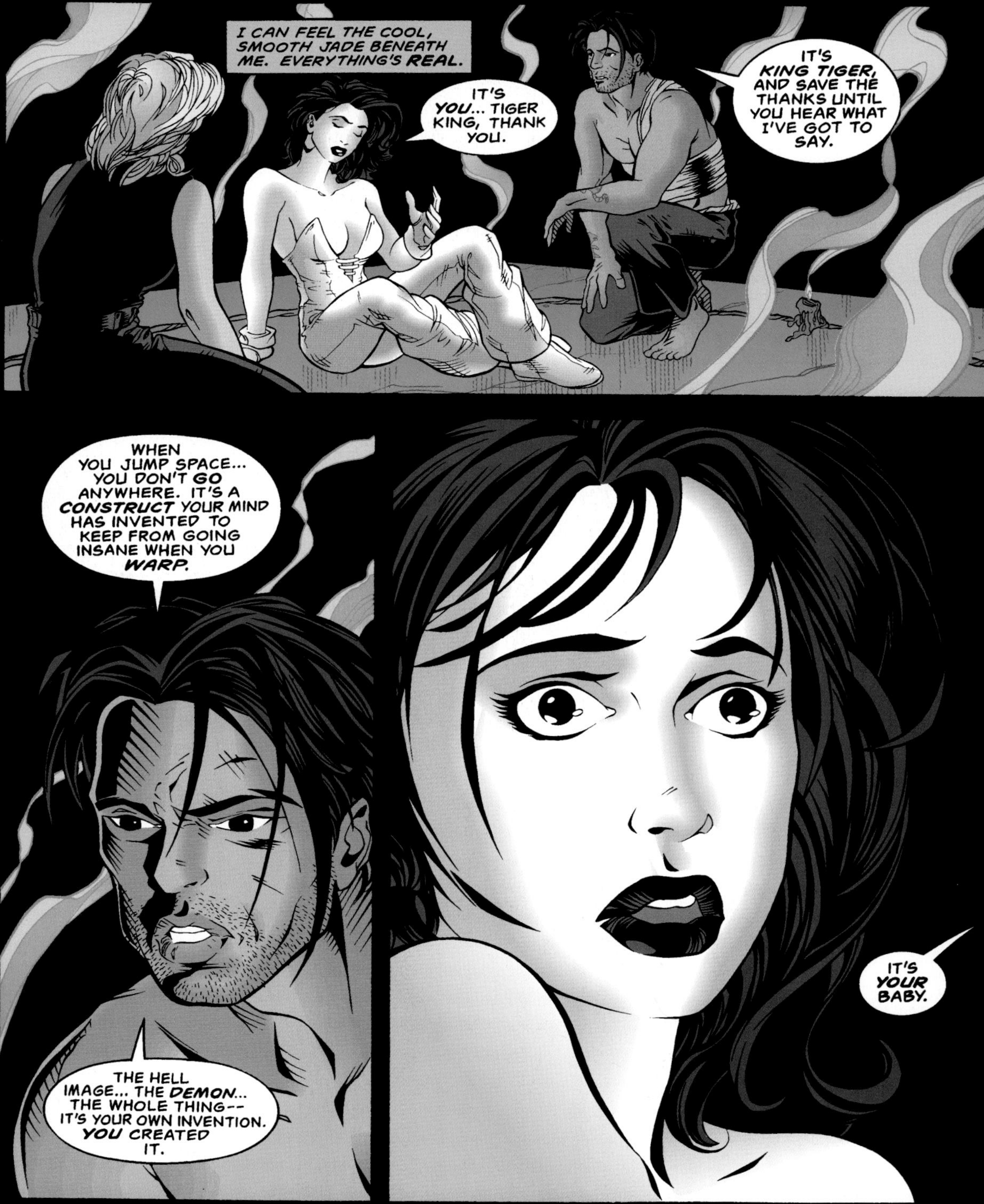
I CAN FEEL THE COOL, SMOOTH JADE BENEATH ME. EVERYTHING'S *REAL*.
IT'S *YOU*... TIGER KING, THANK YOU.
IT'S *KING TIGER*, AND SAVE THE THANKS UNTIL YOU HEAR WHAT I'VE GOT TO SAY.
WHEN YOU JUMP SPACE... YOU DON'T *GO* ANYWHERE. IT'S A *CONSTRUCT* YOUR MIND HAS INVENTED TO KEEP FROM GOING INSANE WHEN YOU *WARP*.
THE HELL IMAGE... THE *DEMON*... THE WHOLE THING-- IT'S YOUR OWN INVENTION. *YOU* CREATED IT.
IT'S *YOUR* BABY.

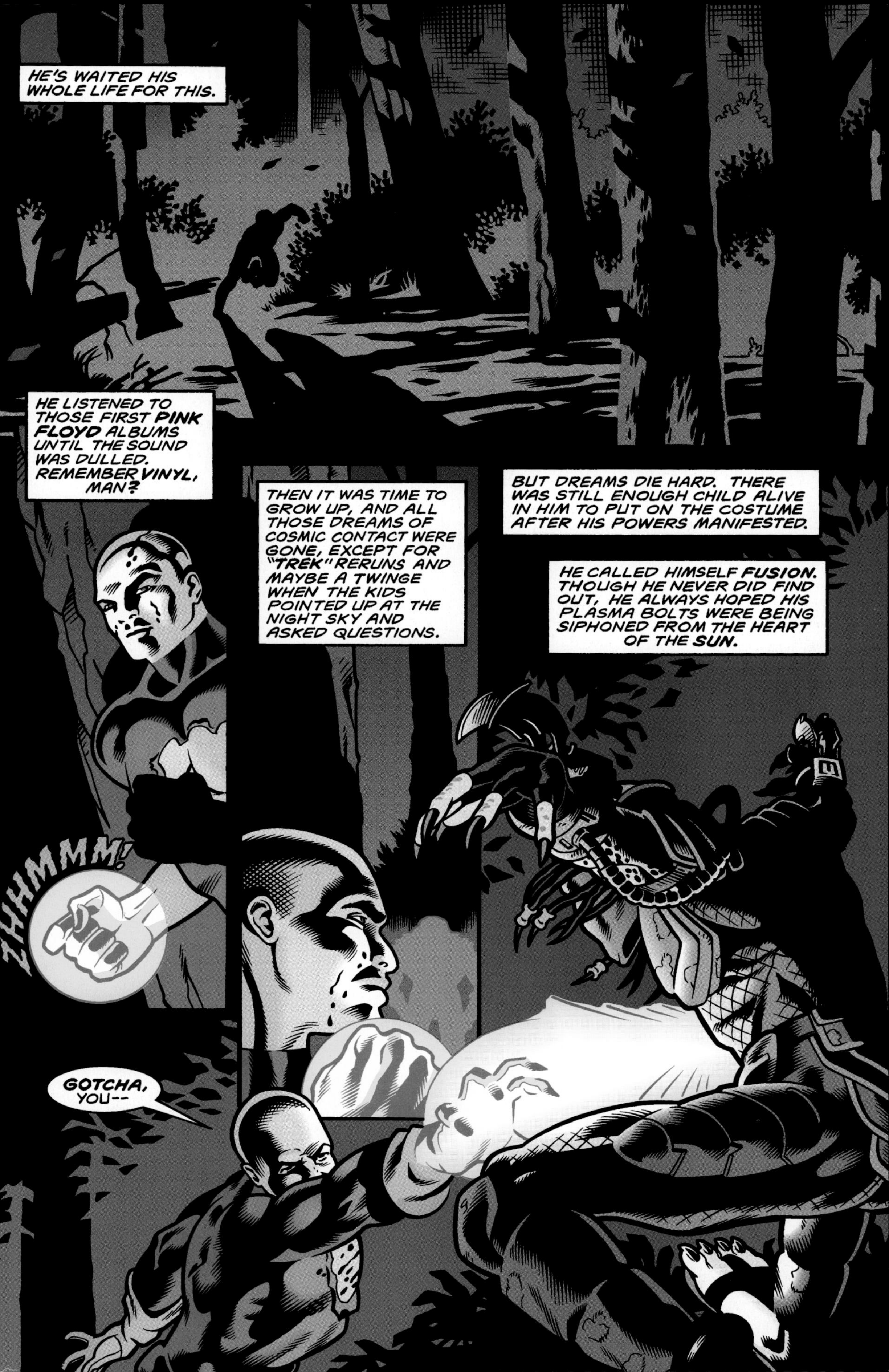
HE'S WAITED HIS WHOLE LIFE FOR THIS.
HE LISTENED TO THOSE FIRST PINK FLOYD ALBUMS UNTIL THE SOUND WAS DULLED. REMEMBER VINYL, MAN?
THEN IT WAS TIME TO GROW UP, AND ALL THOSE DREAMS OF COSMIC CONTACT WERE GONE, EXCEPT FOR "TREK" RERUNS AND MAYBE A TWINGE WHEN THE KIDS POINTED UP AT THE NIGHT SKY AND ASKED QUESTIONS.
BUT DREAMS DIE HARD. THERE WAS STILL ENOUGH CHILD ALIVE IN HIM TO PUT ON THE COSTUME AFTER HIS POWERS MANIFESTED.
HE CALLED HIMSELF FUSION. THOUGH HE NEVER DID FIND OUT, HE ALWAYS HOPED HIS PLASMA BOLTS WERE BEING SIPHONED FROM THE HEART OF THE SUN.
ZHHMMM!
GOTCHA, YOU--

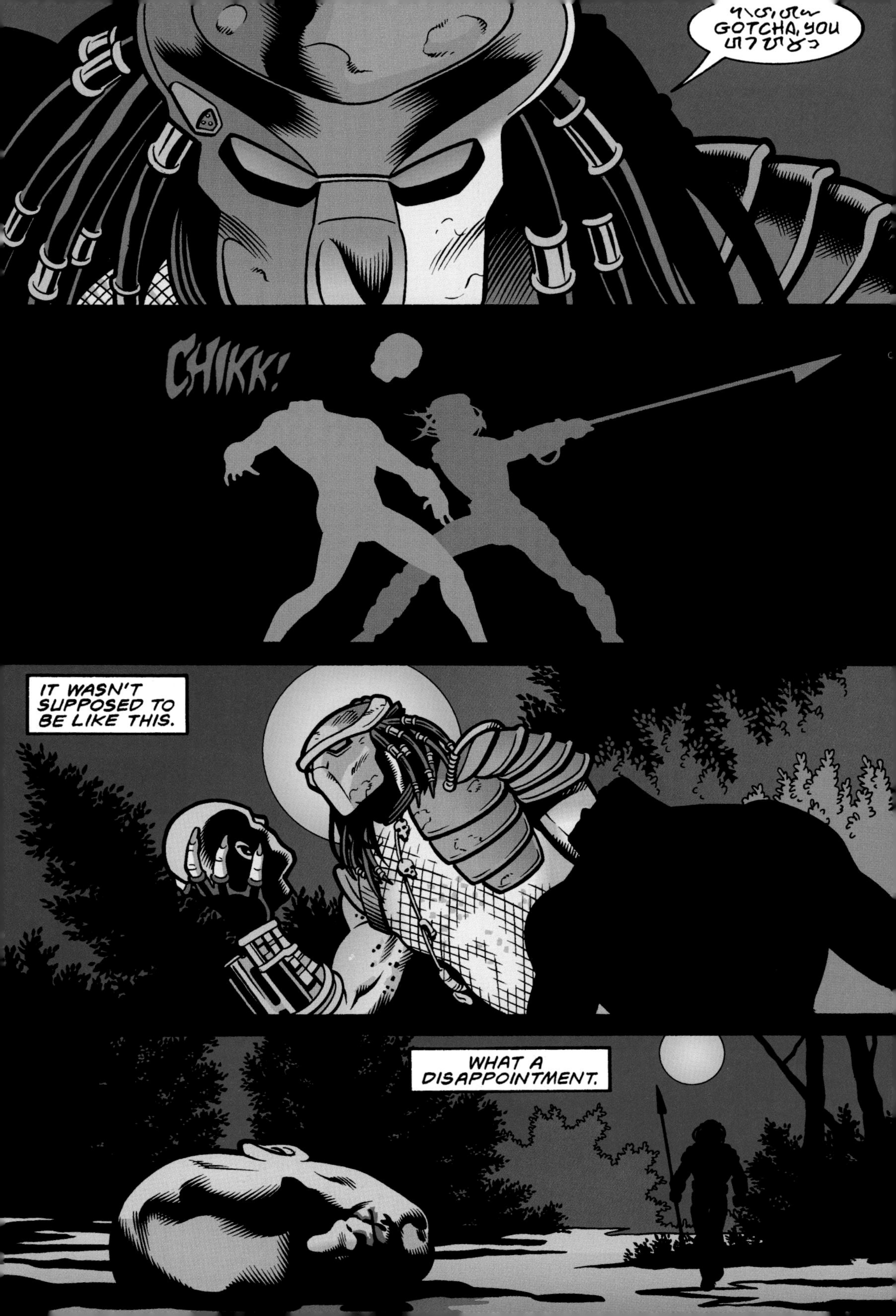
GOTCHA, YOU
CHIKK!
IT WASN'T SUPPOSED TO BE LIKE THIS.
WHAT A DISAPPOINTMENT.

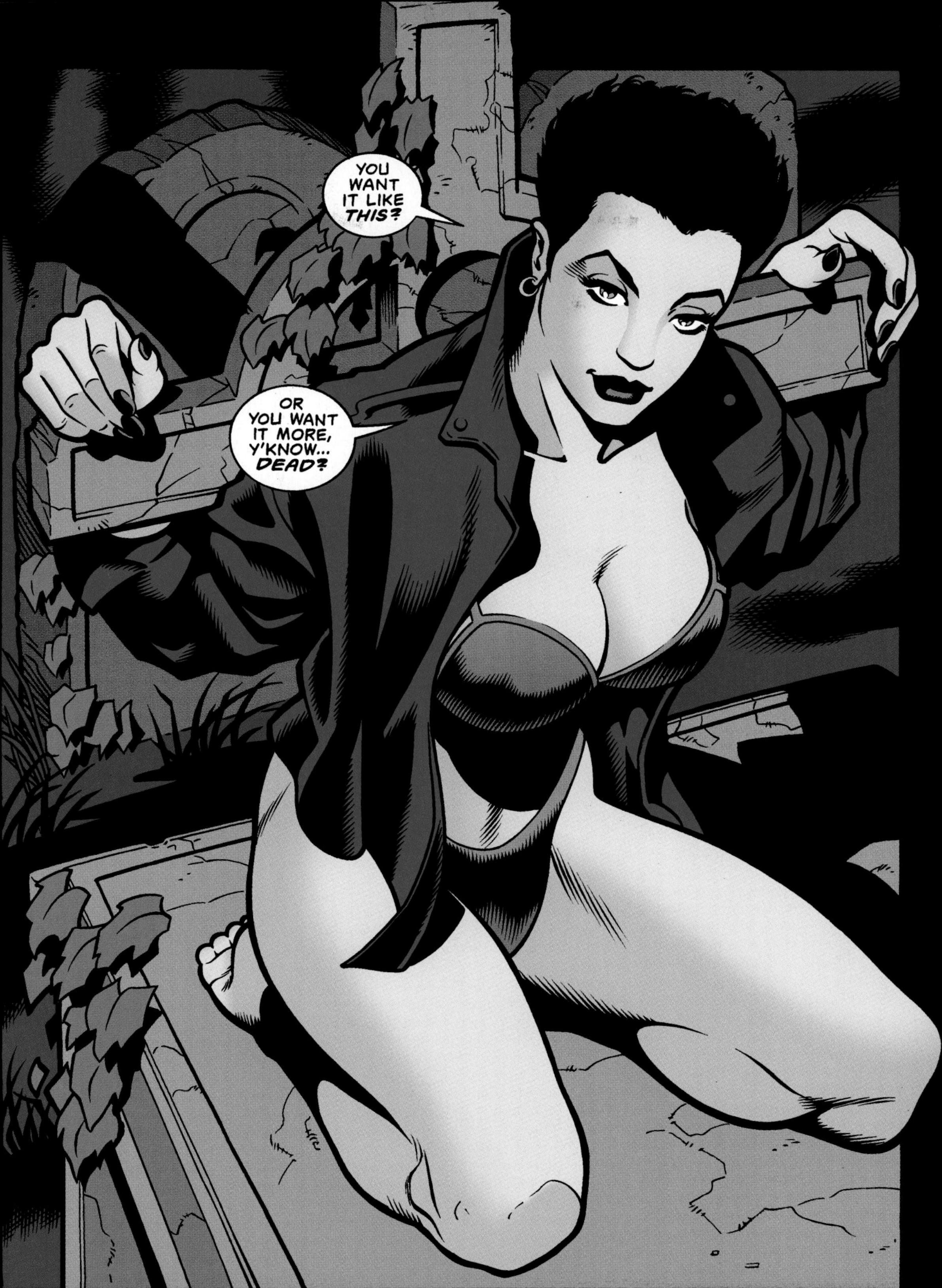
YOU WANT IT LIKE THIS?
OR YOU WANT IT MORE, Y'KNOW... DEAD?

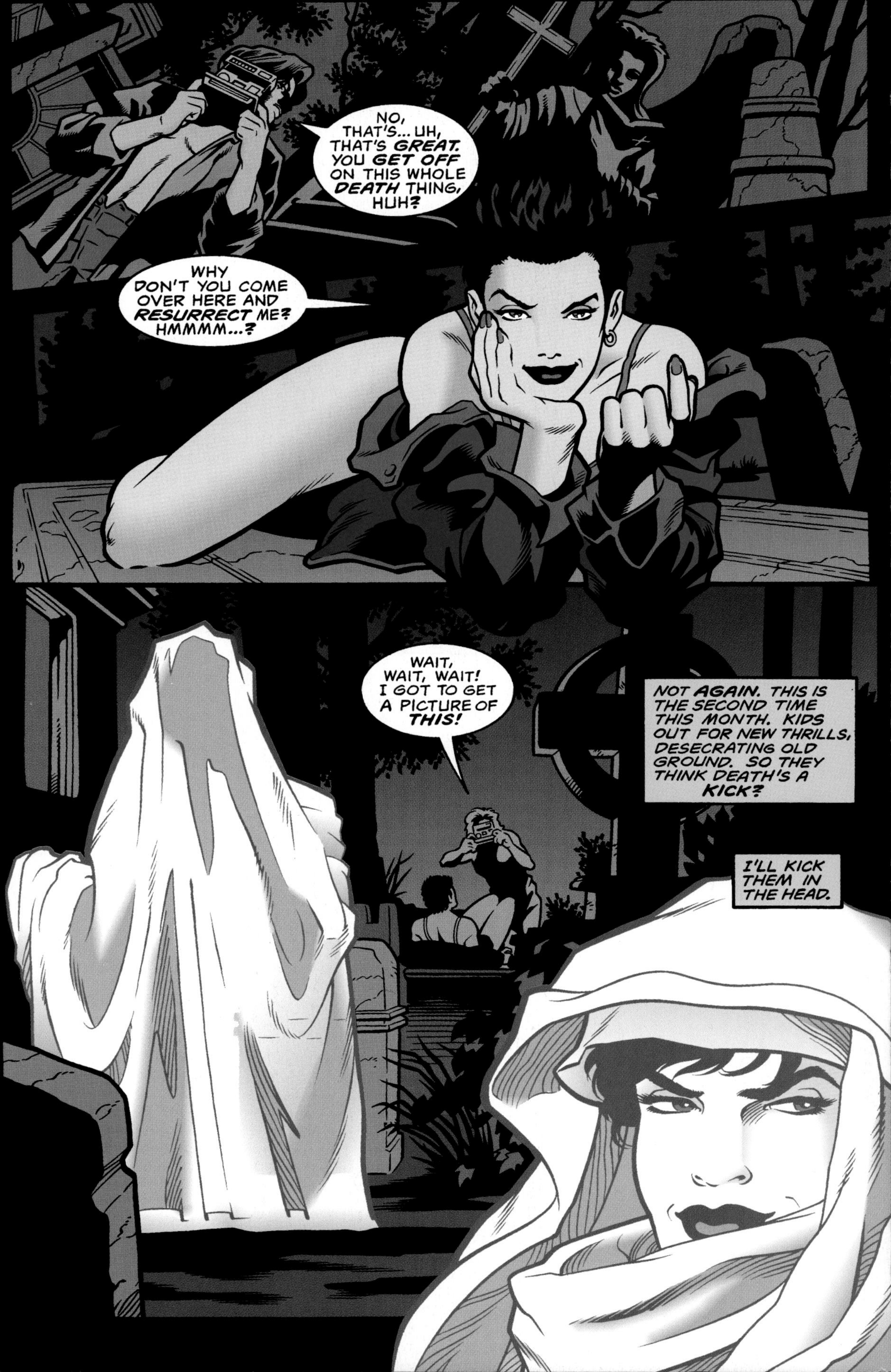

NO, THAT'S... UH, THAT'S GREAT. YOU GET OFF ON THIS WHOLE DEATH THING, HUH?
WHY DON'T YOU COME OVER HERE AND RESURRECT ME? HMMMM...?
WAIT, WAIT, WAIT! I GOT TO GET A PICTURE OF THIS!
NOT AGAIN. THIS IS THE SECOND TIME THIS MONTH. KIDS OUT FOR NEW THRILLS, DESECRATING OLD GROUND. SO THEY THINK DEATH'S A KICK?
I'LL KICK THEM IN THE HEAD.

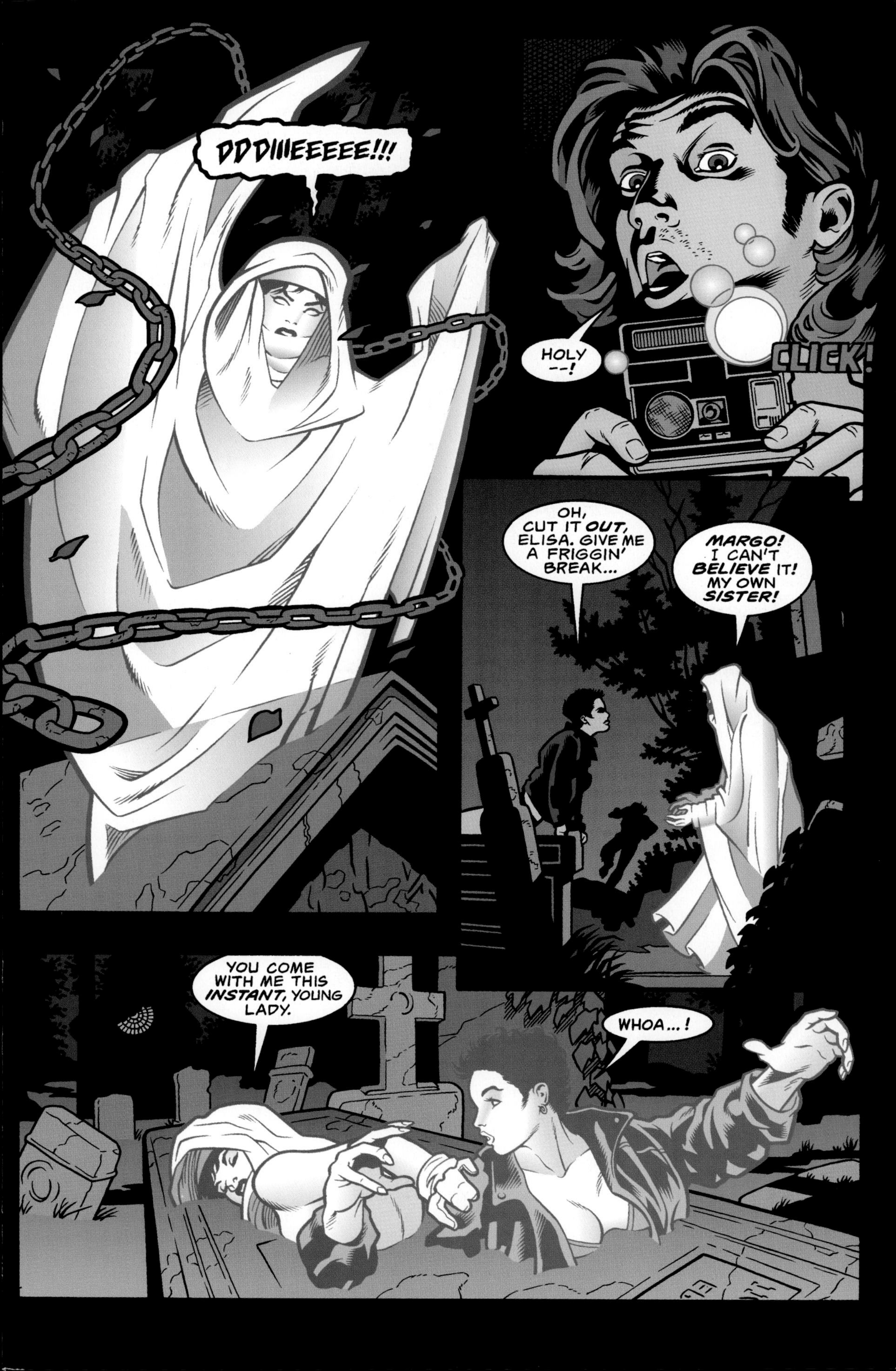
DDDIIIEEEEE!!!
HOLY --!
CLICK!
OH, CUT IT OUT, ELISA. GIVE ME A FRIGGIN' BREAK...
MARGO! I CAN'T BELIEVE IT! MY OWN SISTER!
YOU COME WITH ME THIS INSTANT, YOUNG LADY.
WHOA...!

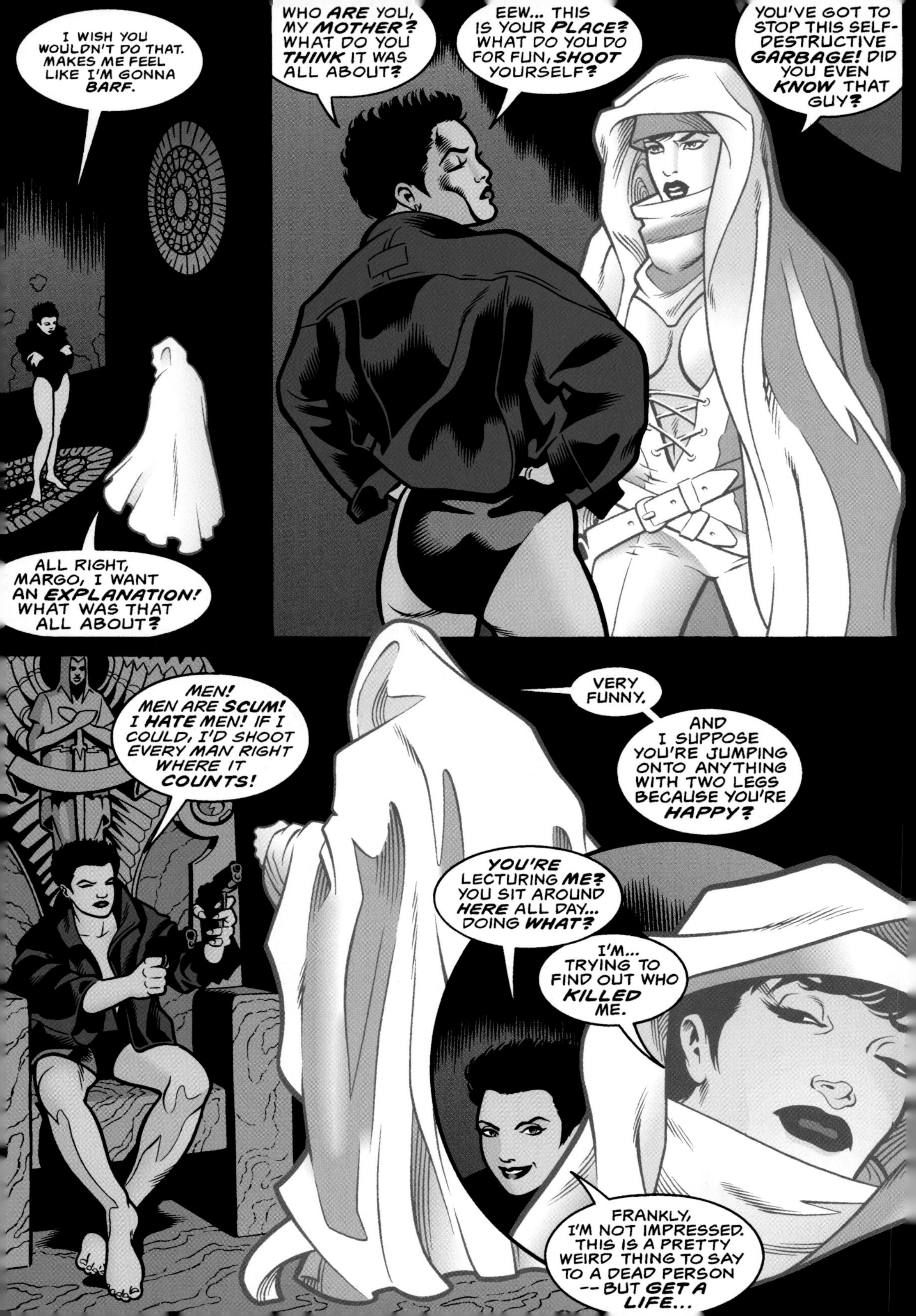

I WISH YOU WOULDN'T DO THAT. MAKES ME FEEL LIKE I'M GONNA BARF.
ALL RIGHT, MARGO, I WANT AN EXPLANATION! WHAT WAS THAT ALL ABOUT?
WHO ARE YOU, MY MOTHER? WHAT DO YOU THINK IT WAS ALL ABOUT?
EEW... THIS IS YOUR PLACE? WHAT DO YOU DO FOR FUN, SHOOT YOURSELF?
YOU'VE GOT TO STOP THIS SELF-DESTRUCTIVE GARBAGE! DID YOU EVEN KNOW THAT GUY?
MEN! MEN ARE SCUM! I HATE MEN! IF I COULD, I'D SHOOT EVERY MAN RIGHT WHERE IT COUNTS!
VERY FUNNY.
AND I SUPPOSE YOU'RE JUMPING ONTO ANYTHING WITH TWO LEGS BECAUSE YOU'RE HAPPY?
YOU'RE LECTURING ME? YOU SIT AROUND HERE ALL DAY... DOING WHAT?
I'M... TRYING TO FIND OUT WHO KILLED ME.
FRANKLY, I'M NOT IMPRESSED. THIS IS A PRETTY WEIRD THING TO SAY TO A DEAD PERSON -- BUT GET A LIFE...

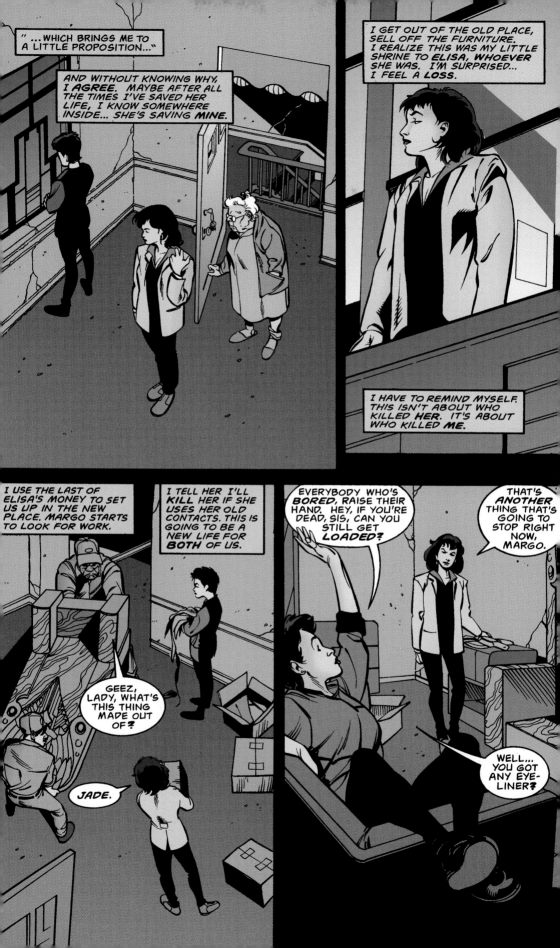

"...WHICH BRINGS ME TO A LITTLE PROPOSITION..."

AND WITHOUT KNOWING WHY, I AGREE. MAYBE AFTER ALL THE TIMES I'VE SAVED HER LIFE, I KNOW SOMEWHERE INSIDE... SHE'S SAVING MINE.

I GET OUT OF THE OLD PLACE, SELL OFF THE FURNITURE. I REALIZE THIS WAS MY LITTLE SHRINE TO ELISA, WHOEVER SHE WAS. I'M SURPRISED... I FEEL A LOSS.

I HAVE TO REMIND MYSELF. THIS ISN'T ABOUT WHO KILLED HER. IT'S ABOUT WHO KILLED ME.

I USE THE LAST OF ELISA'S MONEY TO SET US UP IN THE NEW PLACE. MARGO STARTS TO LOOK FOR WORK.

I TELL HER I'LL KILL HER IF SHE USES HER OLD CONTACTS. THIS IS GOING TO BE A NEW LIFE FOR BOTH OF US.

GEEZ, LADY, WHAT'S THIS THING MADE OUT OF?

JADE.

EVERYBODY WHO'S BORED, RAISE THEIR HAND. HEY, IF YOU'RE DEAD, SIS, CAN YOU STILL GET LOADED?

THAT'S ANOTHER THING THAT'S GOING TO STOP RIGHT NOW, MARGO.

WELL... YOU GOT ANY EYE-LINER?

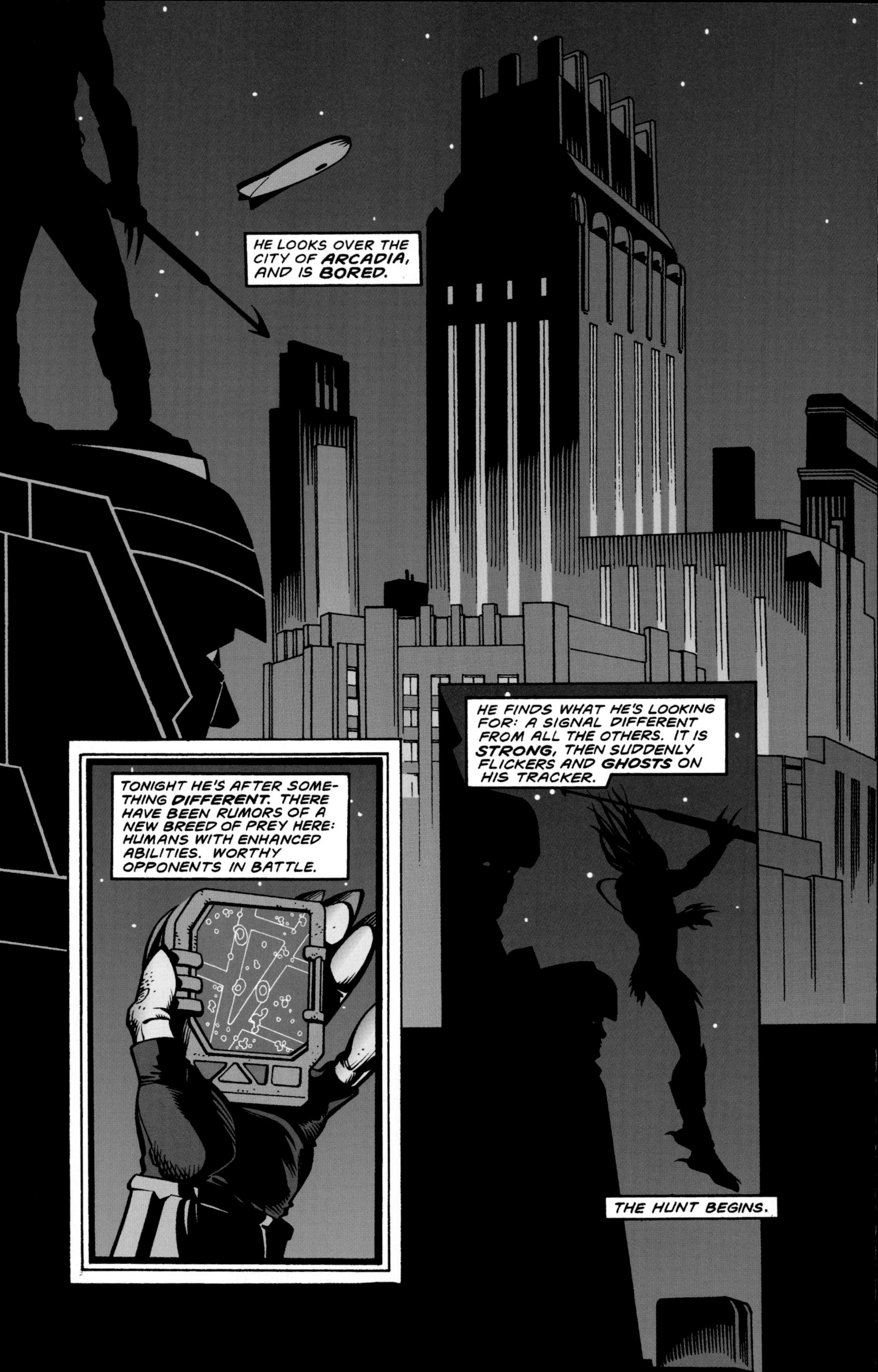
HE LOOKS OVER THE CITY OF ARCADIA, AND IS BORED.
TONIGHT HE'S AFTER SOMETHING DIFFERENT. THERE HAVE BEEN RUMORS OF A NEW BREED OF PREY HERE: HUMANS WITH ENHANCED ABILITIES. WORTHY OPPONENTS IN BATTLE.
HE FINDS WHAT HE'S LOOKING FOR: A SIGNAL DIFFERENT FROM ALL THE OTHERS. IT IS STRONG, THEN SUDDENLY FLICKERS AND GHOSTS ON HIS TRACKER.
THE HUNT BEGINS.

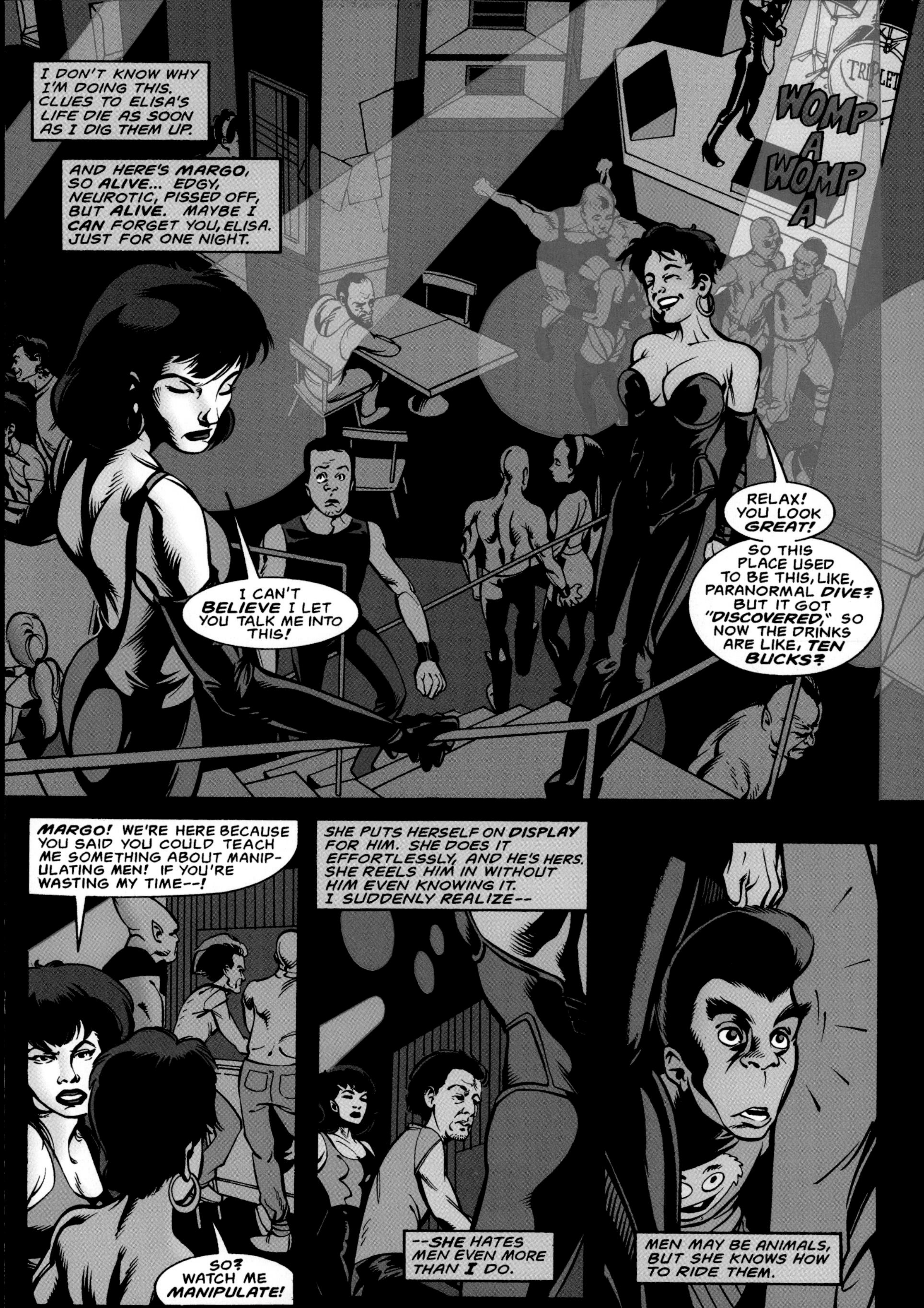

I DON'T KNOW WHY I'M DOING THIS. CLUES TO ELISA'S LIFE DIE AS SOON AS I DIG THEM UP.
AND HERE'S MARGO, SO ALIVE... EDGY, NEUROTIC, PISSED OFF, BUT ALIVE. MAYBE I CAN FORGET YOU, ELISA. JUST FOR ONE NIGHT.
TRIPLET
WOMP A WOMP A
RELAX! YOU LOOK GREAT!
I CAN'T BELIEVE I LET YOU TALK ME INTO THIS!
SO THIS PLACE USED TO BE THIS, LIKE, PARANORMAL DIVE? BUT IT GOT "DISCOVERED," SO NOW THE DRINKS ARE LIKE, TEN BUCKS?
MARGO! WE'RE HERE BECAUSE YOU SAID YOU COULD TEACH ME SOMETHING ABOUT MANIP-ULATING MEN! IF YOU'RE WASTING MY TIME--!
SO? WATCH ME MANIPULATE!
SHE PUTS HERSELF ON DISPLAY FOR HIM. SHE DOES IT EFFORTLESSLY, AND HE'S HERS. SHE REELS HIM IN WITHOUT HIM EVEN KNOWING IT. I SUDDENLY REALIZE--
--SHE HATES MEN EVEN MORE THAN I DO.
MEN MAY BE ANIMALS, BUT SHE KNOWS HOW TO RIDE THEM.

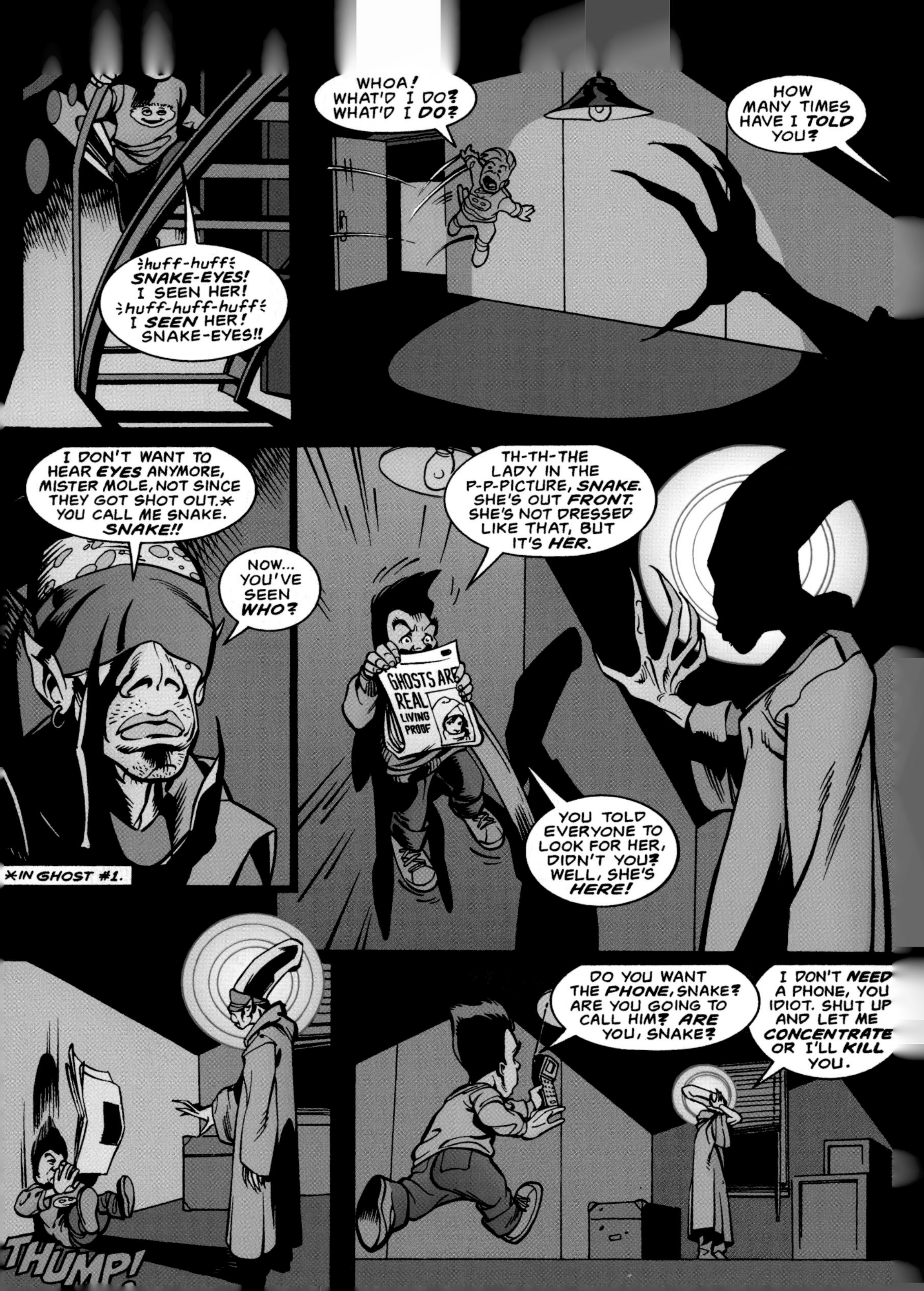

WHOA! WHAT'D I DO? WHAT'D I DO?
HOW MANY TIMES HAVE I TOLD YOU?
huff-huff SNAKE-EYES! I SEEN HER! huff-huff-huff I SEEN HER! SNAKE-EYES!!
I DON'T WANT TO HEAR EYES ANYMORE, MISTER MOLE, NOT SINCE THEY GOT SHOT OUT.* YOU CALL ME SNAKE. SNAKE!!
NOW... YOU'VE SEEN WHO?
*IN GHOST #1.
TH-TH-THE LADY IN THE P-P-PICTURE, SNAKE. SHE'S OUT FRONT. SHE'S NOT DRESSED LIKE THAT, BUT IT'S HER.
GHOSTS ARE REAL LIVING PROOF
YOU TOLD EVERYONE TO LOOK FOR HER, DIDN'T YOU? WELL, SHE'S HERE!
THUMP!
DO YOU WANT THE PHONE, SNAKE? ARE YOU GOING TO CALL HIM? ARE YOU, SNAKE?
I DON'T NEED A PHONE, YOU IDIOT. SHUT UP AND LET ME CONCENTRATE OR I'LL KILL YOU.

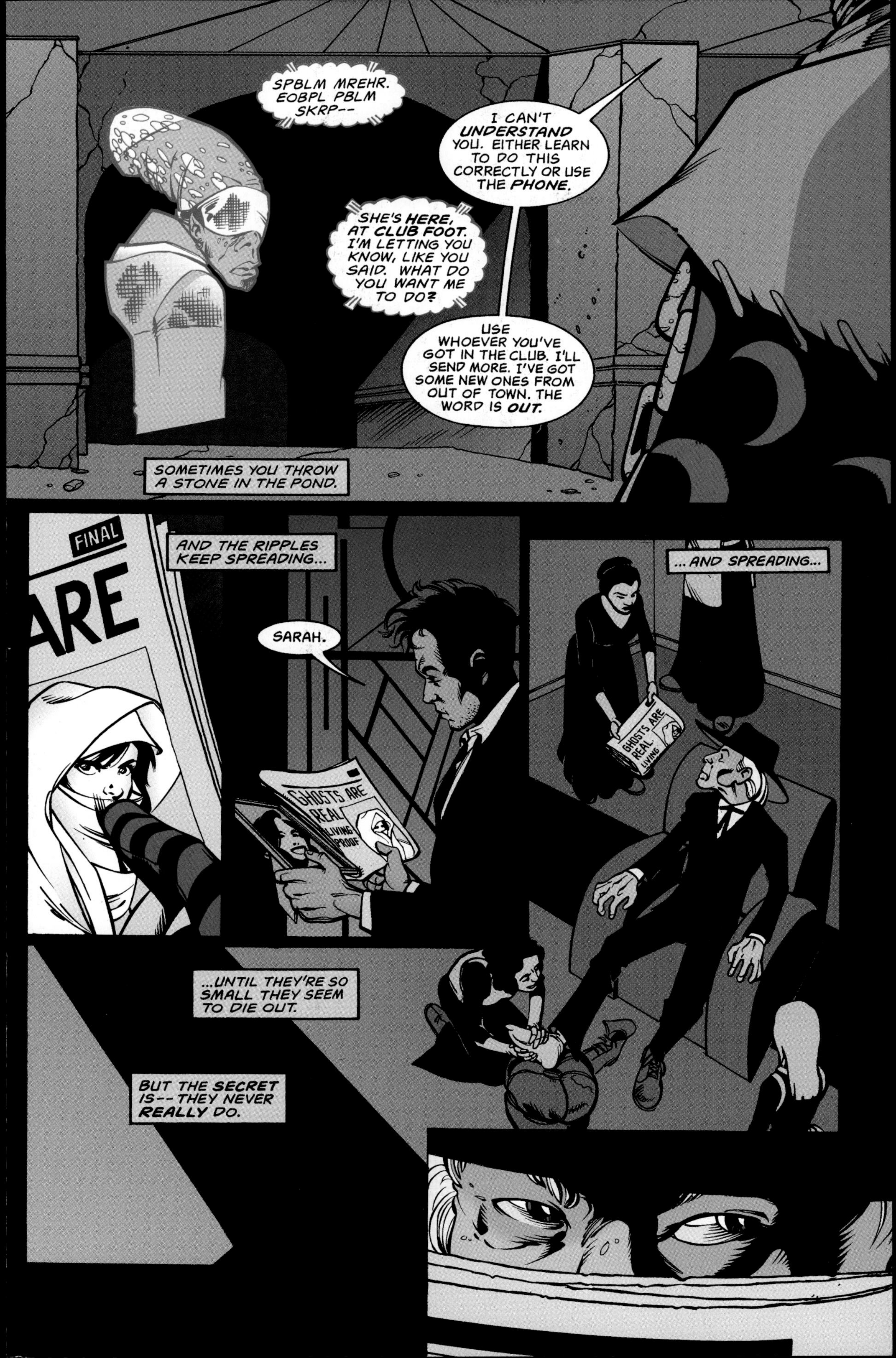

SPBLM MREHR. EOBPL PBLM SKRP--
I CAN'T UNDERSTAND YOU. EITHER LEARN TO DO THIS CORRECTLY OR USE THE PHONE.
SHE'S HERE, AT CLUB FOOT. I'M LETTING YOU KNOW, LIKE YOU SAID. WHAT DO YOU WANT ME TO DO?
USE WHOEVER YOU'VE GOT IN THE CLUB. I'LL SEND MORE. I'VE GOT SOME NEW ONES FROM OUT OF TOWN. THE WORD IS OUT.
SOMETIMES YOU THROW A STONE IN THE POND.
FINAL
ARE
AND THE RIPPLES KEEP SPREADING...
SARAH.
GHOSTS ARE REAL LIVING PROOF
...AND SPREADING...
GHOSTS ARE REAL LIVING
...UNTIL THEY'RE SO SMALL THEY SEEM TO DIE OUT.
BUT THE SECRET IS-- THEY NEVER REALLY DO.

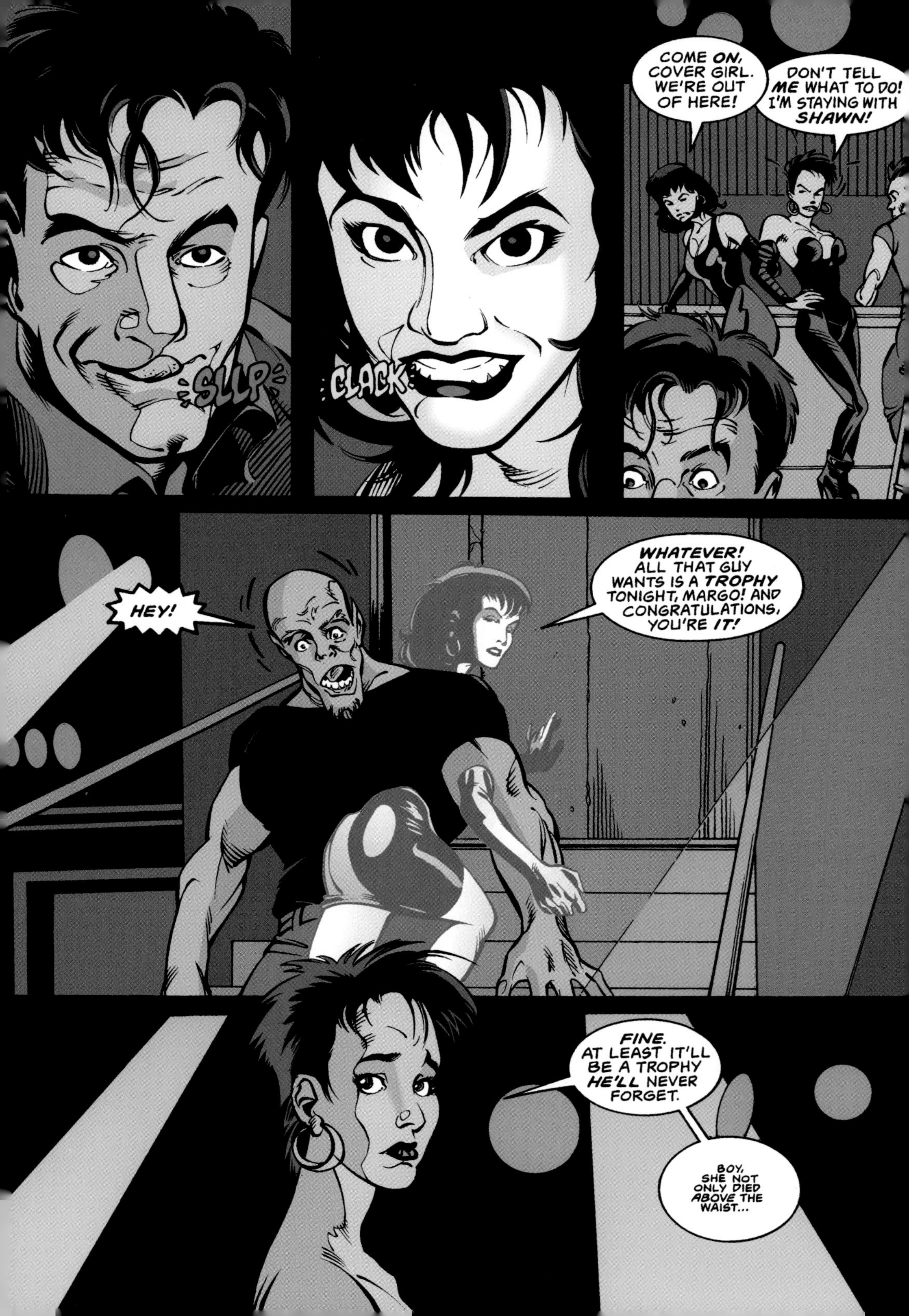
SLLP
CLACK
COME ON, COVER GIRL. WE'RE OUT OF HERE!
DON'T TELL ME WHAT TO DO! I'M STAYING WITH SHAWN!
HEY!
WHATEVER! ALL THAT GUY WANTS IS A TROPHY TONIGHT, MARGO! AND CONGRATULATIONS, YOU'RE IT!
FINE. AT LEAST IT'LL BE A TROPHY HE'LL NEVER FORGET.
BOY, SHE NOT ONLY DIED ABOVE THE WAIST...

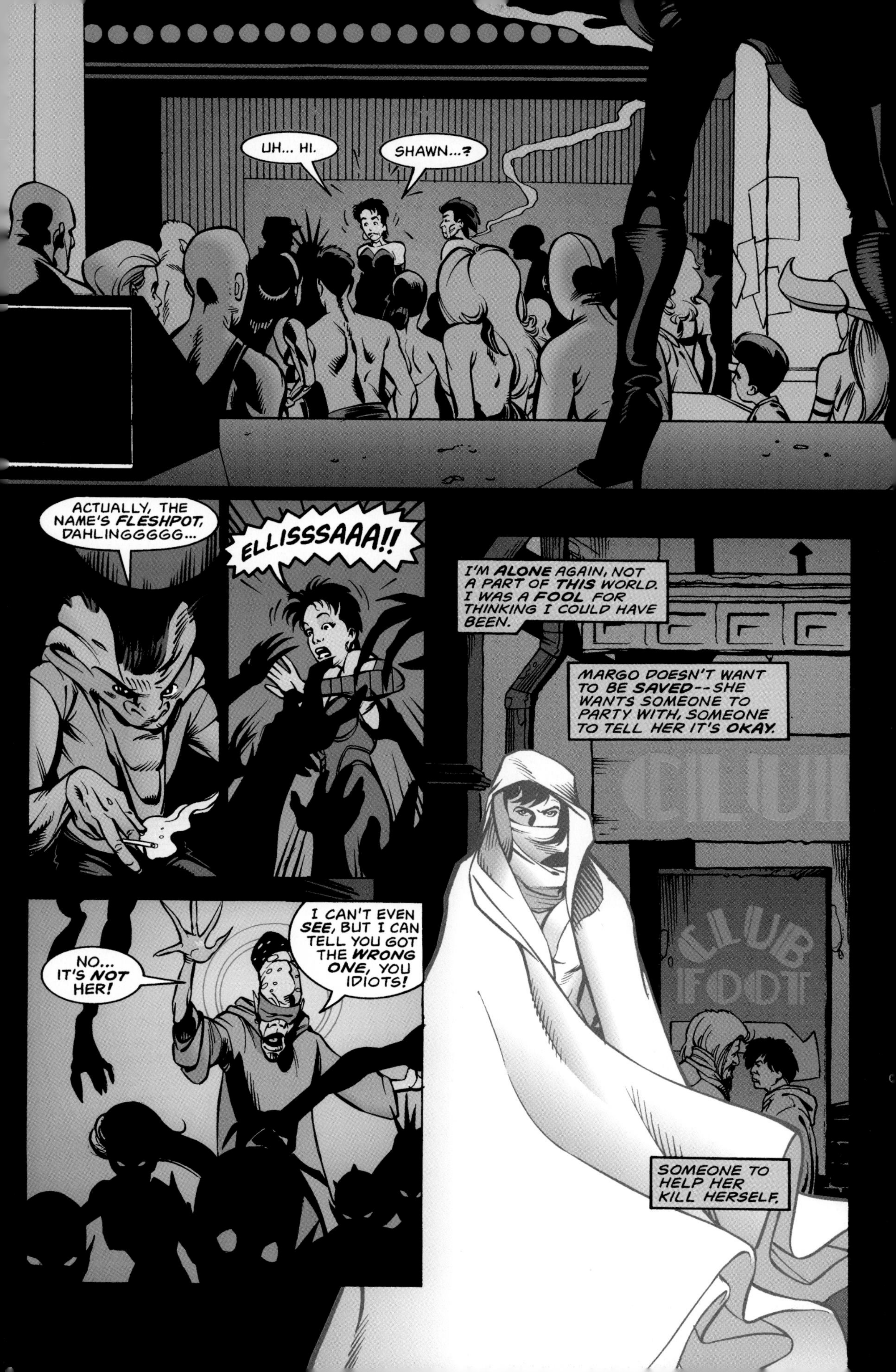

UH... HI.
SHAWN...?
ACTUALLY, THE NAME'S FLESHPOT, DAHLINGGGGG...
ELLISSSAAA!!
I'M ALONE AGAIN, NOT A PART OF THIS WORLD. I WAS A FOOL FOR THINKING I COULD HAVE BEEN.
MARGO DOESN'T WANT TO BE SAVED--SHE WANTS SOMEONE TO PARTY WITH, SOMEONE TO TELL HER IT'S OKAY.
CLUB FOOT
NO... IT'S NOT HER!
I CAN'T EVEN SEE, BUT I CAN TELL YOU GOT THE WRONG ONE, YOU IDIOTS!
SOMEONE TO HELP HER KILL HERSELF.

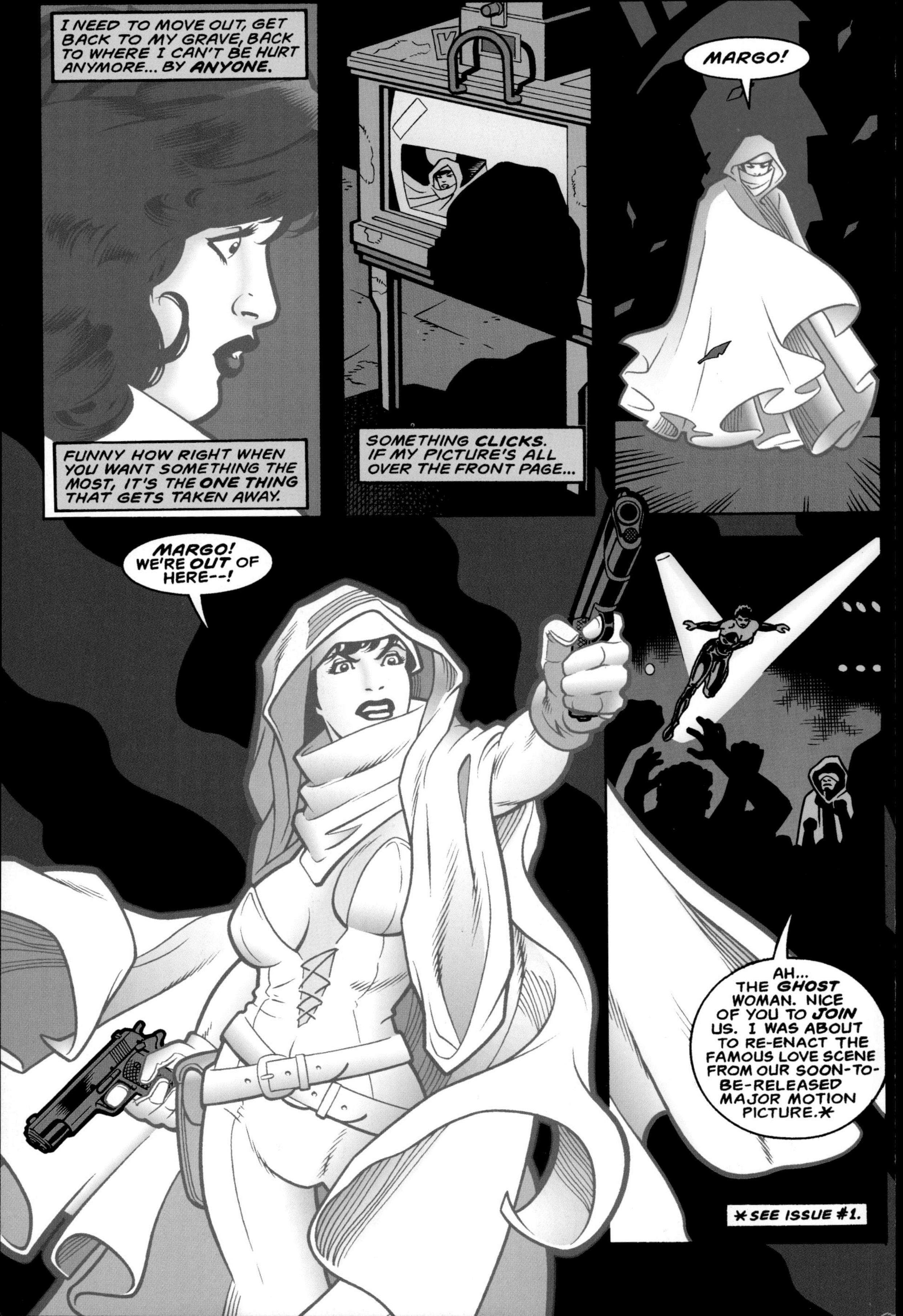
I NEED TO MOVE OUT, GET BACK TO MY GRAVE, BACK TO WHERE I CAN'T BE HURT ANYMORE... BY ANYONE.
FUNNY HOW RIGHT WHEN YOU WANT SOMETHING THE MOST, IT'S THE ONE THING THAT GETS TAKEN AWAY.
SOMETHING CLICKS. IF MY PICTURE'S ALL OVER THE FRONT PAGE...
MARGO!
MARGO! WE'RE OUT OF HERE--!
AH... THE GHOST WOMAN. NICE OF YOU TO JOIN US. I WAS ABOUT TO RE-ENACT THE FAMOUS LOVE SCENE FROM OUR SOON-TO-BE-RELEASED MAJOR MOTION PICTURE.*
*SEE ISSUE #1.

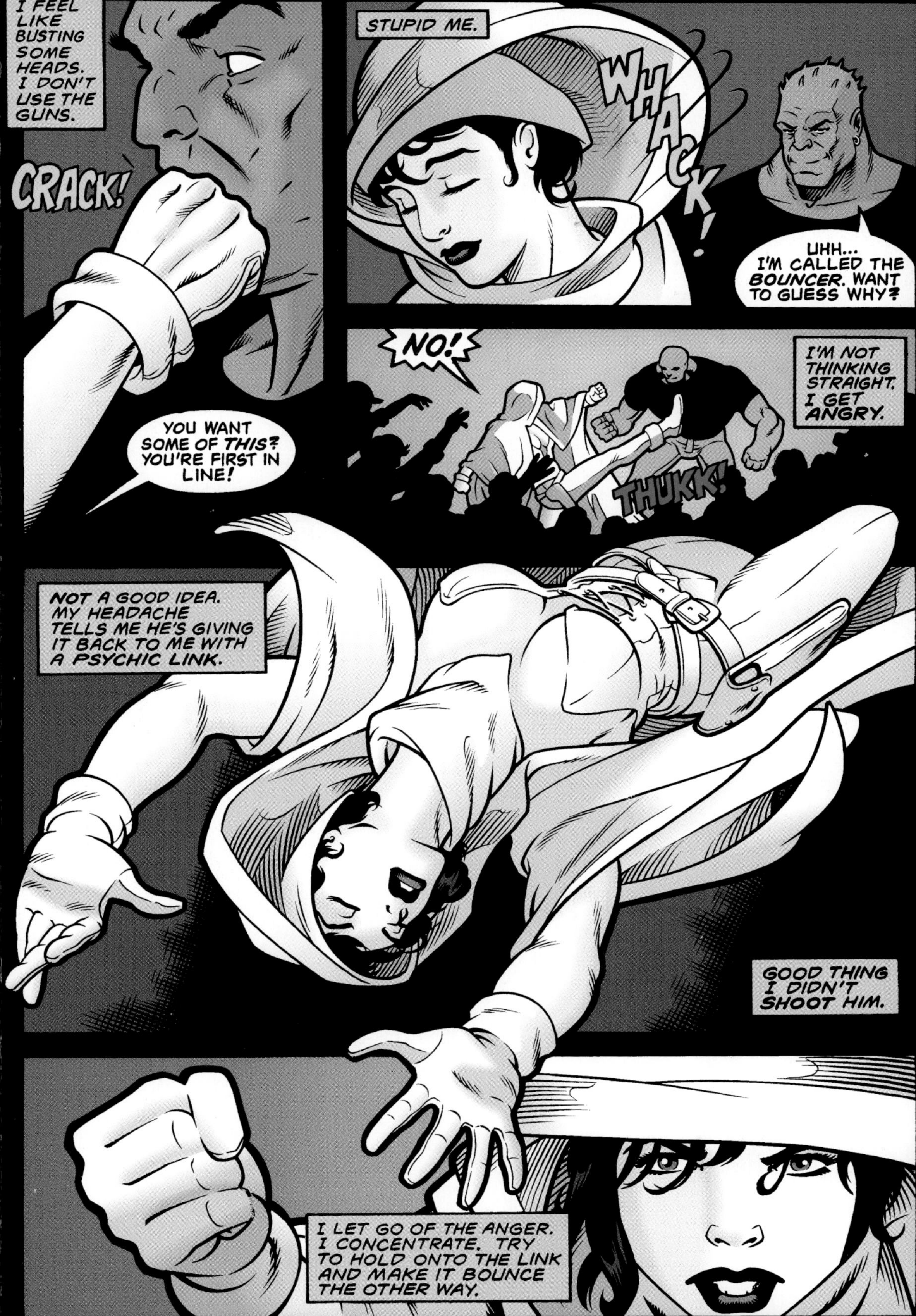

I FEEL LIKE BUSTING SOME HEADS. I DON'T USE THE GUNS.
CRACK!
STUPID ME.
WHACK!
UHH... I'M CALLED THE BOUNCER. WANT TO GUESS WHY?
NO!
I'M NOT THINKING STRAIGHT. I GET ANGRY.
YOU WANT SOME OF THIS? YOU'RE FIRST IN LINE!
THUKK!
NOT A GOOD IDEA. MY HEADACHE TELLS ME HE'S GIVING IT BACK TO ME WITH A PSYCHIC LINK.
GOOD THING I DIDN'T SHOOT HIM.
I LET GO OF THE ANGER. I CONCENTRATE. TRY TO HOLD ONTO THE LINK AND MAKE IT BOUNCE THE OTHER WAY.

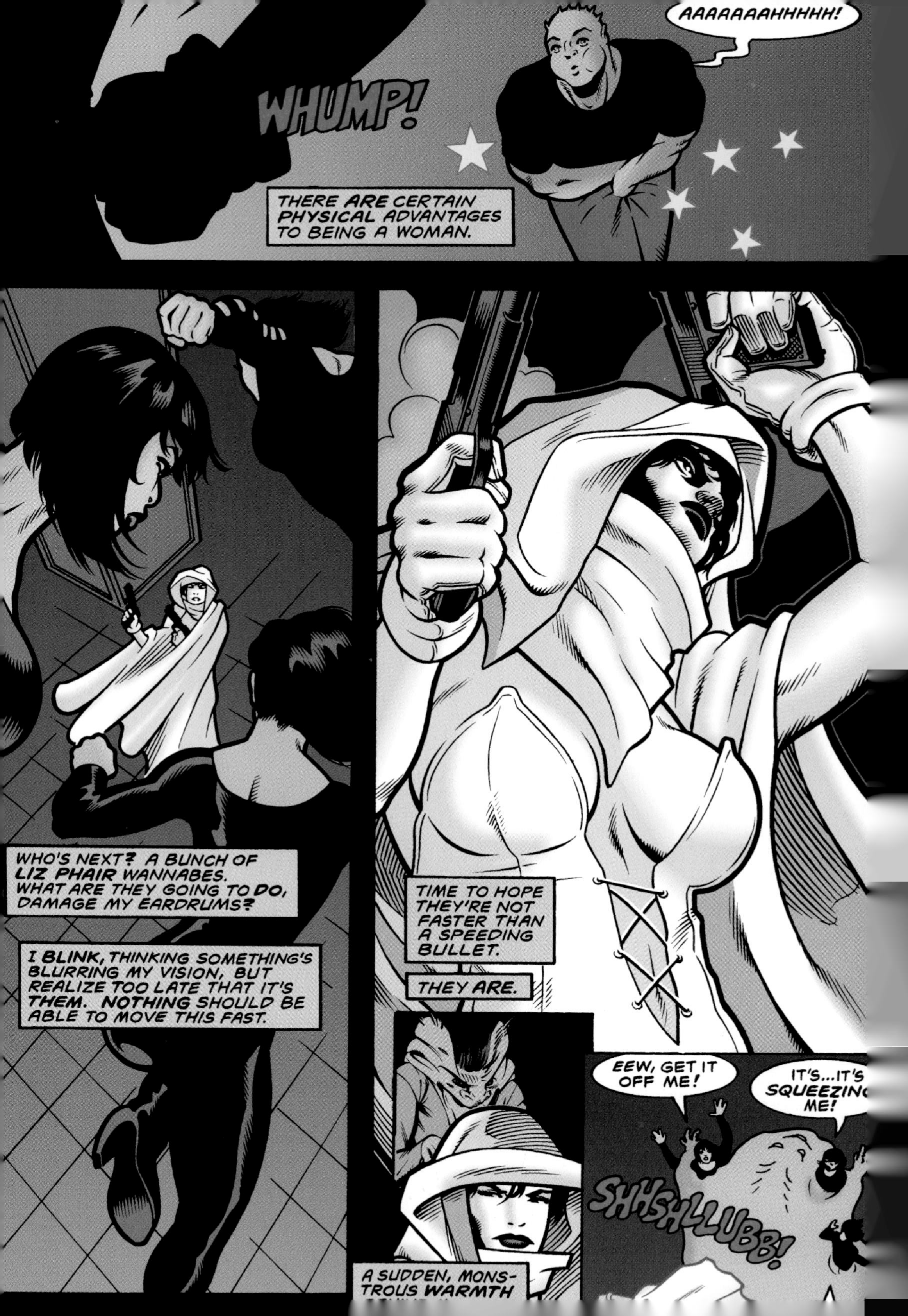
AAAAAAAAHHHHH!
WHUMP!
THERE ARE CERTAIN PHYSICAL ADVANTAGES TO BEING A WOMAN.
WHO'S NEXT? A BUNCH OF LIZ PHAIR WANNABES. WHAT ARE THEY GOING TO DO, DAMAGE MY EARDRUMS?
I BLINK, THINKING SOMETHING'S BLURRING MY VISION, BUT REALIZE TOO LATE THAT IT'S THEM. NOTHING SHOULD BE ABLE TO MOVE THIS FAST.
TIME TO HOPE THEY'RE NOT FASTER THAN A SPEEDING BULLET.
THEY ARE.
A SUDDEN, MONS-TROUS WARMTH
EEW, GET IT OFF ME!
IT'S...IT'S SQUEEZIN ME!
SHHSHLLUBB!

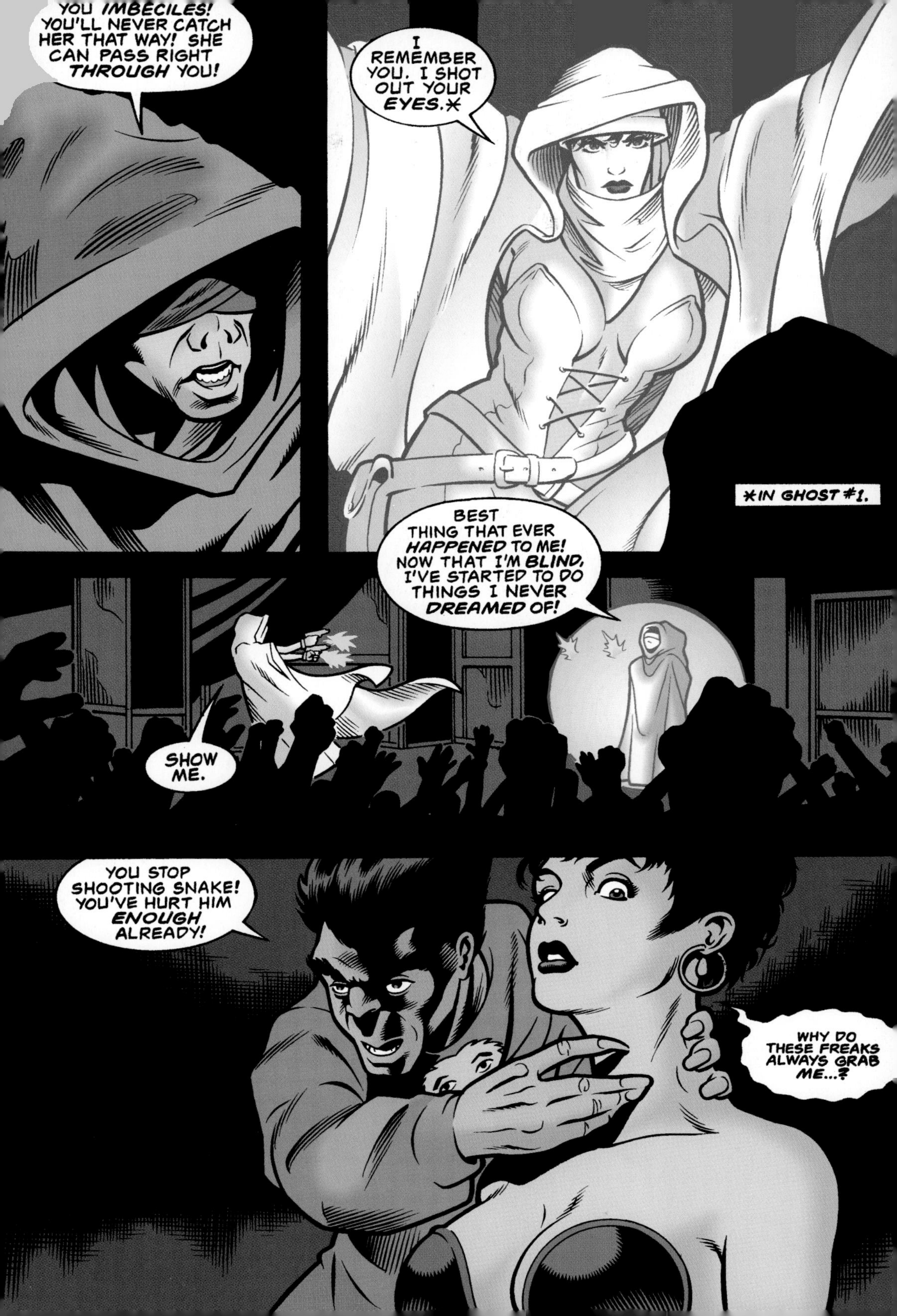
YOU IMBECILES! YOU'LL NEVER CATCH HER THAT WAY! SHE CAN PASS RIGHT THROUGH YOU!
I REMEMBER YOU. I SHOT OUT YOUR EYES.*
*IN GHOST #1.
BEST THING THAT EVER HAPPENED TO ME! NOW THAT I'M BLIND, I'VE STARTED TO DO THINGS I NEVER DREAMED OF!
SHOW ME.
YOU STOP SHOOTING SNAKE! YOU'VE HURT HIM ENOUGH ALREADY!
WHY DO THESE FREAKS ALWAYS GRAB ME...?

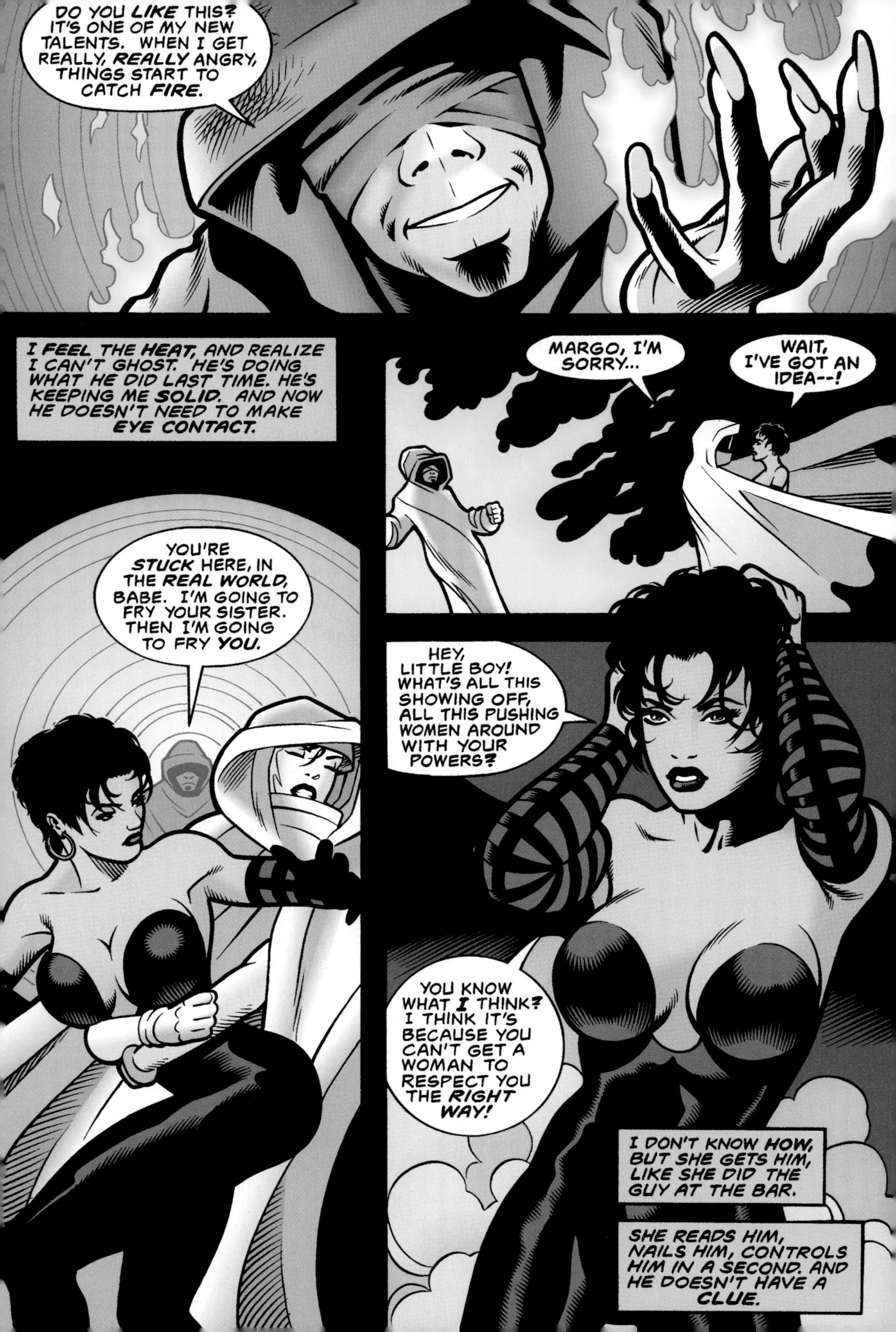
DO YOU LIKE THIS? IT'S ONE OF MY NEW TALENTS. WHEN I GET REALLY, REALLY ANGRY, THINGS START TO CATCH FIRE.
I FEEL THE HEAT, AND REALIZE I CAN'T GHOST. HE'S DOING WHAT HE DID LAST TIME. HE'S KEEPING ME SOLID. AND NOW HE DOESN'T NEED TO MAKE EYE CONTACT.
YOU'RE STUCK HERE, IN THE REAL WORLD, BABE. I'M GOING TO FRY YOUR SISTER. THEN I'M GOING TO FRY YOU.
MARGO, I'M SORRY...
WAIT, I'VE GOT AN IDEA--!
HEY, LITTLE BOY! WHAT'S ALL THIS SHOWING OFF, ALL THIS PUSHING WOMEN AROUND WITH YOUR POWERS?
YOU KNOW WHAT I THINK? I THINK IT'S BECAUSE YOU CAN'T GET A WOMAN TO RESPECT YOU THE RIGHT WAY!
I DON'T KNOW HOW, BUT SHE GETS HIM, LIKE SHE DID THE GUY AT THE BAR.
SHE READS HIM, NAILS HIM, CONTROLS HIM IN A SECOND. AND HE DOESN'T HAVE A CLUE.

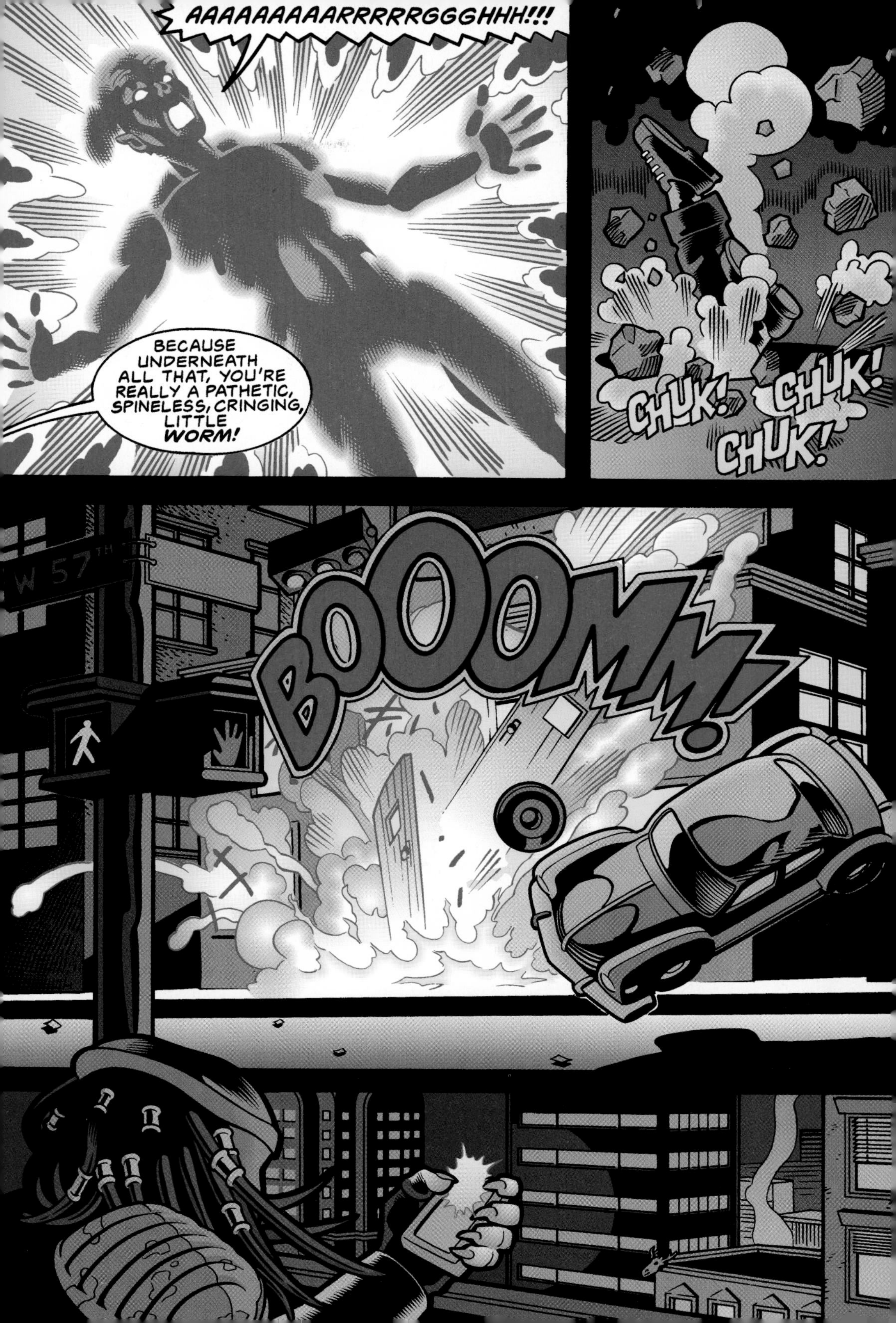
AAAAAAAAARRRRRGGGHHH!!!
BECAUSE UNDERNEATH ALL THAT, YOU'RE REALLY A PATHETIC, SPINELESS, CRINGING, LITTLE WORM!
CHUK! CHUK! CHUK!
W 57TH
BOOOMM!

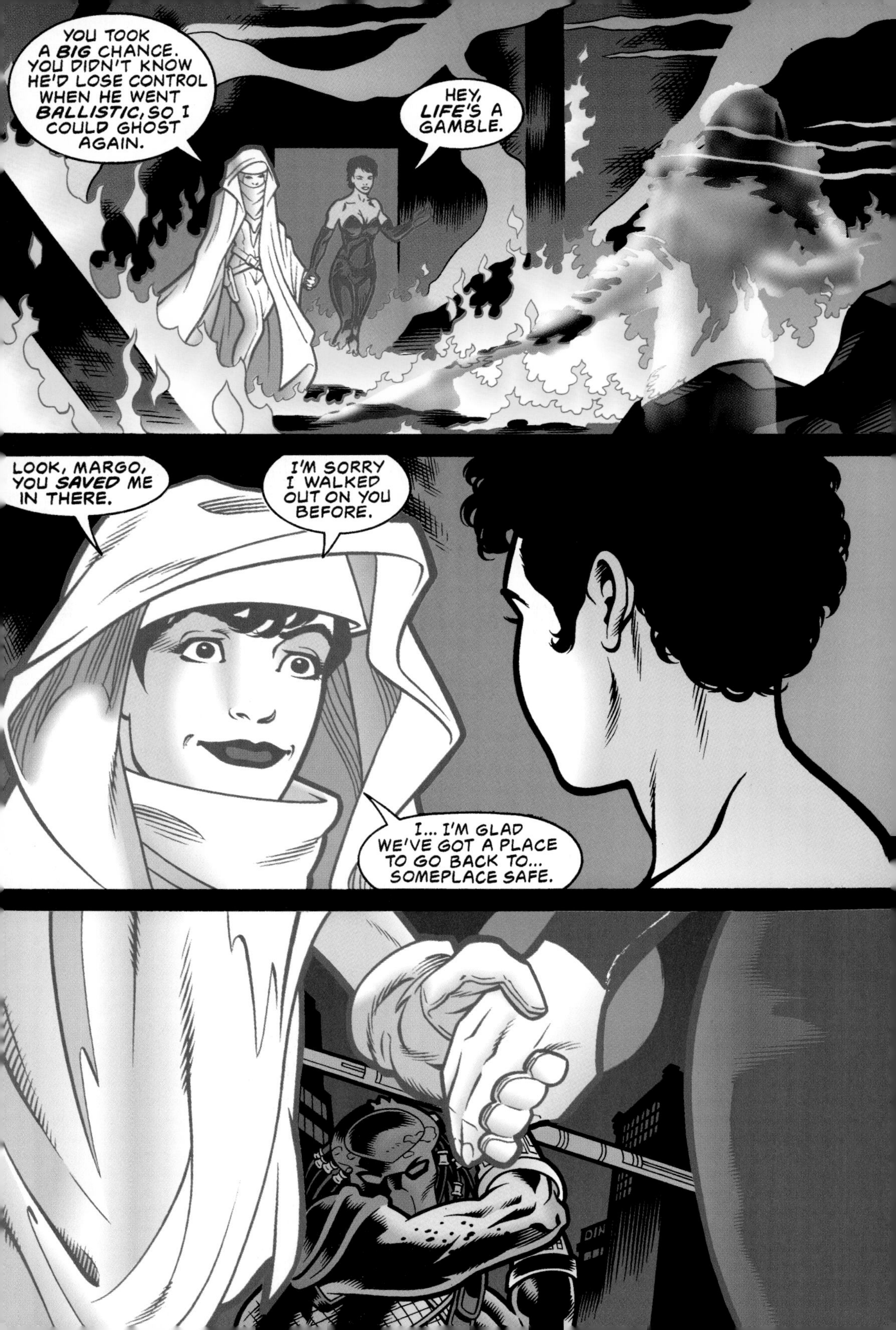
YOU TOOK A BIG CHANCE. YOU DIDN'T KNOW HE'D LOSE CONTROL WHEN HE WENT BALLISTIC, SO I COULD GHOST AGAIN.
HEY, LIFE'S A GAMBLE.
LOOK, MARGO, YOU SAVED ME IN THERE.
I'M SORRY I WALKED OUT ON YOU BEFORE.
I... I'M GLAD WE'VE GOT A PLACE TO GO BACK TO... SOMEPLACE SAFE.

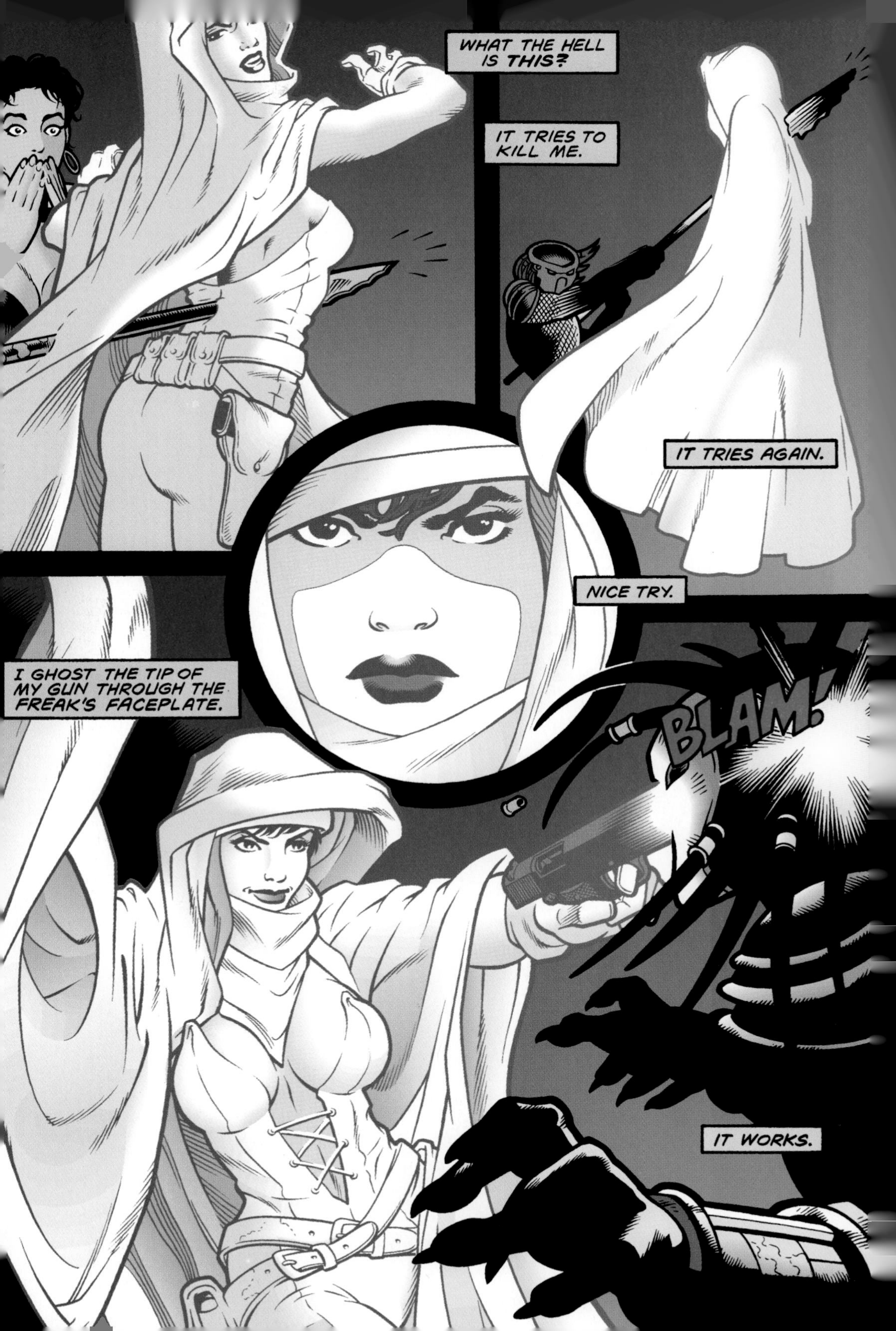

WHAT THE HELL IS THIS?
IT TRIES TO KILL ME.
IT TRIES AGAIN.
NICE TRY.
I GHOST THE TIP OF MY GUN THROUGH THE FREAK'S FACEPLATE.
BLAM!
IT WORKS.

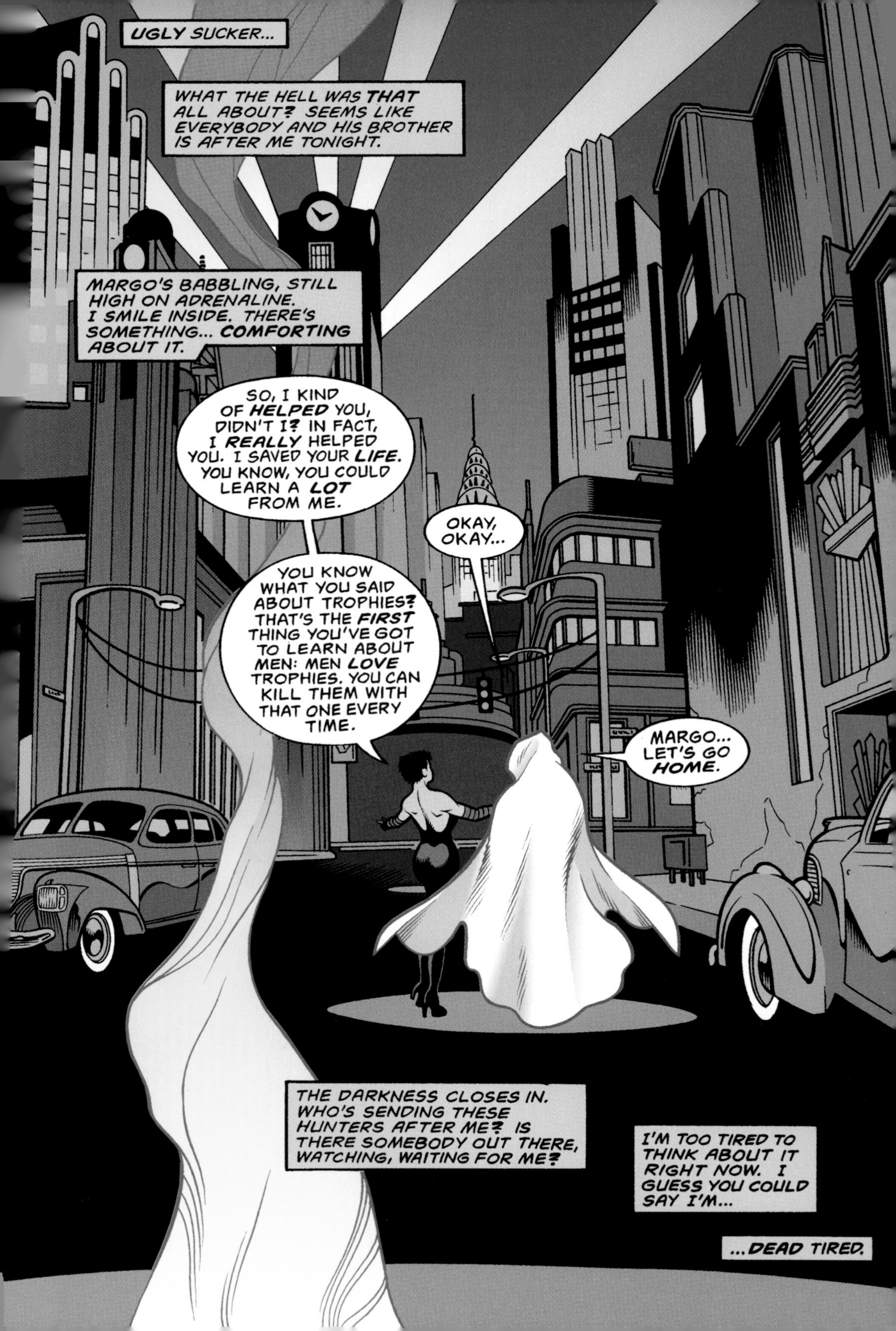
UGLY SUCKER...
WHAT THE HELL WAS THAT ALL ABOUT? SEEMS LIKE EVERYBODY AND HIS BROTHER IS AFTER ME TONIGHT.
MARGO'S BABBLING, STILL HIGH ON ADRENALINE. I SMILE INSIDE. THERE'S SOMETHING... COMFORTING ABOUT IT.
SO, I KIND OF HELPED YOU, DIDN'T I? IN FACT, I REALLY HELPED YOU. I SAVED YOUR LIFE. YOU KNOW, YOU COULD LEARN A LOT FROM ME.
OKAY, OKAY...
YOU KNOW WHAT YOU SAID ABOUT TROPHIES? THAT'S THE FIRST THING YOU'VE GOT TO LEARN ABOUT MEN: MEN LOVE TROPHIES. YOU CAN KILL THEM WITH THAT ONE EVERY TIME.
MARGO... LET'S GO HOME.
THE DARKNESS CLOSES IN. WHO'S SENDING THESE HUNTERS AFTER ME? IS THERE SOMEBODY OUT THERE, WATCHING, WAITING FOR ME?
I'M TOO TIRED TO THINK ABOUT IT RIGHT NOW. I GUESS YOU COULD SAY I'M...
...DEAD TIRED.

THE END

GHOST™
GALLERY

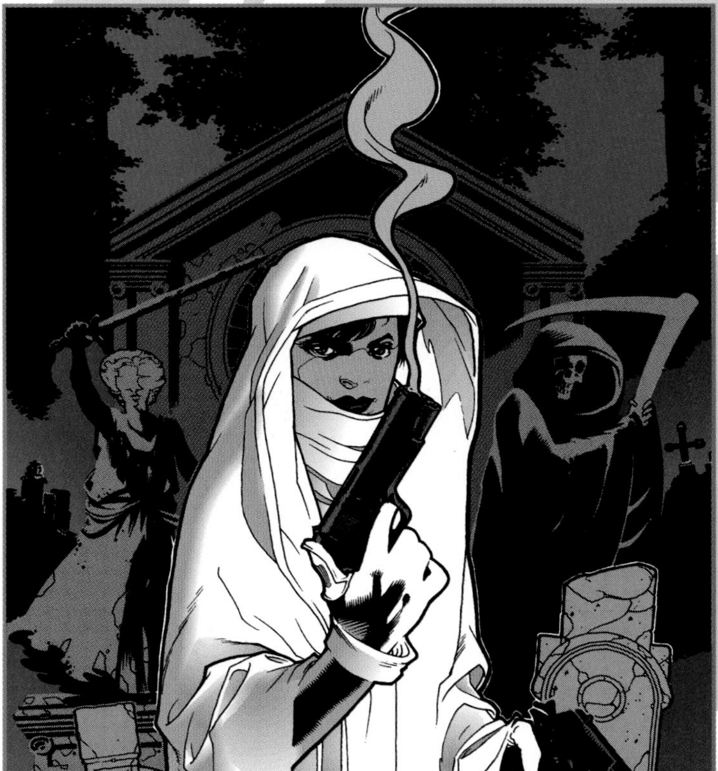
MEMENTO
MORI

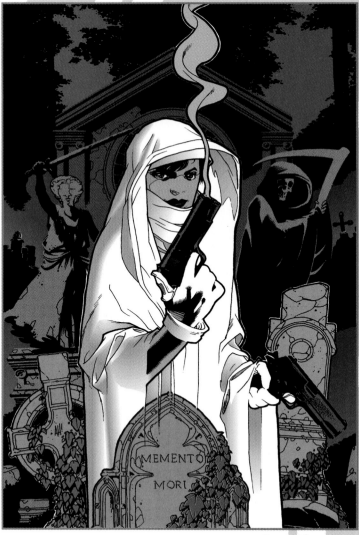

Cover art from issue #1

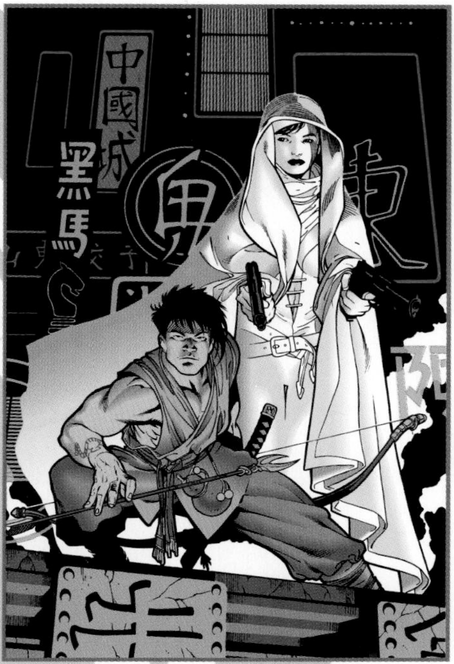
中國城
黑馬

Cover art from issue #2

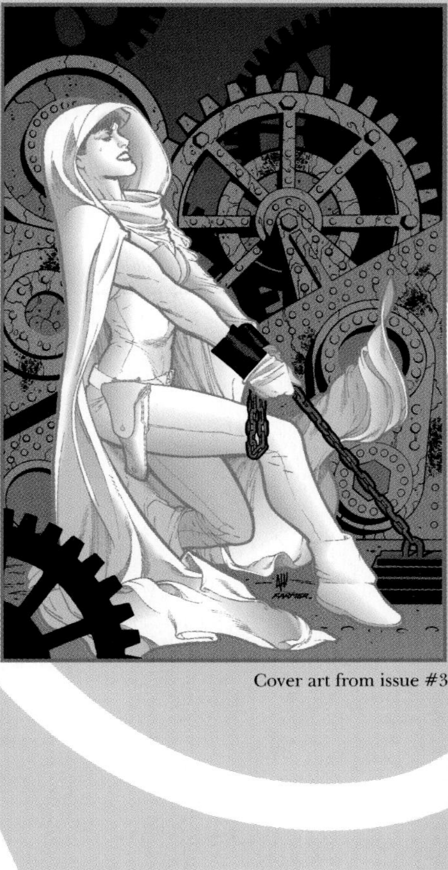

Cover art from issue #3

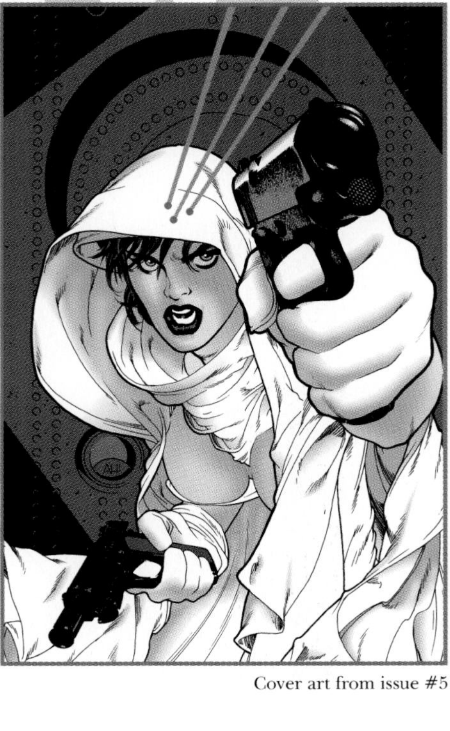

Cover art from issue #5